PLEASING A CLIENT

Lord Edmund Barry might be young in years and boldly handsome, and a picture of up-to-date elegance as well. But he had no sympathy with Juliana's modern notions of what a mansion should be.

"There is nothing wrong with the past," he declared. "I admire the past very much."

"Well, then we will build you a nice Doric temple on that rise over there. It will be lovely," Juliana assured him.

"You are humoring me, aren't you," he said, the tone of his voice causing Juliana to take a step back from him.

She swallowed carefully, then shook her head. "No, that is not it in the least. I want to please you."

His expression changed, and she did not know what to make of it. Until she found herself swept into his arms and kissed with a thoroughness that put previous attempts in the pale.

When he released her he growled again, but more softly, "You do please me. . . ."

Lord Barry's Dream House

Emily Hendrickson

A SIGNET BOOK

SIGNET
Published by the Penguin Group
Penguin Books USA Inc., 375 Hudson Street,
New York, New York 10014, U.S.A.
Penguin Books Ltd, 27 Wrights Lane,
London W8 5TZ, England
Penguin Books Australia Ltd, Ringwood,
Victoria, Australia
Penguin Books Canada Ltd, 10 Alcorn Avenue,
Toronto, Ontario, Canada M4V 3B2
Penguin Books (N.Z.) Ltd, 182-190 Wairau Road,
Auckland 10, New Zealand

Penguin Books Ltd, Registered Offices:
Harmondsworth, Middlesex, England

First published by Signet, an imprint of Dutton Signet,
a division of Penguin Books USA Inc.

First Printing, February, 1996
10 9 8 7 6 5 4 3 2 1

I would like to acknowledge several books I found particularly helpful when writing this novel.

The Elements of Style by Stephen Calloway and Elizabeth Cromley

Life in the English Country House by Mark Girouard

The Sheraton Director arranged by J. Munro Bell

Craftsmen and Interior Decoration in England 1660–1820 by Geoffrey Beard

Regency Design by John Morley

Architectural Drawings of the Regency Period by Giles Worsley

Life in the Georgian City by Dan Cruickshank and Neil Burton

Chapter One

66 "That bottled spider, that foul bunch-back'd toad!" Lady
Juliana Hamilton brushed back a strand of soft brown
hair from her forehead, streaking soot across her fair skin, and
compressed her lips in righteous wrath as she surveyed the
ruins of a storage hut that had been built close to the house
under construction. " 'Tis a blessing the fire did not spread to
the house. It likely could have, had you not happened to stay
around here later than you usually do."

She nudged a charred timber with the toe of her half-jean
boot and sighed. This was another in a long chain of misfor-
tunes that had plagued her since she took over the building of
the house following her architect father's death. She strongly
suspicioned who was behind her ill luck. "I wish the man to
Jericho."

"Now, Lady Juliana, we cannot prove that it was *him* that
did this." Henry Scott gave her a commiserating look while
striving not to acknowledge that the man they both suspected
of foul play was responsible for the fire. That they both immediately thought of the same man, baronet Sir Phineas
Forsythe—gray fringe ringing his balding head, a hawkish
look to his face, especially his eyes—was not remarkable. The
amateur architect had made it clear he intended to take over
the late Lord Hamilton's project.

"And I cannot prove the sun rises in the east and sets in the
west," she snapped, then gave her worthy assistant and cousin
an apologetic look. "I am sorry, Henry, but will he never
leave us in peace to finish this house? Why can he not con-
cede, admit I am doing a good job of completing what must
be my father's finest work?" She bestowed a fond look at the

house that soared behind her. Every line was known to her
like the back of her hand.

She eased her tired self down onto a pile of wood destined
for wainscoting and studied her outstretched boots that peeked
from beneath the dusty hem of her oldest gown. She really
ought to buy new half-boots, she supposed. Her attire when
working at the house was sufficient to give her mother the vapors, did she chance to see her eldest daughter before she
slipped off to the site. However, it was not practical to come
to the work site garbed in delicate muslin. Juliana had donned
a serviceable corded muslin in faded blue with a simple
spencer over it, figuring the workmen neither noticed nor
cared what she wore.

That was probably the only practical streak in Juliana. She
was a dreamer, an adventuress on paper. She wanted to design
and build just as her papa had. She had studied his books and
learned all she could from him before a bout of pneumonia
snatched him from his loving family.

Being a woman had distinct drawbacks, for she could never
achieve her dream. Her mother insisted Uncle George chaperon her, but never bothered to see if he always tagged along.
But she *could* finish this house for the patron who had con-
tracted with her father for a large home, suitably decorated
and furnished, to be situated on a splendid knoll on his fine
property. He would likely never notice that she had made subtle changes and additions. But, she stubbornly insisted, they
were for the better; they made a more livable and far more
new-fashioned house.

"Your being a woman likely galls the man," Henry said
with a wry smile. "It would be a feather in his cap to claim he
completed the work on this mansion."

"True, the odious toad," Juliana murmured in response. She
studied the smoking ruins and continued. "Thank heavens we
have managed to conceal most of the *accidents* around here,
or those who are superstitious would refuse to step on the
property. Can you imagine what would happen were the patron to catch wind of them? The longer he stays in Jamaica,
the better. Father always said that patrons proved to be the
greatest problem in building. They go sticking their noses into

every corner, demanding silly changes that inevitably increase the costs, not to mention the work, and utterly refusing to understand the need for the improvements you incorporate."

"I fancy you mean those new-fashioned water-closets you ordered," Henry said musingly.

"*And* the latest design in ranges for the kitchen—a Rumford rather than a Bodley, I think. A man would likely think it extravagant, never mind it would result in better cooking, not to mention making the kitchen more convenient and pleasant for the kitchen staff. No, I can do quite nicely without his lordship around." Juliana gave her assistant and trusted friend a tired smile. "Although I must confess he writes a very nice letter."

She drew up her legs, tucking her skirts closely about her, then rested her chin on her knees. An approaching sound caught her ear, and she glanced in that direction. "I suppose that is our carriage. Mama persists in sending it for me, even when I ride over."

"She worries about you."

"Uncle George says it is because I am the cement that holds our family together." Juliana grimaced at the burden her uncle would place on her slim shoulders.

"George Teynham says a lot of things, most of them outrageous," Henry said with a smile. While most assistants would never give voice to such a thought, Henry was somewhat a member of the family, being a distant cousin and having been trained by Juliana's father to ably further his work. Now Henry remained with his late patron's daughter because he would see the project to its conclusion and . . . because he could not leave her.

"I do believe he has memorized every insult ever written by Shakespeare and simply dotes on shocking people." Juliana smiled when she thought how she had slipped into the same usage, for she dearly loved that quote from *Richard III,* the one about the foul bunch-backed toad. It so aptly fit their neighbor, the nasty Sir Phineas Forsythe.

Henry straightened as a stranger turned the corner of the great house and walked toward them. The chap was studying everything about him in a very considering way—examining the mortar between the stone, the joints, and fitting of the windows. He paused to look upward at the cornice that crowned the windows, an exquisitely classical feature of the house design and one that Juliana had added. A frown crossed his brow, then he continued toward the two who sat by the ashes of the fire.

At the sight of a leather case tucked under the stranger's arm, Henry murmured, "Another damned salesman to plague you."

Tired and annoyed past all politeness—Juliana rose and militantly advanced upon the stranger. He was unusually tall and quite dark-skinned, as though he spent much time in the sun; his eyes flashed a surprisingly bright blue at her as she neared. Dark he might be; he was a handsome man. Broad shoulders admirably filled out his coat, which looked to be the latest thing in fashion. How odd for a salesman. He must represent a superior company. And his pantaloons were impeccably cut and fit to him like a glove. Young ladies of quality were not supposed to notice things like that. She hurriedly turned her attention.

She gave a pointed glare at the leather case and spoke in her best daughter-of-the-mansion manner. "Good day, sir. Whatever it is you are selling we want none of it. We purchase all our goods from none but our chosen sources." She made a point of studying all available information and carefully ordered her materials based on what she learned and with Henry's guidance. She believed in sensible economy— abhorring waste, yet demanding the best quality in everything that mattered.

Her toes curled in her half-jean boots at the lazy—and most superior—smile he bestowed on her. Perfectly splendid teeth parted, and in a rich, deep voice he said, "And who are you, may I ask? I seek Julian, Lord Hamilton. Where is he, and why do *you* talk of ordering goods? Does Lord Hamilton employ a female assistant!" He seemed vastly amused by the idea.

A look of anguish flashed across Juliana's face as she thought of her talented father who was no more. She half turned to motion Henry to silence before answering. "May I inquire as to whom *you* are, my lord?" she bestowed a title on him, figuring that whether he was or not, he would be flattered by it. He certainly looked and acted the part.

"Since you correctly address me, I gather you have surmised I am Barry." Edmund, Lord Barry bowed most faintly in her direction.

"Lord Barry! All the way from Jamaica?" Juliana exclaimed softly and with a sinking heart. What a perfectly dreadful time for him to make an appearance. Lord Barry was in for a few surprises. He would soon learn of her duplicity, not to mention all the changes she had made.

"I have in my case a wealth of correspondence from Lord Hamilton. I thought all was going as I wished when I received a letter from his neighbor claiming that Lord Hamilton had died some time ago and his daughter had taken over the building. This in spite of efforts by a capable architect to assume control of the works. Yet I continued to receive letters and information from Lord Hamilton all this while. I decided it time to return to England and see for myself what is going on."

Juliana shifted uneasily under that penetrating gaze. She sensed that there was no gentle man to cozen with sweet words and guile as her sister Barbara liked to do. He possessed a hard polish over his aristocratic manner, most likely from giving orders on his Jamaica plantations. This situation was not likely to please him in the least.

"I am Lady Juliana, Lord Hamilton's daughter," she replied with an air of hauteur at odds with her appearance. She attempted to draw him away from the house. She wanted him to see it at its best, not at half-light and when he was tired from travel. "Perhaps you would come with me to our home where we can discuss this in comfort and out of the evening chill. It is growing late, and I feel certain you would appreciate a good meal. You must have traveled a long way this day," she concluded with hope. "I know my mother would be pleased to meet you."

"*You* are Lord Hamilton's daughter?" He could not have looked more astounded if a toad had jumped up to kiss him.

"Indeed, sir," she admitted with a faint smile. "I have written you a good many letters over the past years, for I have served as my father's assistant and secretary. Papa said I have

a good hand and excellent understanding of construction."
She hoped this tiny clue might lead Lord Barry step-by-step to
the truth of the matter.

He stared down at her, eyes narrowed and the smile gone
from his oddly sensual mouth. "I have a feeling there is a
great deal more to this than I know at the moment." He
looked behind her then, catching sight of the still-smoking
ruins of the hut. "What's this? A fire? So close to the house?
It does not seem prudent to do away with rubbish in such
proximity."

A breeze ruffled the skirt of Juliana's gown, emphasizing
how dangerous such action might be, for a wind carried em-
bers a fair distance. He frowned at Juliana, and she wished
she were a mile away from this man. He was odiously arrogant, and she would wager he ate young women like her for
breakfast.

"Henry came upon the blaze—having remained later than
usual—and put it out." She crossed her fingers behind her
back and continued. "I feel certain it was a mere accident,
most likely by one of the workmen, who left, thinking it
safely out. I chanced to come over here as well—wishing to
check on things—so between our efforts the fire did not
spread." She did not like the speculative expression that entered his lordship's eyes at her words. Surely he did not think
she would have an assignation with her works supervisor!
Dismissing the thought as silly, Juliana said, "No great harm
was done, but I suspect we should have a guard here day and
night." These last words she directed to Henry, who nodded in
understanding. To Barry she added, "This is Henry Scott, our
works supervisor. I do not know how we would manage without him."

Lord Barry acknowledged the other man's presence with a
nod of his head and murmured, "Scott."

"We are pleased to see you here at long last, my lord,"
Henry said, ignoring Juliana's glare. "I believe it a good thing
for a man to watch his home being built."

Dusk crept across the fields, and a setting sun illuminated the
house with warm rays of peach and gold, giving the Portland
stone a beautiful glow, highlighting the Ionic capital at the

corner of the portico with a blaze of color. She looked at the house with fond pride in her eyes, then turned toward the rough drive that had been laid out before the house.

"I know you must long to explore your home," Juliana said hesitantly. "However, I suggest you wait until tomorrow. There is scaffolding about, and pots of paint and buckets of paste lurk for the unwary, not to mention piles of lumber and sawdust elsewhere. The house is close to completion, I feel sure you will be happy to know. I have designed . . ." and here Juliana halted her flow of words, fearing she had uttered far too much already.

"Yes?" he queried smoothly. "You have designed what?"

"Nothing, my lord. Come, let us go." She placed a dainty— if somewhat sooty—hand upon the arm held out for her, then turned to Henry. "I shall see you first thing tomorrow."

"Aye," Henry replied. Only when Juliana had turned away from him did a wistful longing slip into his eyes. It disappeared immediately, quite as though he remembered how impossible any yearning in her direction might be. He resolutely headed for his pleasant and empty home.

Juliana chattered about the weather all the way to where Lord Barry's traveling coach awaited him. Here she stopped.

"I had best take my mare and lead the way. Even with excellent directions, these roads can be deceptive."

"Like a number of other things around here, it seems," he murmured. He climbed into his coach and leaned out of the window to signal his coachman.

She had swiftly mounted Beauty and motioned to the driver with no outward sign of her fluttering heart. While the coach rumbled along the lane away from the house being built for Lord Barry, she tried to think of what she should say to him. Would he possibly understand?

It was not as though she sought a future as an architect. She knew better than that. She merely wished to complete the home her father had designed and of which he had been so very proud. And she would, too—if Lord Barry permitted and that odious toad of a Sir Phineas Forsythe would keep his nose to home.

True, she had not a shred of proof that Sir Phineas was behind all the ills that had plagued her since she had assumed responsibility for the completion of the house. But she felt in her bones that he was the one answerable. "He has not so much brain as ear-wax!" she seethed softly, adopting one of her uncle's many favorite expressions from Shakespeare. Sir Phineas heard only what he pleased.

With a few turns along the lovely Oxfordshire country roads, they entered what was one of the minor estates belonging to the late Lord Hamilton. While his newly married son and heir resided at the principal estate in Kent, the Dowager Lady Hamilton, Juliana, her younger sisters Barbara and Kitty, and Lady Hamilton's brother, Uncle George, preferred to live in Oxfordshire. Juliana suspected her mother hated to leave the place where her dear husband had died, quite as though he was yet close to her in the home he had designed and built for her pleasure.

She handed Beauty's reins to the groom who ran to meet her in front of the house, then turned to face Lord Barry as he exited his coach. "Welcome to Beechwood Hall, Lord Barry."

He gave the house a cursory glance, then joined her in the walk up the flight of stairs that led to the front door. They entered the high-ceilinged hall, ushered in by the longtime family retainer, the venerable Dalston.

"Your father designed this house, I presume?" Lord Barry said to Juliana as he glanced about the beautifully proportioned room.

"Indeed," she replied with a gracious nod, wondering precisely how it was that Lord Barry had come to engage her father to design his house. She murmured a few words to Dalston regarding Lord Barry, then turned to catch sight of her uncle looking down from the first-floor landing.

"Well, the ministering angel returns to soothe the family spirits." Uncle George paused at the top of the stairs before strolling down to join Juliana and the unwanted guest.

"This is Edmund, Lord Barry," she announced to her uncle, hoping he might curb his more outrageous tendencies. To her guest she added, "My dear uncle, George Teynham, is the buttress of our family regardless of his frippery words." Juliana patted her uncle on the arm, then said, "Perhaps you would show our guest to a room where he might refresh himself while I seek out Kitty to inform her of the news." After receiving an assenting nod, she curtsied prettily, then hurried in the direction where she thought Kitty most likely might be found.

George looked after her disappearing figure, then motioned to Lord Barry. "Welcome to this house, Lord Barry. I fancy I know just where my sister would place you, for you must stay with us, you know. It would never do for you to stop in that country inn, clean though it may be. Come along with me, dear sir, and you shall fortify yourself before you meet this passel of womanhood." They began their walk up the lovely stone staircase, and George continued his conversation. "I believe I knew your father a long time ago. Dashing fellow. You have the look of him. I seem to recall that Susan, my sister, admired him very much before she married Julian."

With scarcely a lift of his brows Lord Barry murmured suitable replies, joining Uncle George in a sauntering walk up the stairs, pausing every now and again to examine a fine bit of detailing. Although the house was not immense, it was a jewel of architectural design; anyone of taste would see that at once.

Back on the ground floor Juliana whirled into the sitting room and then relaxed to see Kitty in the corner of the window seat, trying to read by the fading light and one lone candle. She crossed to touch her younger sister on the shoulder. When assured she had her attention, she spoke carefully, enunciating clearly.

"We have a guest. Lord Barry is come to see how his house goes on. You had best join me in changing for dinner."

"Oh, dear. Must I join you? Strangers always fuss at me, and I hate that." Kitty put down her book, frowning at her elder sister. But she obediently gathered her skirts, preparing to do as bid. People tended to heed Juliana.

"You are not deaf; you merely require a clear voice. No mumblers will do for you, my dear," Juliana joked. "Lord Barry has an excellent voice and speaks distinctly. Come along, do. I must pass the word along to Cook and to Mother. I do not know who will be the more flustered."

Then Kitty stared at Juliana and giggled. "Truly, you did never allow him to see you looking like that! Why, you look a veritable fright. Oh, my." She placed her book on the window seat, joining Juliana in the exodus to the upper regions with much giggling and shaking of her head.

"I promise to make myself respectable before dinner," Juliana said with a smile at her precious sister.

"We would never wish Mama to have a fit of the vapors," Kitty replied with a twinkle in her pretty gray eyes.

In his room, a most elegant and tastefully furnished abode, Edmund strolled to the window, gazing off into the fading light in the direction of his new home. Every sense he had told him that something was distinctly havey-cavey with the construction. Could Sir Phineas be correct? Would the daughter of an earl, albeit the architect earl who had designed and presumably overseen the construction of the house to this point, have lied to him in her letters?

It seemed most unlikely that a young woman would attempt the completion of a house such as he had specified. The letters had been most detailed as to what was being done at the moment. The drawings were exquisite, beautifully executed, and sent to him in a tube so as not to crease them. He had kept every one of them, and now he decided he would study them, comparing them to the actual house. Something the daughter had said—oh, yes, she had begun to explain about her designs. Surely she would not have attempted to change her father's excellent plan!

Unthinkable! Yet . . .

Edmund restlessly paced about the room, then turned to greet his valet when he slipped inside with the valise containing the things that would be needed to restore Lord Barry's less than pristine condition.

"Melton, I should like you to keep your ears open and try to find out what has been going on around here. I imagine the best tack would be to admire everything, particularly the earl and his eldest daughter. People are more apt to be open if they believe you a friend, not a foe."

"And what are we, my lord?" the valet said, keeping his face carefully neutral.

"At the moment I do not know. I think Lady Juliana a shocking bit, dressing as she did in a rag of a gown and parading around the building site with the works supervisor. Perhaps the family needs the money?" He gave Melton a meaningful look.

"I doubt that, for the place has the air of prosperity, and there is not a picture missing from any wall I chanced to see." The valet referred to an oft-used means of raising funds by way of selling assets.

"True. The uncle was dressed quite well, considering they are a country family. Dinner ought to prove most interesting." He permitted Melton to assist him from his traveling clothes and into proper garb for a dinner in the country with the family of an earl. Where that earl might be was a matter for conjecture, but Edmund began to suspect the man would be found in his grave, not at the dining table.

"Would that your father were alive to handle his patron," Lady Hamilton exclaimed as she dithered about near her dressing table. She gave Juliana an accusing look, then sniffed into an exquisite scrap of black-bordered linen before continuing. "How I permitted you to convince me that you be allowed to complete that house I shall never understand."

"You wished it to be finished as a tribute to Papa's memory and great talent. You know that if Sir Phineas took over, he would ruin Papa's design and turn the place into a Gothic horror," Juliana reminded her mother.

Lady Hamilton sank down on a velvet bench placed at the foot of her vast and cleverly canopied bed. "I trust you have the right of it. It will be in your hands to convince Lord Barry that it was a proper thing to do, for I suspect he will not be best pleased with this turn of events. Who ever heard of a woman doing architectural work, much less contracting!" The last word was said much as though Juliana had begun dabbling in smuggling, or possibly murder.

"You must admit that I have donned my best for the evening," Juliana offered by way of appeasement, turning about for her mother's inspection.

Her mother rearranged her modest necklet of diamonds before graciously giving Juliana her hand and joining her in the exodus to the drawing room. This room was located on the ground floor, contrary to city plans, and vastly convenient for all.

When they entered the room, they found Barbara and Kitty, along with Uncle George, awaiting them. Kitty gave Juliana an encouraging smile. Lady Hamilton hurried to instruct her second daughter, the beauteous Barbara of the ash blond curls and limpid blue eyes, regarding the guest.

In a quiet voice Lady Hamilton said, "Now, dear, this is a highly eminent gentleman, one who is likely to be much sought after by all the mamas with daughters to marry off. I think it would be nice if you were to catch his eye, for you are undeniably lovely, and if he is anything like his father, he must be a handsome man."

"Yes, Mama," Lady Barbara answered dutifully. She had heard this speech so often she might have matched it word for word.

Further directions were denied when Lord Barry entered the room and brought all conversation to a halt. The man was simply too elegant for words, Juliana thought. None of his garments were of themselves the sort to draw attention, but the whole, on him, captured the eye and interest of the beholder. Barbara was speechless.

"Welcome to our home, Lord Barry," Lady Hamilton said with practiced ease. "I regret that my husband is not here to greet you. He came to an untimely end last winter." Her manners were impeccable, her black sarcenet dress fitted her with queenly grace, and her smile was most genuine. "I knew your father well," she said simply, without elaboration as some might have given.

"Fine man," Uncle George chimed in. "I gather you have been minding the plantations in Jamaica. How goes it there?"

"Quite well, thank you," Lord Barry replied with an elegant show of manners to the elder members before turning to face the lovely Lady Barbara and Lady Kitty, now introduced as Katherine.

Lord Barry scarcely noticed the younger girl, concentrating on the exquisite Barbara instead. "Charmed, my lady."

Juliana placed a protective arm about her youngest sister's shoulder and said, "I believe dinner is ready. Following that, I had best have a meeting with our guest, if you will permit, dear Mama."

Lady Hamilton, for once seeming flustered, nodded, then gestured to the guest. He immediately offered his arm, and they walked to the dining room, the others falling in behind.

"Are you nervous, puss?" Uncle George murmured in her ear before seating her at the table.

She nodded, not trusting herself to speech.

The meal went off well, considering the tense strain present in all but Barbara, who managed to look demure and flirtatious at the same time. Lord Barry parried her social chatter with practiced ease for one who had been off across the ocean in the wilds of Jamaica.

Once the covers had been removed and a tasteful dessert served, Lady Hamilton rose and gave Juliana a significant look. "I shall withdraw along with Barbara and Kitty. George, you may do as you please. You always do. Juliana, I expect you to give Lord Barry a full accounting."

"I propose we forgo the customary port after dinner and retreat to the library," Uncle George suggested as he rose from the table. Juliana slipped from her chair to join him. Lord Barry had risen the moment that Lady Hamilton had announced her intention to leave them, and now he strolled toward Juliana.

She gulped and hurried to the door, leading the way down the hall to the pleasing confines of the library, which held many books on architecture and construction. The room was a favorite one, furnished with comfortable chairs, and had a pleasant fire in the grate. Once they were settled in those chairs, Lord Barry studied Juliana, then said, "I believe I am due a few explanations."

"Yes, my lord," Juliana replied in her most conciliatory manner. "When Papa died, I could not bear to see another take over the project, especially the man who sought to do so. I had served as Papa's assistant and secretary—as I mentioned before—and felt that with Henry's help I could finish the house. I wished to honor my father's talent and memory. Should someone else have intruded, I feared the plans might be altered drastically and not for the better." She gave Lord Barry a defiant look.

"So you failed to mention his passing, but continued to write me as in the past and carried on with the construction? Did it not occur to you that I deserved to know this?"

Juliana gave him a guilty look and nodded. "I see now that I ought to have informed you. I did not look at things quite that way before."

"She is as capable as many a man in this field," George inserted, earning an anxious look from his niece. "Her father trained her as well as he might his son, had he been interested. He was not, hence Juliana became an apprentice at an early age. When other girls were playing with dolls or doing needlework, Juliana was practicing her drawing—of house plans—and studying the books in this library. You could do much worse than Juliana," he concluded.

Lord Barry rose and strode to the window, looking out into the darkness before turning to face Juliana. "I shall not give comment to the situation until I have seen the house for myself. *If* I find all is well, I may permit the arrangement to continue. I have the plans with me and shall do a walk through the house with them on the morrow."

Juliana thought of all the subtle changes she had made in those plans, and her heart sank to her toes. Gallantly facing the challenge, she nodded and said, "I shall be at your side, if you please."

She couldn't figure out what his answering look meant, but she felt a tiny bit of hope growing within. Perhaps . . .

Chapter Two

The following morning Edmund walked into the break-fast room to find George Teynham seated with his cup of coffee in hand. Seated next to him, Edmund was surprised to see Henry Scott enjoying a hearty breakfast. His surprise must have been revealed on his face, for Mr. Teynham offered an explanation of sorts.

"Good morning, Lord Barry. I trust you slept well. Henry has joined me in breaking my fast. We frequently discuss the coming day over our coffee."

The two men exchanged looks, and Edmund wondered what had been said before he entered the room. He helped himself to various selections displayed on the sideboard, then also seated himself at the oval cherry table. From their gilded frames, assorted portraits of past ancestors looked down on him with varying degrees of approval.

"Indeed," Edmund agreed, "I sleep better when in England. It is pleasant to have wool blankets atop me at night. I missed that while in a warm climate. It is one of the many things I look forward to enjoying once established in my own English home."

"You intend to remain here, then?" George said, holding his cup in both hands while studying their guest and patron. He exchanged another glance with Henry Scott.

"I do. I also intend—in due time—to find myself a pleasant English bride and live the good country life of a solid English citizen." Edmund gave the two men a wry look, then sipped the hot coffee. He grimaced at the knowledge that he sounded more than a little stuffy. But he had longed for a comfortable, pleasant home in the English countryside for so long it had become an ache within him. And he knew he needed a wife—not only to run the house but to provide him with an heir. Wives were necessary items.

"An English home, an English bride, and an English life. Methinks you have had a surfeit of life in foreign parts," George said with a half smile. "You must wish that to be kept mum. I warn you that every matchmaking mother within miles will seek you out otherwise."

"I'd prefer a peaceful existence—without that sort of thing, thank you." Edmund tucked into his meal with a hearty appetite. The food was excellent—a typical English breakfast, the sort he had dreamed about while in Jamaica.

"We shall take care it is not bruited about, then." If George thought it unlikely that Edmund would be spared the husband-hunting female, he didn't give voice to the thought. Edmund felt he was more than capable of finding a wife on his own.

"Good morning, Uncle George, Henry," Juliana sang out as she entered the breakfast room with a light step. She stopped suddenly when she discovered the third occupant. "Oh."

"Good morning, Lady Juliana," Edmund said smoothly. The chit was most presentable this morning—as she had been last night, to be perfectly honest. The blue gown she'd worn at dinner had brought out a sky blue in her candid gaze. This morning she wore a green sprigged thing that might cover that delightful bosom, but nicely hinted at her curves and gave her eyes the color of a tropical sea.

"G-good morning, my lord," she stammered. She accepted a cup of tea from the butler, then sank down on the closest chair to contemplate Edmund. She peeped over the rim of the cup with an amusingly concerned look. It pleased him that she was worried about the trip to his building site. He had studied the plans most carefully last evening, and he was primed for the day.

Juliana contemplated the unwelcome guest with a speculative gaze. Would he make a fuss and bother about those trifling changes she had made in the plans? Worse yet, would he demand she restore the original—and impractical—details to the house? What would be his position on water-closets?

Or the Rumford range? She decided she would wait a while to spring the Etruscan room on him. Not to mention the Chinese dairy. Surely he would appreciate hot and cold running water, and the steam engine to pump water to the house? Would he also like central heating? Much as she loved her parent's house, she could not deny it was cold and drafty in winter. If he desired comfort, central heating looked to be the thing.

Juliana had found an excellent account of the scheme Sir John Soane had used to provide central heating for a mansion and its offices in Tyringham. If they could do this off in Buckinghamshire, it could certainly be accomplished here. She had long ago firmed her intention of trying it out in the new house.

But . . . *he* had come. Oh, how she wished him a thousand miles away. What a pity those good looks were wasted on a patron. Her intuition told her this man was nothing but trouble, and her intuition had never been wrong.

Somehow food had no appeal this morning. She managed a few nibbles of toast and one bite of buttered eggs. Dalston frowned down on her, and she returned his look with a shrug. He glanced beyond her to the stranger and gave her a barely perceptible nod of understanding.

The conversation was of the weather and the probability of rain. With the lead on the roof, the house was safe from water now, but not all the windows were installed, and she blessed every sunny day until then.

There came a lull in the conversation, and Juliana sat tensely, wondering what might come next.

"Shall we depart for the house?" Lord Barry said, dropping his napkin on the table and pushing his chair back an inch or two. He thus established his intent to be in control of the situation. Juliana supposed he had that right since he was footing the bills, but it rankled her that he did not permit her to lead the way in this instance. Good manners ought to have prevailed here.

"By all means, we shall go at once if you like," Juliana replied evenly, popping up from the table with nicely feigned enthusiasm.

Lord Barry immediately came to her side, walking close to her so she had no chance to speak with Henry about anything. His lordship could not possibly know that she needed to compare stories with Henry so they would not contradict one another. Had she thought at all, she would have planned for this. Who had expected Lord Barry to turn up out of the blue, demanding to see his home?

The procession out to the carriages brought to mind her dear papa's funeral; thus she had little enthusiasm or desire for this particular jaunt.

"Here, my lord," she said hastily, "you must drive with Uncle George. I will ride my mare over." And have that chance to talk with Henry, she added to herself.

Edmund could do little else but nod acceptance at this point. The mare stood at the ready and, the green sprigged muslin aside, Lady Juliana was eager to mount and be off. A faint smile lingered on Henry Scott's face. Edmund wondered at that. What were those two hatching? Or did the chit merely seek a chance to have a romantic word or two with her smitten swain? Edmund decided he did not care for Henry Scott—on general principles, of course.

As the coach set off along the avenue, Juliana followed behind, Henry close by her.

"Henry, I must speak to you. Did Uncle George tell you what happened after dinner last evening? We met in the library where Lord Barry informed us that he had studied the original house plans—brought them with him, as a matter of fact—and intends to go through the house with an acute eye, no doubt hunting for changes. What am I to do?" she cried in true distress.

"He's a sharp one, make no mistake," Henry said with a slow nod. "I suspect you will wish that you either had not made changes or at the very least consulted with him over them."

"That would have taken precious time, and things are slow enough as it is," Juliana said with a rueful shake of her head. "Were it later on, it would be far too late to make changes. Now it can be done, and I believe he has the right to make me pay for any work that must be done to make corrections—if they are my fault."

"I noticed that he watched you rather carefully just now—before he entered the coach. I don't know what to do about the changes you have made," Henry said with a glance at the vehicle that preceded them down the lane.

"Well, you must try to match your story to mine," she said with a frown. How complicated this all was. Her main desire was to build a house, and she wanted nothing to interfere with that. At the moment it was her entire life. Or it had been. Lord Barry had changed everything, the dratted man.

For the remainder of the ride, the two compared notes and decided what they would say on every matter either could think of should one or the other be asked.

"I fear we have forgotten something," Juliana said with a worried glance at Henry.

"You will simply have to do the best you can. You are rather clever. Just twist him around your finger as you do every other male who crosses your path," Henry said with a resigned air.

"Do not be absurd," Juliana said absently, watching the coach draw to a halt before the construction site. "Barbara is the one who captures attention, not me."

Henry shook his head as though to say that Juliana ought to pay more attention to those around her. She would not, of course. She had her head in the clouds, or was far too deep in contemplation of a problem with the construction to notice that a man had given her his regard.

"Here we are, my lord," Juliana sang out in what she hoped was a gay voice.

He left the coach and stood, feet planted firmly on his own bit of English soil, to gaze his fill at the front of the house. It was an elegant structure. Solid Portland stone gave the house a feeling of permanency, while the divided stairs winged upward to meet before the central door with an airy grace. This sense was enhanced by the elegant wrought iron balusters just partly installed.

Four pillars graced the portico before the front entry, their Ionic capitals nicely picked out in the morning sun. Workmen swarmed about the place like so many ants, each intent on his own particular mission, paying only slight heed to the visitors. Lady Juliana was far too familiar to cause the least comment; and strangers came to see the work in progress too often to spark curiosity from the carpenters who chanced to be near the front door.

The group walked at a leisurely pace toward the house, Juliana darting swift glances at Lord Barry, trying to catch every nuance of change in his expression. The man gave away nothing of his inward feelings; his face was a mask of polite interest.

"Fine house," Uncle George commented at long last when the suspense became too much for them all.

"Indeed," Lord Barry replied in an undertone.

He walked on ahead of the others, striding up the stairs, his heels clicking on the stone floor as he crossed the portico. Inside the great entry hall he came to a halt. It was magnificent in reality. He had not been able to acquire a grasp of the immensity of the room from a mere floor plan. Even the watercolor rendering of the room had not the impact of actually seeing the place. The ceiling soared upward to high above where the plasterers, standing on the scaffolding, were at work. Lady Juliana had cautioned him regarding that scaffolding yesterday. The plasterwork looked to be coming along nicely.

"They have been in residence for a year now," Lady Juliana murmured at his side. "I truly wonder how they manage to work at that height, given the amount of wine charged to their account. Oh, dear," she exclaimed, her cheeks pinkening, "I ought not have said that."

"Quite understandable. I understand they are weaned to red wine in infancy. How much longer will they be up there?" He craned his neck to inspect the details he could see and wished he might climb the scaffolding to see it all better.

"Well," she replied in a considering way, then turned to her works supervisor. "Henry, should they finish soon?"

"I believe so. They have the central figure to complete, but the decoration around the ceiling perimeter is done, and very well, I must say."

"You see, my lord? Soon," she said with a sigh of what sounded like relief.

Edmund made no comment, but strode on ahead to the dining room. In here carpenters were at work on fitting in the two bookcases he had required be added. He wanted books throughout the house, not just in a library and rarely looked at. In his opinion a good book ought to always be available if one wished to read.

"And here," Juliana said with a gesture to an alcove in which niches had been created, "is the area for the china cabinets to be installed when finished. Father and I thought it would be nice to have your china on display when not in use. I trust you have a suitable pattern in mind? Wedgwood does a very nice design incorporating initials, with a discreet gold border."

He merely looked at her, and it gave Juliana the feeling that she had been silly and rather female in her observation, not to mention intruding where she was not wanted. She resolved to remain silent regarding any future helpful suggestions she might wish to offer.

"Actually, I ordered a set of Sèvres while in London. It will have English flowers centered on each plate and a border of celadon and gold." Edmund did not know why he so carefully explained his selection to Lady Juliana. Perhaps it might assist her in other matters regarding the dining room, but he found he was interested in her reaction to his taste.

"English again," Uncle George muttered while looking at the niches created for those china cabinets. *"Thou are not altogether a fool."*

"We could paint the walls the same celadon, if you wish, and use accents of gilt on the ceiling," Juliana said politely, ignoring her uncle's foray into Shakespeare. "And of course you will want another set of dishes for daily use." She studied her patron. Sèvres was far too expensive for common usage, even if the gentleman was as rich as reputed. "Queens Ware is lovely, and much used by the royal family."

"English, too," Uncle George chimed in from his place across the room where he now stared out of the windows.

"I shall attend to that in due course." Relenting a trifle, he added, "Perhaps a representation of my family crest would be possible."

Juliana again felt put in her place, although he had been polite in his speech. Perhaps he failed to realize that an architect did not merely design a building and halt with that. Her father, and Juliana as well, had felt it important to be concerned about all aspects of the dwelling. She had made her own sketches for furniture, china, just about everything, including color and fabrics. Whether or not she might offer them to her patron would remain to be seen.

"Juliana, what is that man doing?" Uncle George inquired.

She glanced at Lord Barry to find him absorbed in the detailing of the trim around the doors. Swiftly crossing to her uncle's side, she raised her brows in silent query.

George pointed out of the window to where a man prepared to cut into a long piece of lumber. Juliana gasped and darted from the room without another word to anyone.

"Shall we proceed, milord?" George said patiently. "It seems my niece is momentarily required elsewhere."

Edmund frowned, then joined the other men in exploring the remainder of the ground floor.

Juliana rushed out the central door and flew down the stairs and across the grounds, reaching the carpenter who had placed his saw upon the length of wood.

"Precisely what do you think you are doing, my good man?" she demanded, hands on hips.

He hiccuped and said, "Was told to cut this in one-foot pieces. Walls too short in the stables."

Juliana boldly took the saw from his unresisting hands and subtly guided him away from the spot. The man was slightly foxed—not the first time this had occurred to one of the carpenters.

"I do believe there are ample short pieces of lumber here for you to use without resorting to cutting up a long—and rather expensive—piece." She led him to a pile of lumber containing perfectly good—if short—pieces remaining from lengths that had been used in the main house and were quite usable for his purpose.

"Oh." The man was not quite so befuddled that he couldn't realize that Juliana meant him to work here and leave the other timber alone.

"Who told you to work with that good piece?" she asked, trying not to sound as annoyed as she felt. There had been entirely too many incidents of this sort. They continued to drive up the cost of the building, something she sought to avoid if at all possible.

"Fellow over there." The carpenter pointed vaguely in the direction of the main building, and Juliana sighed. It was clear to her that the culprit would be impossible to identify if all the men banded together to maintain silence. Had she not needed the lot of them, she would have fired the crew and hired others. That was impossible, for they were skilled—in spite of their fondness for ale—and had been excellent workers in the beginning when her father was still living. But Juliana felt that unless she or Henry were in constant attendance, the construction would suffer greatly.

"Try to use common sense," she murmured, hoping the man would not take silent umbrage at her words and do worse. "I should like to know why the stable walls were built too short in the first place." She felt guilty, for she should have inspected them the day before, and she had merely glanced from a distance, depending upon Henry to catch any wrong.

"Dunno," the man replied carefully. "Henry Scott looked at 'em."

Juliana murmured something, then marched away in search of Henry. She could not believe that he would undermine her work on this house. He had always given her to understand that it was as important to him as to her.

Then she wondered if this was another attempt upon the part of Sir Phineas to subvert the work on the mansion. She would not put it past him to supply strong ale to the carpenters, slipping it to them when she was not present. The men would likely seek to place the blame on Henry, hoping to divert attention from their own wrongdoing.

When she entered the house again, she was met by Lord Barry, who looked ready to explode.

"Is there something the matter, my lord?" she said in a brisk, businesslike manner.

"I would ask about the little rooms scattered here and there in the house. Henry Scott informed me that a number of water-closets are planned, that you have actually ordered the fixtures!" Lord Barry sounded as though he had not believed his ears, and he waited for her to deny this incredible assertion.

"I firmly believe the design that Joseph Bramah developed is the best at present. My father experimented and felt he had improved slightly upon the original design, and that change was included with our order. But yes, the plumbing pipes have been installed, and we merely await the fixtures. Once the painting is finished and perhaps some decoration added, they will be set in place. It is so disagreeable to seek a privy in the midst of a rainstorm or in the cold of winter. I felt certain that you would wish a modern convenience for your home." Since he had said he wished comfort, that was what she intended to give him.

"But they are not on the plans," he countered. "Someone ought to have consulted with me."

Of course he was right, she admitted to herself. "Time constraints," she replied, taking refuge in the distance that had made correspondence a long, time-consuming matter. She took a militant stance knowing that this was the first of many obstacles she had to face. If she failed at this one, she might as well hand over the reins of the building to Sir Phineas and watch the place become a Gothic pile.

Lord Barry blinked, taking a step back, no doubt because of her aggressive attack. Juliana congratulated herself on her approach. If she might win this particular battle, the remainder should follow.

"And drainage?" he queried in a faintly ominous tone.

"They drain to a point some distance from the house. It is a better system than prevails at Osterly House, where, as you must know, Lady Jersey wishes the finest of things installed." Juliana clasped her hands behind her, hoping he would not notice how nervous she was. This was not a time for vapors or weakness of any kind. It was difficult enough to discuss a subject like water-closets with a strange man without going into the matter of proper drainage—a matter that a young lady usually knew nothing about.

Steps were heard on the portico, and moments later Sir Phineas entered the vast hall, a smirk on his lean, hawkish face. He doffed his hat to Lord Barry, revealing that fringe of gray below his balding pate.

Juliana performed the introductions with grace, her anger at the nasty Sir Phineas for daring to show his face in this house causing her to forget her nervousness.

"Well, my lord, is it not as I told you? This chit of a girl has the nerve to assume the direction of the beautiful home being built for you, when you thought you had the services of a capable architect—Lord Hamilton. Surely you will wish to make some changes." He bestowed a smug look at Juliana, and she longed to kick him in the shins, or perhaps nudge him off a ledge. She *knew* he was responsible for her problems, yet she could not prove a thing against the man.

Edmund glanced at Lady Juliana and noted the tightening of her lips, her determined stance. It seemed clear to him that she had not the least liking for this intruder. And what did this old neighbor stand to gain by his action? This aspect intrigued Edmund not a little.

"And what would they be, Sir Phineas?" Edmund inquired in a dangerously quiet voice that echoed through the room.

Above them the plasterers were silent, pausing in their work. The carpenters had moved to a distant part of the building, and not a hammer could be heard. Edmund, Henry Scott, George Teynham, and Lady Juliana all stared at the newcomer until he shifted uneasily and gave a false-sounding laugh.

"Why, find yourself a truly capable architect to oversee the remainder of the work, of course—one who will add some life to the building, give you the very latest in style and design," Sir Phineas said persuasively. "I believe that I am capable of giving you a first-rate home."

"I have promised Lady Juliana that I will give her some time before I reach any decision regarding the future of the house. I have not yet inspected the building from top to bottom. Once that is accomplished, I will have a better idea what I intend to do."

At that moment several workers entered the room carrying what appeared to be a fireplace surround, extravagantly sculptured and exquisitely finished. The white marble gleamed in a shaft of sunlight before it was placed against an opening on the far side of the room.

Edmund strode across the room, making short work of the distance. Before him was the creation of one of the premier sculptors of the day. To either side of the rounded center opening an angel held what appeared to be a spear, with the handle extended upward. In the center of the piece was carved a wreath. It looked quite magnificent.

"The design comes from Thomas Hope," Lady Juliana said. She had hurried after Edmund and now stood poised at his elbow, ready to answer questions. "He has such a one at Deepdene. It is a beautiful design, perfect for this hall. A matching surround will be placed on the opposite wall." She gestured to the gaping hole on the other side of the room. "The over-mirrors will have the same rounded shape as the French-inspired mantel."

"Are all the mantels like this?" Edmund asked, while taking note that Sir Phineas was chatting rather familiarly with one of the carpenters who had just entered.

"No, most are elegantly simple, keeping with the style of each particular room," Juliana replied, which was certainly true enough. The Etruscan room would have a mantel with beautifully carved palm leaves. And the bedrooms had the very latest design that used canted sides in the fireplace opening to increase burning efficiency. She hoped he would appreciate her efforts on his behalf, but doubted it. Patrons were notoriously ungrateful.

"It will do," Lord Barry said.

What Juliana might have replied to such understated approval was never to be known, for her sister Barbara fluttered into the house. She was delicately dressed in pale pink muslin and brought the scent of roses with her. A more soberly garbed Kitty followed her.

Barbara floated across the room to join Lord Barry and the others. Kitty hung back, watching all from a careful distance.

"La, sir, I trust you do not intend to spend this glorious day cooped up in the house," Barbara cried in that beautifully cultured manner she'd developed with her mother's help. She toyed with the ribands of her exquisite bonnet and bestowed a devastatingly attractive smile on his handsome and dangerous lordship.

"I must," he said, smiling at Barbara in a way he had never looked at Juliana or anyone else since he'd arrived. That smile was quite a revelation to Juliana. She sighed slightly and shared a look of understanding with Kitty.

"Well, Mama sent me along to tell you that we are going to have a bit of entertainment to please you. Since you are staying with us, it is only proper, is it not?" There was no clue in her trill of laughter that she had carefully practiced it to achieve that lovely lilt.

"I shall be certain to return to your home in ample time, in that case. And I shan't permit myself to be detained by anyone," he added with a look at Sir Phineas.

The discussion became general after that, with Barbara charming every male in sight, especially the Italian plasterers, who clambered down for a better look at her.

Sir Phineas sidled up to Lord Barry and spoke briefly, then took himself off, after first demanding in a bantering way that he be invited to the party as well.

Juliana stared after his departing figure and frowned.

"You do not care for the gentleman?" Lord Barry queried smoothly at her side.

"To borrow one of Uncle George's favorite quotes, *His brain is as dry as the remainder biscuit after a voyage*. He fancies himself an architect, and I suppose he is one, should you like the Gothic style."

"I imagine it has merit," Lord Barry said, watching Barbara flutter about the room. She exclaimed over the new fireplace mantel, and he strode to her side to discuss it, smiling at her with a look of fond amusement that set Juliana's teeth on edge.

"There may be a way out of our troubles, Henry," Juliana said to him when he joined her off to one side. "If only his lordship likes what he sees in the rest of the house. Barbara can enchant him out of any doldrums into which he might fall. Perhaps I should have her come along? She will distract him from all those changes I made."

She exchanged a look with Henry, then turned to study her patron. She was in trouble, all right, and she feared it was not going to be a simple matter to solve.

Chapter Three

*A*ctually, the tour through the upper regions of the house went far better than Juliana had hoped, much less expected. Each time Lord Barry paused to examine a bit of some architectural detail, Barbara would offer an enchanting smile and a small comment, then draw him on to the next room or point of interest. Her laughter bubbled out—pleasing and delightful. She clearly amused his lordship, who gazed upon her with a most tolerant eye.

Juliana had never been jealous of her younger sister in the past, counting it wonderful that Barbara would easily find an excellent match when she went to London for her Season. Now Juliana gave her sister a thoughtful frown. Was it *quite* necessary for her to smile at his lordship in *quite* that way? Or must she be *quite* so engaging?

He indulged the sparkling minx with a lenient smile, as was the wont of every gentleman who encountered the second of Lady Hamilton's three daughters. Yes, Barbara would undoubtedly be a diamond of the first water when she went to London for her come-out next Season, with a highly suitable marriage to an eligible peer following.

However, Juliana felt that Lord Barry would not be the right one for her sister. There was something about the man that set pulses to racing, and whimsical Barbara would never be a match for him. For while she didn't want for sense, she was a trifle featherheaded. Most men might not give a fig about that, given a pretty bride. Juliana felt Lord Barry would find her bird-witted ways a trifle wearing.

Juliana made a rueful moue, thinking of how she had given up her Season to finish this house, afraid Sir Phineas might do great harm while she was gone. And to think the patron would never know, much less appreciate her efforts on his behalf. Well, her father had often commented on the subject of patrons, so she had been prepared. Only, the reality was more hurtful than she had expected.

Lord Barry would most likely return later full of unanswered questions. But for the time being, she and Henry had a reprieve. She could query her assistant while Lord Barry's attention was fixed on the size and arrangement of his dressing room—a neat room off his bedchamber fitted with shelves and compartments Juliana had considered very clever and his own water-closet.

"Henry, what is this about the stables?" Juliana asked in an undertone. "The walls are too short? I found a slightly foxed carpenter about to saw a long and expensive piece of lumber so the walls could be raised to a proper height. What happened? And why didn't the chap use wood from the pile of odds and ends left over during construction?"

"The carpenters claim it was all a mistake, that the plans were unclear and they had misread your notations. Since they had no problem reading the house plans, I give leave to doubt their lame excuses. I would fire them if I could. However, I need their labor and cannot easily replace them at the moment." Henry gave her a look that plainly reflected his anger at the man he felt responsible.

"I have never known such a feeling of frustration," Juliana said quietly. "I thought that all my drawings were sufficiently detailed so as to prevent precisely that sort of confusion."

"They are, indeed." Henry looked at her, understanding and sympathy in his eyes. "I would give anything to be able to force Sir Phineas to admit what he is doing, accuse him of his dastardly deeds."

"And the toad dares to request an invitation to our little party for Lord Barry," Juliana said with disgust. "I depend on you to keep a watch on him. Needless to say, I cannot trust him an inch."

"Look on it this way—you *will* be able to keep an eye on Sir Phineas while he is there," Henry offered with a grin.

"Aye, but he never does a thing on his own," she pointed out with simple logic. "He hires another to do his dirty work."

Lord Barry turned to face them, a quizzical expression on his handsome face. Juliana murmured an excuse to Henry and hurried to where Lord Barry now inspected the dressing room that led off the opposite side of the master bedchamber.

"May I answer a question for you, my lord?" she inquired in dulcet tones.

"I do not recall the dressing room for my future wife being quite this large. On the set of plans that *I* have, it is no larger than mine." He studied Juliana with a gaze that had her clasping her hands before her lest she betray her nervousness.

"I believe there was a decision to add a fixed bath in that room. I trust you have not changed your mind?" Juliana frowned at the mere thought of the time and expense involved with such a change.

Lord Barry gave her a bland look that offered not the least clue as to what might be in his mind. She continued without waiting to find out what it might be.

"However, it does seem to me that your lady wife will appreciate a generous dressing room," Juliana said persuasively. "And note that each of you will have your own sitting room beyond." She felt her cheeks warm as she doggedly continued. "And your wife's sitting room leads through to the nursery. This creates a lovely family suite."

"I trust my wife will appreciate your thoughtfulness."

She caught sight of a gleam in his eyes before he turned to inspect the intricately carved molding that had been placed above the door.

Juliana wondered if he had selected his bride yet. The way he was looking at her sister made it unlikely, but one never knew. Think of all the married men who flirted with ladies not their wives!

This thought pushed her from the master suite out into the hall. Henry followed her. Foot tapping impatiently, she waited for the others to join them. Oh, for this ordeal to be over! She had worked so hard to incorporate the very latest in design into this house. Now it seemed that her patron was steeped in tradition, wanting the old styles.

"The rest of the bedrooms are quite ordinary; he can see them another time." She glanced at the door that led to the attic stairs. "Nor shall I show him the attics."

The attics were in such disarray that little could be discerned from a casual walk-through. Juliana doubted he would understand the meaning of the layout of the partitions anyway. Few people seemed to grasp the elements of transferring the lines of a floor plan into reality. The sizes of rooms were especially baffling to most. What seemed adequate on paper usually turned out to be far too small once built. Rarely did it work the other way.

The rustle of skirts could be heard before Barbara and Lord Barry came around the corner.

"La, sir, I believe you have inspected enough for the day," Barbara teased while avoiding a pile of sawdust, revealing a fetching dimple when she beamed a smile at his lordship. "Why do we not return for a dish of tea and a stroll in my mother's rose garden? It is truly pretty this time of year."

"By all means, lovely lady," Lord Barry replied as they joined Juliana in the first-floor hallway. Then he gallantly escorted Lady Barbara down the incomplete and wood-strewn staircase with a look on his face that led Juliana to understand her reprieve was but temporary.

At the foot of this potentially elegant fixture he paused, staring at the right and left wings as they soared to the first floor. He turned to an uneasy Juliana, forbidding look on his face.

"I shall speak to you about this later—in private," he added with a glance at Henry.

"Henry has been a faithful assistant, first to my father and now to me," Juliana said with a snap. "There is nothing in this house about which he is not knowledgeable."

"But *you* have the ultimate responsibility for translating the plan into reality. It is *you* with whom I wish to speak." His words were quiet, but uttered in a manner that brooked no denial. He was the patron. He paid the bills and was to be heeded if at all possible.

"Yes, Lord Barry." She stood at the foot of the stairs, hands folded, watching as he joined her sister by the entry door. When he realized she would not be going with them, he turned and gave her that quizzical look again. "What? Do you not come with us?"

"I have work to do here, my lord. I shall see you later," Juliana replied. Much later if she could manage it. He was one to avoid if possible.

He said nothing, just studied her a few moments, then turned and left the house, listening to Barbara's chatter with every evidence of pleasure.

Outside of the house where the beginnings of the avenue had been begun, Edmund paused before joining Lady Barbara in the carriage. He gazed at his future home for some moments, studying the classical lines of the house, the elegant simplicity of it. While it seemed most acceptable, he had strong reservations about some of the innovations he suspected Lady Juliana had introduced after her father's death. That young woman had a goodly number of questions to answer later, and he would not permit the charming Lady Barbara to deflect them.

Reluctantly, he turned his back on the construction and entered the carriage. Listening to his companion's talk with half an ear, he considered his lady architect. Sir Phineas was right. Had Edmund known of the earl's death, Edmund would have demanded another qualified architect replace him. Yet, it seemed that the daughter sought—with no little determination—to complete the house. Perhaps she intended it as a monument to her father's genius. Edmund could understand such sentiment. He would most likely feel the same, given the circumstances.

What he did not know was how he would deal with the attractive young woman on a businesslike basis. Women didn't belong in business. They should marry and produce babies with proper regularity. It was deuced awkward and not a little distracting to try to be forceful, demand to know what he wished, with a delectable armful as his opponent.

What qualifications did she possess to make changes? Had she any notion what they would look like in reality? He very much doubted it. In his experience architects spent a great deal of time producing piles of contract drawings for each edifice they designed. His smile became rather feline as he considered requesting that the enticing Lady Juliana produce her little stack of such details—the staircase, for example. It seemed to him that those cantilevered stair treads were far too thin to last any length of time. He did not want a main part of his house tumbling to ruin in short order.

"We have arrived, Lord Barry," Lady Barbara said, shifting in the carriage to remind him that he ought to be attending her.

"Indeed. If you do not mind, I shall not come in with you just now. I have to discuss a small matter with my groom. I shall see you shortly in the drawing room. Thirty minutes, perhaps?" He assisted her from the vehicle, then bowed politely.

Those limpid pools of crystalline blue smiled at him, concealing any curiosity she might have had.

He watched as she gracefully walked to the house, blond curls peeping from under a saucy bonnet and her shawl draped elegantly over her shoulders. Some man might appreciate her, but not him. Nor was Lady Juliana his sort. That young woman might drive him mad with frustration, but Juliana would never lie in his bed as his wife. Then—quite unbidden—came an image of the self-possessed Lady Juliana in the stately bed he intended to purchase. She was tucked beneath linen sheets and wore a radiant expression on her face as she turned to him.

"No," he muttered to himself, causing the gardener planting some annuals to replace a few late-blooming bulbs to glance up in alarm. Edmund knew he must not think of Juliana as a woman—that way led to disaster. She must be no more than an architect in his eyes.

Indeed, he decided as he strolled around to the stables to check on a few of his things, he would discuss all matters relating to the construction of the house with his lady architect in a rational way. And, he concluded, he would *not* allow that willowy body nor the soft dark cloud of hair to distract him. Never! Now, if he could manage not to be swayed by a pair of most fetching blue eyes that brought to mind a tropical sea, he would be quite fine. They were, he admitted, disconcertingly honest eyes.

With that decision reached, although why it had to require so much debate he most likely could not have said, Edmund left the stables and returned to the drawing room without having consulted with his groom on a thing.

"My lord, we are so pleased to have you join us," Lady Hamilton said. "Do accept a cup of tea, perhaps a ratafia biscuit?" She sat poised at the tea table, seemingly bent on pleasing his every whim. Her manner was most gentle, yet Edmund found himself obeying her in an instant, for there was that thread of steel lurking within her tone. To his surprise, he found the tea most welcome. He wondered if Lady Juliana managed a cup of tea while working at his house. He also wondered as to what Lady Juliana called work.

The damask-covered armchair proved to be surprisingly comfortable. Sipping his excellent brew and listening to the amiable chatter of the two women—for Lady Katherine said nothing at all—his thoughts returned to Lady Juliana. She needed someone to look after her he decided when he took note of the elegant garb worn by the other women of the family. Why, Lady Juliana was years out of fashion, even he could tell that. He had observed the clothes in London on his way through the city, and his lady architect was by way of becoming a dowd! Pity, that.

"We have sent invitations to all our friends and neighbors to join us in a bit of festivity in your honor, my lord," Lady Hamilton said, unknowingly intruding on Edmund's reflections on the state of Juliana's dress.

"How kind," Edmund remembered to reply just in time. "I hope I may do you justice in my attire. I ordered several coats and other items while in London and pray they will be delivered in time. It is difficult to be *au courant* with fashion while off in the islands," he concluded with a smile at them all.

The youngest of the girls, Lady Katherine, had been staring at him most intently. At his last words she spoke. "What is it like on the island? Is it truly so hot and humid? And are the flowers as exotic as reputed?"

"Our Katherine, or Kitty as we call her, likes flowers, my lord," her mother explained with a confused look on her face, as though she did not quite know what to make of her youngest child when she chanced to recall her presence.

"I have read a great deal about island flowers, but I confess they seem amazing." Kitty watched him with that same flattering, steadfast look.

Edmund smiled at her eagerness and spent some time entertaining her with descriptions of all the flowers that had grown around the plantation. He remembered more than he would have believed possible, and the minutes slipped by quite unheeded with such an enthralled audience.

At last Lady Hamilton rose from her chair, gesturing to Lady Katherine that the conversation must conclude. To Edmund she said, "We offer a simple collation in the breakfast room about this time of day. Should you wish, you may join us there."

Edmund had been thinking that it had been some time since he broke his fast and welcomed the thought of food. He offered his arm to his hostess and strolled along at her side in perfect amiability to the breakfast room.

He had to admit that the young Hamilton girls were well-bred and quite charming. If he found Lady Katherine's intent regard a trifle disconcerting, it was also flattering.

Following the light repast, he explained his desire to return to the construction site.

"We quite understand, dear sir," Lady Hamilton said. "We shall expect you later."

Rather than take a carriage, Edmund strode to the stables and ordered his horse saddled. While he waited, he inspected the stables and surrounding area. It was well laid out and maintained in top condition. There could not be a shortage of funds here, for no reduction in staff or horses had occurred as far as he could see.

So why, he wondered as he swung on his horse, did Lady Juliana persist with her efforts at his house? Were he a vain man, he might be tempted to think she wished to entrap him, catch him as a husband. Considering the looks she sent his way, she would be more inclined to dump a basin of water

over his head, should he come too close to her. He cantered
along the lane, negotiating the twists and turns of the road
with absentminded skill.

Approaching the building site, he entered the partially completed avenue to catch sight of Lady Juliana and Henry, heads
together over a set of plans. As he neared, he could see the
crude table also held a stack of what appeared to be drawings.
The detailed working drawings he had wondered about earlier, perhaps?

He swung himself down, tied the reins to a tree, then
walked over to join them. Their start of surprise amused him.
Why would they *not* expect his return?

"I have a number of questions that perhaps you could answer for me—providing you have the time, of course." He
suspected his bow was a trifle mocking, but it had seemed to
him that Henry had been gazing at Lady Juliana with more
than a businesslike eye.

"I shall tend to the matter we discussed at once," Henry
said, then absented himself with a polite bow.

"You wished to discuss the stairway, as I recall," Juliana
said, promptly attacking Edmund's concern. Her troubled
gaze followed Henry until he disappeared. Then she focused
her full attention on her patron. Willing herself not to chatter
or annoy him with unnecessary explanations, she waited for
his questions to begin.

He strolled to the house, studying everything in sight. Once
inside, he paused, looking closely at the interior.

Juliana walked past her patron with a roll of plans in her
hand. At the foot of the central part of the stairs she came to a
stop, unrolled the paper, and glanced at him. She was more
than a little nervous. There was something about him that fas-
cinated her even as she was disturbed by the feelings he
aroused in her. Henry did not have this effect on her at all.

She cleared her throat, then turned to the far safer view of
the staircase as it winged upward. "As you may know, this is
the very latest in design for a staircase. The handrail is to be
mahogany—some of the very wood you sent from your plantation. The balusters will be made in cast iron, simple uprights
alternating with delicately carved panels. See, here is my . . .

er, the design." Holding out the paper for his inspection, she hoped he would concentrate on the lovely curving lines of the delicate S-shaped baluster and not what she had said.

Wordlessly, he went over to examine the central portion of the stairs, then to study the two wings that soared on either side. "It does not seem sufficiently substantial," he said at last.

"They are in accordance with the finest principles of staircase design. My father consulted the works of Batty Langley and Abraham Swan, as well as the geometrical calculations by Blondel. I assure you, Lord Barry, you and your future wife will find the stairs pleasant to use as well as to look upon. Note there are only twelve steps until the landing, and that each step is carefully calculated to be an easy ascent."

Juliana repressed the smile that longed to surface when he gave her a look that expressed his frustration. It seemed he was not quite satisfied, but did not know how to counter her explanation. She clearly knew of what she spoke; she had studied and was well informed. He was not.

"We shall see," he muttered in an ominous way.

Pleased by her success, she gained confidence and walked with him, her sheaf of plans in hand, to the next point of contention—one of the many water-closets she had ordered installed.

"Now this seems the height of nonsense," he said after inspecting the simple room with its utilitarian purpose.

"I think you will find it of interest that every home of any size and pretense is now being fitted with such conveniences. Why, I recently read of a London home that has such for the servants." With a wry expression she added, "I fear that it is not helpful here, for the country girls are terrified of such contrivances."

"The drains?" he said with the air of one who is pouncing on a vulnerable topic.

"As before, the best manuals have been consulted, the experts in the field. While there is a deal of controversy in this matter, common sense prevailed and the drains go away from the house, down a slope, and empty into a bed of gravel. I believe they will do nicely."

The look he bestowed on her was unfathomable, but Juliana was glad that she clutched the roll of plans in her hand as a sort of protection, little as it might be. She swallowed carefully, then said, "Perhaps you would wish to see the kitchen area and other estate offices?" Not waiting for an answer, she led the way.

"The butler's pantry has a small bedroom behind it and a plate room next to it, as customary. And here"—she gestured at a long, narrow room with several small windows—"is the servant's hall." She quickly walked along a passage down several steps to a connecting building not a part of the main house, yet adjoined to it by a short passage. "The kitchen. I consulted with our cook and butler to improve past designs."

The wait was agonizing while he strolled about the room in total silence. Not a word about her careful design, done after lengthy consultations with the servants.

"What is this?" he asked in a seemingly bland voice that didn't fool Juliana in the least, now that she had a better idea of his reasoning.

"The latest in stoves, my lord. Cook and I went over the newest design and selected this one, the Rumford range." Juliana pointed out how the water would always be hot in the boiler off to one side, then said, "The fire will keep the oven at an even temperature as well, yet enable the cook to use a hot plate on top. You certainly desire to have good meals, my lord," Juliana concluded in what she hoped would be a telling point. It had been her observation that a man might forgive much if he were well fed.

"And what did the butler say?"

"He advised on the best way to improve service and make the various jobs easier. Happy servants are better servants, he says."

"Pity he will not be here," Lord Barry murmured as he strolled along the hall, pausing to inquire what each room might be with merely a lift of his brow.

Juliana decided that she was coming to detest this lordly man, and that feeling was heightened by the peculiar stirrings within her whenever he drew close to her. The scent of his linens and shaving lotion was alien to her. Certainly Henry never smelled of anything but soap or sweat.

Somewhat nervous at the direction of her thoughts, she fluttered into speech. "The scullery is there with a pantry and larder close by," she pointed out. "The washhouse, laundry, and brew house are located along in this area as well, just beyond the house, but low enough so that they do not interfere with the views from the principal rooms."

"Practical and most likely as done in most homes in England and probably abroad."

Juliana felt the blush creeping over her cheeks and prayed he would not take note of it. She had been presumptuous and a little condescending, quite forgetting he was her patron and a world traveler, to boot.

"The water for the baths is heated down here so it may be piped up whenever you desire. And, since your wife will have a fixed bath in her dressing room, I wondered if you might enjoy a shower bath in yours?" Juliana said with great daring. Bathing was not a topic of conversation between a gentleman and a lady. However, she was not a lady, she was an architect, and as such she had jolly well forget the vapors. The plumbing was in place, so she was quite safe in making the suggestion. She had planned ahead for such.

"A shower bath? Novel idea," he said with arched brows and a touch of sarcasm. "Cleanliness appears to have become of great interest while I have been gone. I suppose it would be nice—if not too costly—although what my father would have said would singe the ears."

She turned back to the central house, not waiting to see if he followed her. Even if she had not heard his boots on the stone floor, she could sense him directly behind her.

"And now to the upper regions," he said with an anticipatory air.

Juliana half expected to see him rubbing his hands together in expectation of a good battle. Instead, he held his roll of plans like a weapon.

"You carry a roll of papers with you, too. The plans, of course," he said in a deceptively smooth manner.

"Plans and detailed drawings," she replied, pleased he had asked what she had wished.

"Lighting," he murmured as he inspected his set of plans after they had reached the entry hall once again.

"Do you wish a staircase standard with an oil lamp at the base of each staircase?" Juliana asked, backing away from him to stand by the bottom of the steps. "I believe they would offer excellent light and a finishing touch to the staircase as well."

He rolled up his set of plans and crossed to tower above her, making her realize how powerful he was—how vulnerable she felt facing him. Why had the carpenters disappeared? Not even the Italian plasterers were around. She was utterly alone with her patron, who was a very handsome gentleman, to be sure.

"How much of this house is your design? And just where did you receive any training? Precisely why did you not turn to a competent architect after your father died?" He reached out with his free hand to clasp her upper arm, drawing her closer to him.

Juliana sought the words even as she gazed into those eyes of deepest blue, darker than she had seen before. Her lips trembled, and she wanted to say something that would please him, but what would give him peace of mind? "Your lordship . . ." she began.

His eyes had assumed a hungry, yearning look that set off an alarm in her mind.

"Indeed." He bent his head, seeming intent upon kissing her, and she found it impossible to move, or speak, or deny him anything he wished. She took a tiny step forward, to her dismay.

"Hello, is anyone about?"

Chapter Four

"**R**osamund!" Juliana whispered. How vexing, yet how providential, to be interrupted at such a point! Juliana had the presence of mind to step away swiftly from the intimidating figure who had hovered over her in such a threatening manner. Surely it was an overactive imagination that made her think he was about to kiss her. Gentlemen simply did not do that sort of thing—particularly her patron. Quite impossible. It was more likely that he intended to berate her.

She walked toward the entry with every evidence of pleasure on her face as she greeted the most unwelcome Lady Rosamund Purcell, the local reigning beauty. She was only a trifle prettier than Barbara, but as the daughter of a marquess, she took precedence over the daughter of an earl, and in addition was reputed to have considerable wealth. The slender and most elegant blonde, whose hazel eyes seemed a trifle predatory at the moment, smiled in return.

"We were just studying the staircase. Lord Barry wished to see the detailed sketches of the balusters and railing." Juliana noted that Uncle George had come along with the beauty, so she must have found her quarry—for word of the eligible peer would have spread like fire—absent when she called at Beechwood Hall and decided to hunt him down. Bless Uncle George for insisting he escort her, for Juliana had no doubt that was the way it happened. Uncle George was far better company than Lady Rosamund's plump and somewhat overbearing mother.

"My, you constantly amaze me, dear Lady Juliana. I would never be able to read a set of house plans, much less draw objects as you do. It seems such a *masculine* thing to do," Lady Rosamund purred. She twirled her furled, tulip-shaped parasol around, knowing full well how feminine she looked in her rosebud-sprigged muslin and a bonnet with roses arranged artfully beneath the brim.

The latest word in style, she made Juliana feel the veriest dowd. Although, she reminded herself, it would never do to come to the building site attired in delicate muslins and fragile bonnets. Still, she'd had little time for such things, nor had her mother lavished the interest on Juliana that had fallen on the more rewarding and obedient Barbara.

George wandered across the entry hall, glancing at Juliana, then at Lord Barry. When he drew close to his lordship he darted a glance at Lady Rosamund and muttered, "'She speaks, yet she says nothing'."

Edmund looked at George Teynham, then back at the newcomer. She was most likely a featherbrain, as so many beautiful women seemed to be in England. It was as though someone had decreed that no woman should reveal any sign of intelligence. Why did every woman he met persist in giving him the impression that she lived only to reflect his words back to him? He was certain there must be intelligent women who also looked charming. He had yet to find one—other than his architect, and she did not count.

He turned away to study the drawing he held in his hand, ostensibly trying to visualize the final results. But inwardly he berated himself for almost losing his head. What had happened to him? For a few moments his wits had gone begging, and he had actually been tempted to kiss that female architect! What was there about her that enticed him so? She was attractive, but so was Lady Barbara, and he had scarcely paid her more than polite attention. No more than he would give to Lady Rosamund Purcell. Yet Lady Juliana—

"You find the design acceptable?" George inquired at Edmund's elbow, peering over his arm at the sheaf of drawings, the one for the baluster being topmost.

"What? Oh, indeed. Quite so." Edmund collected himself and put the peculiar sensation he'd felt toward Lady Juliana in the back of his mind to be examined later.

"Juliana spent hours over that particular drawing, trying to achieve the right touch that would complement the rest of the entry. Her father died before he reached the minor details, you see. She has attempted to fulfill his vision for the finished house." George smiled fondly at his niece with undisguised pride.

"It must have been difficult for her," Edmund said with another look at Lady Juliana while she coaxed her guest across the entry, then off toward the first of the public rooms. The murmur of feminine chatter mingled with the distant hammering of the carpenters. Not far away could be heard the impact of something heavy being moved about.

"She is not one to shirk her duty, nor would she wish another to step in, changing everything her father had conceived," George cautioned. "I think this house must be the highlight of her father's achievements. It will be magnificent when it is completed, you know," George concluded with a gesture. "Why do we not join the young women?"

Edmund willingly walked along with his host—at least he supposed Mr. Teynham served as host if his sister was the hostess.

"Have you gone over the plans for your private rooms yet?" Mr. Teynham inquired. "Juliana made a few changes there, as she may have explained. Personally, I like the notion of a shower bath rather than a fixed tub. Let the women soak if they please. I like the idea of brisk flow of water over me come morning. I know a few old-fashioned folks would balk at the notion—think a fellow ought to bathe once a season, if then. Not very progressive, those. Do you not think it clever how she designed the water system? All the best families have hot and cold running water now, you know. Quite the latest novelty. Juliana is very much the new-fashioned woman."

"Hot and cold running water? I have not heard of such a thing—nor has Lady Juliana informed me of it. It must be costly," Edmund muttered. He wondered what else his lady architect had not told him and how the bills might escalate. This house was costing more than he expected.

"Well, if you have an engine to pump the water to the cistern on top of that pretty little water house out there"—

George gestured vaguely off to the distance—"you might as well have it heated for the baths, not to mention the kitchen, once it comes to the house. Dashed practical, I say," he concluded. Then with a glance out of the window, he added, "There's to be a fountain out in front of the house that promises to be right pretty, and I believe she planned a buffet in the dining room where running water could be used to rinse hands, faces, or glasses. Dashed clever girl, my niece. Has thought of everything." George put his hands behind him and strolled ahead, leaving Edmund in deep thought.

Not only was Lady Juliana clever, she had providentially neglected to inform him of these novelties she'd added to his house. Hot and cold running water, a buffet, a shower bath, not to mention a fountain in front of the house—like some blasted monument? What would be next? He fairly steamed with annoyance.

All he had wished for was a solid English house on his own English land in which he might install a suitable English wife to raise his English children. He desired a conformable wife with traditional taste. It seemed he'd acquired a lady architect determined to give him every folderol and fancy whether he wanted it or not! Novelties! Well, he would see about that. And he would not allow this pretty miss to wind him around her finger.

He slowly followed George Teynham into the dining room to come to a halt at the sight of a vast piece of marble being eased into place by means of several stout workmen. When finished, they picked up a wooden platform with rollers on the underside, then quickly left the room after darting anxious looks at Lady Juliana and himself.

"La, my lord," Lady Rosamund simpered as they stood before the newly installed buffet. "I vow you will be the envy of everyone around. I saw one not unlike this in a recent issue of *Ackermann's Repository*," she said, referring to that arbiter of Regency taste.

Edmund surveyed the monstrosity with hostile eyes. It was huge, of white marble veined with pink and gray. Above it a shell design in the same marble was set into the wall over a series of shelves—for glassware, he supposed. The large basin in the center of the buffet was flanked by small niches to either side—separate pieces of the identical marble. He presumed the hot and cold water would spout from the mouths of the fancy and quite unidentifiable animal heads of shining brass. He hated the thing on sight.

"Indeed? I was unaware that the buffet as you call this, would be so desirable." He produced his quizzing glass so to inspect it more closely.

Juliana looked at her patron with dismay. His voice fairly froze one. She had not expected him to balk at something so mundane as a mere buffet. How would he accept the marble shower bath she had planned for his dressing room? She hoped to expand on the subject and prepare him for the results. This discouraging inspection of the buffet did not bode well for the next innovation she intended to introduce. Or the others to follow, for that matter.

"My lady," said an anxious workman who had hesitantly entered from the side hall. His face was bland, but his hat was being twisted into even worse shape than it had appeared before. Something was obviously wrong, and Lord Barry *would* have to be present when it arose.

"Excuse me. Lady Rosamund, perhaps you might be so kind as to entertain Lord Barry while I see to this matter?"

It was really unnecessary to ask such a silly question. Lady Rosamund eagerly grasped the chance to have the eligible peer at her disposal without the slightest competition—not that *she* considered Juliana in that light.

Juliana hurried along with the workman until they reached the rear entrance of the mansion. She did not have to ask what the problem was. There before her was what would have been the magnificent slab of marble that she intended for Lord Barry's shower bath. It was in pieces, totally fractured. Drat and blast!

"We was real careful, milady. Real careful. I s'pect the marble busted on the way here. Someone had dumped a load of rocks at the turn of the road coming here, and we didn't notice it in time to avoid 'em."

"There is nothing for it but to order another piece from the quarry. Thank goodness it is not too distant. Take the order over at once and demand they cushion the new slab better than they did this one," Juliana said with a faint snap in her voice. "Make certain they send along the other two sections I ordered as well. May as well have them all at once."

"Trouble?" Uncle George said quietly at her shoulder.

"As you can see, the marble shattered. I had hoped to have it installed right away. I need it to finish off the plumbing. The pipes are in, but the marble must come next. How can I demonstrate how wonderful it will be when all I have to show him are metal pipes sticking out of the wall," she wailed.

"Steady on, girl," her uncle said, patting her on the shoulder.

"I wish . . ." Juliana began, then stopped. Of course she wished her father was still alive. But wishing did no good. She had to cope the best she could, and she'd not admit to failure. She squared her shoulders and turned to face the house again. "Best to say nothing about this if you can avoid it."

"Upon my honor as a Teynham," her uncle said quietly as he guided her along the hallway and back to where they could hear voices. Rosamund's laughter trilled through the empty rooms with a hint of forced gaiety.

"Shall we return to Beechwood, my lord?" Juliana inquired of Lord Barry, ignoring Lady Rosamund for the moment. She had come unbidden and could jolly well fall in with whatever plans were made for the patron's benefit.

"I do not wish to leave here just now. Although," he said with a melting smile at Lady Rosamund, "it is a great temptation to forgo my inspection and turn my attention to pleasure. Forgive me, my lady, my house awaits me." Edmund took Lady Rosamund's exquisitely gloved hand and placed the most delicate of kisses somewhere above it.

"I shall look forward to your company, Lord Barry. Until then." Lady Rosamund swept a lovely curtsy, then accepted Uncle George's arm for her return to the carriage. The scent of lavender lingered in the air after she had left.

Juliana awaited Lord Barry's attention with no little trepidation. She suspected she would soon learn what manner of temper the man possessed.

"The buffet," he began.

"I do hope you like it," she said with enthusiasm. "It was the last piece my father designed and has so many clever innovations in it. I vow it will become quite a point of interest for your guests. As Lady Rosamund said, it is quite the latest design—an improvement on the old."

Edmund looked down at her innocently beaming face and found he simply could not tell her that he hated the dratted thing and that he wished it was in any house but his own. Now, if the architect had been a man, he could have expressed himself forcefully, and the blasted buffet would have been sent on its way to buffet heaven.

"I see," he replied lamely. The buffet stayed. He was defeated. He could admit it, but not without a sigh. "Well, regarding this shower bath you mentioned earlier. I was under the impression *I* was to choose if I wished one." That rankled him, and how he longed to berate her with a tongue blistering. But she was a lady, more's the pity.

"Come with me, and I will attempt to give you an idea as to how it will be," Juliana said with eagerness. "I think that once I explain it to you, it will seem most excellent." She omitted the news of the fractured piece of marble. With any luck at all the replacement ought to be here in a couple of weeks—perhaps sooner.

Lord Barry followed her up the stairs, avoiding the chunks of wood and piles of sawdust in his path. When they reached his dressing room, she walked over to where pipes emerged from the plaster wall at slightly above his height. She had not pointed them out when they were here before, hoping to see the marble in place first. Now there was no reprieve.

"Now stand right here," she commanded nicely, positioning him where he would stand beneath the flow of water. Never mind that she found the touch of his arm beneath her fingers to be shocking, yet enticing. "See, the water will come out from this pipe, and below it will be cocks with which you may regulate the flow." She touched one of the two smaller pipes that protruded slightly from the wall. "Think of it—no more footmen carting buckets of water up and down the stairs whenever you wish to cleanse yourself. It is far more practical and agreeable. Believe me, one day every house in England will have such convenience."

They were alone again, and Edmund found he had to concentrate on the matter at hand to avoid having his thoughts regarding his lady architect stray into dangerous paths. "I had not intended anything of the sort. It was not in the original plans that I approved," he chided.

"I realize that, and had you been closer to hand I would have consulted you regarding it. But I did feel that as a progressive *younger* man, you would wish the very latest in improvements." She gave him a wide-eyed look, continuing, "You have no idea how difficult it has been to design things for the house when you have been so far away. I have longed to talk with you about ever so many matters. A discussion on paper is not the most satisfactory sort." She clasped her hands before her in an almost supplicating way.

"True." It almost undid Edmund to see her so humble. Though he suspected she was anything but when away from him. Was he being outwitted by a woman?

"My father was an excellent architect, but I fear he did not welcome the latest in innovations for the home. I felt certain that you appreciate the value of these progressive features, how they will enhance your home and add to your greater comfort," she said with such persuasion that she nearly convinced him. "I could not imagine that one such as yourself, who has traveled widely and met such a vast number of interesting people, would be provincial in taste."

"However," he said when he remembered a few things, "that is the very reason I hired your father to design my house. You see—in case you do not realize it—I *wanted* a traditional house, one steeped in the very essence of England."

"Oh." It was clear that she had not considered such a possibility. "You mean a house without running water, or an efficient kitchen range, or shower baths, or the latest in buffets?"

She looked so very small and vulnerable that all of a sudden Edmund felt like a monster for telling her what it was that he as the patron and bill-payer wanted. He knew a desire to brush the sad frown from her forehead and see those rosy lips curve in a smile.

"Well, we shall see," was all he could offer at first, then he continued with words that seemed to come from elsewhere. "You may proceed with the shower bath. I would not want to be considered provincial." It seemed to cheer her, for her face lit from within and she marched over to the window, beckoning him to follow her.

"There is the water house." She pointed to a small, rather pretty little building on the side of the hill beyond. "The water tower is some distance above and beyond it. The Savery engine will bring up the water, which will be stored in the cistern over the water house, then brought here on demand, to be heated if necessary. Once the marble is installed for the shower bath, the rest of the marble will be put down on the floor and walls. This will be a very elegant, yet practical room. I feel sure you will find it most pleasurable."

He glanced about him, observing that the ceiling, which he had not noticed before, was of an elegant ornamental design that would be gilded. Another expense. "It seems that I will have any number of devices installed in this house," he said wryly. "The new stove, the shower bath and, oh, yes, the fixed bathing tub in my future wife's dressing room. I had better take another look at that as well."

Juliana hurried after him as he strode from his dressing room, through the main bedchamber, and into the other dressing room. Someone had uncovered the marble bath that had been installed some time before. It gleamed in all its white and pink splendor, creating a focal point of the room.

He came to an abrupt halt, and Juliana nearly ran into him. "Excuse me, my lord," she murmured.

"And well you might," he quietly replied. "I suppose," he added in a voice rife with sarcasm, "that all I need to do is to show a prospective bride through this room and she will fall at my feet in raptures."

Juliana suspected that, given his handsome face and wealth, he would scarcely need to do anything of the kind, but she dare not voice such an outrageous thought.

"Well, it is not so very unusual. Marble floor and walls— like yours. The tub is fine marble as well, and I do think that white with rose veining is especially nice for a lady. She will have every facility at her fingertips."

"Indeed," he murmured. "The lap of luxury."

Somehow, Juliana felt that was not a compliment nor even a desirable reaction. "The niches on the wall will hold pretty sculptures or perhaps some flowers if she desires."

All Edmund could think when he looked about him was the cost of all the extras. He would have to exhort the overseers on his plantations to greater production, he could see that.

"The floor will be cold in winter," he said, hoping to make some sort of point with his architect.

"Rugs exist, my lord," she replied with a sage nod.

"You seem to think of everything." What would be the next thing she had thought of? he wondered. What radical device would be foisted upon him by this scheming woman?

Yet, when he looked at her, he saw a guileless young woman, eager to please. It seemed that all she desired was to enhance her father's design and create the most comfortable house possible. Comfort? Well, he supposed that hot and cold running water would do that.

"And, as to the winter cold, perhaps it will not be so very bad. I have designed a heating system," she revealed eagerly. "There is a steam engine. It will heat the air . . ." She faltered and words ceased, no doubt at the expression on his face.

"I believe I enjoy comfort as much as the next Englishman, but is this not a trifle bizarre?" he demanded, hands on hips and visibly controlling his temper to a slow simmer. "What nonsense is this—a heating system. I never heard of such a thing."

"The Romans first designed them, the hypocaust, you know. And the Earl of Shelburne has steam heating in his library at Bowood, my lord. Put it in back in the 1790s," Juliana demurely answered. "It is not precisely new, you see. Hot-air heating has been used much in Ireland, particularly at Packenham Hall. We would not wish to be thought behind the Irish, would we?" A twinkling smile peeped at him, her lips curving slightly in amusement.

"Heaven forbid!" Edmund gave her a dark look, then strode from the room. If he remained with her in the privacy and quiet of the dressing room, he could not be responsible for his actions. Far from wishing to kiss the chit, he knew a desire to strangle her. Or at the very least, he amended, to shake some sense into her. Shower baths, hot and cold running water, and now hot-air heating! He doubted if there could be any more shocks in store for him, then reconsidered. He suddenly suspected that this was only the beginning and shuddered at the thought of what was to come. Radical! Revolutionary!

Yet, he admitted, he did like his comfort. Any man would appreciate a soothing shower of warm water. He did not hold with the current trend in cold bathing. Too great of a shock to the system besides being dashed uncomfortable.

Comfort. Hmm. Perhaps he might try to look at all these novelties from a different angle?

"Lord Barry, is anything amiss? Do you wish to return to Beechwood Hall? It is growing late, and you must long for refreshment."

Edmund slowly turned around to face the woman who had rapidly become his nemesis. She stood not far away, a worried expression on her face. Good. He had her concerned and intended to keep her that way—on her toes. He had to gain the upper hand somehow.

"We shall return to the hall for now. But I warn you, I take a dim view of all these radical novelties you have introduced into the original plans. Tomorrow I want you to show me the details of the so-called heating system. I suspect it is not only complicated and difficult to operate, but dashed expensive."

With that pithy comment, Lord Barry marched from the room and down the stairs, kicking the blocks of wood out of his way as he went.

Juliana clutched her shawl about her as she quietly slipped down the stairs behind him. It seemed her worst fears had been realized—her patron was a provincial who was opposed to progress. Although he *did* seem attracted to comfort. Then another thought burst upon Juliana that brought a pleased grin. If Lord Barry hated progress and change from the traditional, he would utterly loathe the Gothic that Sir Phineas wished to foist upon him. Pity that, she concluded, feeling rather smug that Sir Phineas would scheme for naught.

The ride home was completed in total silence. Juliana worried that if she said anything, it might irritate him even more than he was already.

Edmund fumed in his corner of the carriage while wondering how best to extricate himself from this mess. If only he could walk away from the house and all its commitments, but he had advanced a great deal of money. He would have been better off to return to England and buy something standing, then modify if necessary. He must not lose his investment. Somehow he would have to reach some sort of understanding with the woman who sat in blessed silence at his side.

The carriage drew up before the house, and Edmund stepped down, then offered his hand to assist Lady Juliana. She gazed at him with a most puzzled expression, one that almost amused him.

"You find me a conundrum, Lady Juliana?"

"Indeed, sir, I do." She gathered her skirts and began to walk up the steps to the front door. Before entering the huge entry door, she paused and turned to study him. "I would have wagered any amount that you would be sharp and progressive, eager for innovations, anxious for the very latest in design. Instead, I find you like an old woman, loath to so much as consider change and clinging to the past." She forgot for the moment that he had capitulated on the shower bath. "One never knows about people, does one?"

With that she marched into the house and up the stairs without hesitation nor a glance to see how her words might have hit him.

I *will* strangle her, Edmund thought, ignoring how the butler might interpret the fierce expression on his face.

"Ah, Lord Barry," Lady Hamilton cried as she came into the entry room, obviously from the regions of the kitchen and on her way to her own rooms above. "I trust your visit to the construction site was edifying?"

"Indeed, my lady. Highly edifying. Illuminating, in fact," he added with wry understatement. He joined her in the walk up the stairs.

"Oh, good, for I know how much this all means to Juliana. Although, mind you, I cannot understand why she will not allow Sir Phineas to assume direction. Do you know he does the most fascinating designs in the Gothic style? Although I cannot appreciate the gargoyles he likes so much. Repulsive creatures, do you not think?"

Without awaiting an answer, she waved at him, then disappeared down the hall in the direction of her rooms.

Gothic style? Gargoyles? Perhaps his plight could be worse, he mused as he entered the room assigned to him.

The party on the morrow might be most interesting should he convince Sir Phineas to put forth his ideas on architecture. Perhaps Lady Juliana had reason to detest Sir Phineas. How would she react were Edmund to pit Sir Phineas and his Gothic leanings against her radical notions? At least Gothic was traditional in design, was it not? Or had it altered like everything else Edmund had held to be sacred?

Puzzled and disconcerted, Edmund allowed his valet to assist him in changing for dinner. If nothing else, life in the coming days and weeks would not be dull. Far from it.

Chapter Five

~

"Oh, Kitty, I have never felt so frustrated in my entire life. That man is absolutely dreadful!" Juliana plumped herself down on the window seat to survey her younger sister, her face quite reflecting her feelings.

"I thought him most polite," Kitty objected mildly.

"Polite! Well, allow me to put you straight on that matter. I will agree that when a pretty woman is around Lord Barry, he is all charm and smooth words and devastating smiles. But when it comes to the wonderful innovations I worked so hard to have installed in his house, well! He is an utter monster. However"—a delighted gleam entered her eyes—"I did convince him that a shower bath would be quite acceptable. And he appeared to accept my drawing for the balusters. I do not think he cares overmuch for the buffet that Papa designed, sad to say. I expect it overwhelmed him." She exchanged a rueful look with her sister.

"I should like to see this buffet. Does it truly have hot and cold running water? The footman will be able to rinse the glasses? Oh, any woman would be pleased with that. Think how it will save on the amount of crystal necessary!" Kitty clapped her hands with delight, then added, "Mama would like it, I feel quite sure."

"Lord Barry does not, not in the least. I could tell, even if he was excruciatingly polite about it."

"I must say, I thought better of the man," Kitty said thoughtfully, subsiding in the window seat close to her sister, watching her face carefully.

"I just know I shall have a battle with him over the matter of the hot-air heating I intend to have completed in a week or two. He does not realize that things are so far along," she confessed with a guilty grimace. "I never dreamed that he would not be pleased to have a warm house in the winter. The pipes are all in place. They must be tested and then connected to the boiler—and I confess I do not understand quite how it all works, but Henry has assured me that he does and will take care of the matter for me. Dear Henry—what would I do without him?"

Kitty studied her sister's face, then said, "You think of Henry as another brother, do you not?"

"Of course," Juliana said simply in a most matter-of-fact way. "Why, he has run tame around here since I can remember. It was Henry who gave me my first drawing lessons. I should think he is dear to us all. With a bit more training he could assume Papa's place as architect. Pity he cannot train in France, as did Papa."

"I believe Rome is the place to go now," Kitty offered.

"Lord Barry wonders what training *I* have had. It is difficult to explain all those years of working at Papa's side, executing drawings for him, accompanying him to various sites. I absorbed every word he said, studied every change in his designs from my earliest days."

"Mama was not best pleased that he took you with him," Kitty reminded. "She felt it highly improper for a young girl to be tramping through houses under construction."

"Poor Mama," Juliana said, looking down at her serviceable muslin that was torn near the hem and sported a spot of paint on one sleeve. "She would have me sit on a cushion and tat lace or flutter over the roses as she does. That sort of life would bore me to tears."

"Do you suppose Lord Barry feels as Mama does? That it is improper for you to be working on his house? Perhaps if Henry spent more time with his lordship, he would be more accepting of all these innovations you propose."

"I see what you mean," Juliana said in a considering way. She rose and brushed down her skirt. "I shall think on it. In the meanwhile I had best change into something more feminine. I suppose Lady Rosamund is to join us for dinner and the evening?"

"And her parents. I confess that Lady Titchfield is frightfully imposing. I scarce dare speak a word when she is
around. I am glad to be as mute as a fish at dinner."

Juliana paused by the door, smiling at Kitty. "At least you
do not have to wonder what *she* says. Her voice booms over
the room above all others."

Kitty giggled and left the window seat to dress for the
evening, feeling more resigned to the company. "I shall wear
blue tonight," she announced. "Rosamund is certain to wear
her rosebuds."

"Perhaps I shall wear my peach silk. It will clash with her
rose, and she will be furious." Juliana winked, then slipped
down the hall to her room, hoping that none of the family
would see her in her dirt.

She did not wear her peach, of course. She was tempted,
but far too well-mannered to be so rude to a guest. Instead,
she donned a simple willow green gown of gossamer satin
that fell in delicate folds about her slim form. There was a
touch of blond lace at the neck, and the sleeves were slashed
to reveal cream satin underneath. It was a becoming gown,
one her mother had bestowed on her when she decided it
would not do for Barbara.

Like her missed London Season, the dress had rankled at
first, then was accepted as being better than nothing. Some
day Juliana fully intended to visit a good mantuamaker. She
would order an entire wardrobe and charge it to the estate.
Since she received no direct payment for her efforts on Lord
Barry's house, she felt something was due her.

Unfortunately, upon entering the drawing room, she found
she was ahead of the others. All, that is, but for his lordship.
"Good evening, Lord Barry," she said with a faint curtsy in
his direction. She almost smiled at his reaction and could not
resist adding, "Did I clean up well?"

He gave her a thunderous look. "Good evening." Obviously
he intended to ignore her outrageous remark, which was probably just as well.

"I gather a few of your London togs have arrived?" She had
noticed his beautifully tailored corbeau coat and biscuit pantaloons the moment she saw him. Drat the man, he certainly

was a treat for the eyes. His stance reminded her of the Grecian statues in that book of etchings in the library. He was quite classical. And that thought brought a blush to her cheeks, for those statues were frightfully unclothed.

"Indeed," he admitted. "It will take time to become adjusted to the change in fashion."

She thought a moment, then it dawned on her. "Pantaloons. Ah, how practical they look."

"I suppose *you* would have women wearing them as well." He strolled over to stand at her side, rather intimidating yet not at all as he had been by the staircase at his house.

A gleeful light entered her eyes, and she nodded demurely. "I should think it would be most practical, my lord. Think of the fabric saved, and how comfortable they would be. We would be able to climb ladders and steps with little worry. I should think they would be warmer in winter as well—for you must know that silks and muslins are dreadfully chilly. Yes, I believe it would be a wonderful idea." She permitted her shawl to slide down from her shoulders to reveal her bare neck and low-cut bodice. She had noticed that Henry frequently stared at her when she wore this gown.

"Do not think of it," Edmund cautioned, having a little better notion now of how she went about things. "Restrain your radical ideas for once." He observed the expanse of creamy skin and swelling bosom that would delight the eyes of any red-blooded male. Egad, the chit *was* fetching. Pity she held such revolutionary notions.

"But I frequently restrain my so-called radical ideas. Why, were I to have my way, I would be free to—"

Her words were cut off, to his apparent annoyance, when Barbara entered the room in a drift of ice blue sarcenet with a white gauze overskirt. She looked like a princess at the very least. Mama had permitted her darling girl to wear a simple sapphire pendant on a gold chain. It totally eclipsed the necklet of pearls that Juliana was allowed.

His annoyance fled fast enough. He advanced upon Barbara with all his consummate charm.

"La, sir, how fine you look this evening. I vow that Weston must have had the making of that coat. 'Tis nothing that would come from a country tailor." Barbara glided to his side and smiled at him. Usually when she did this, it left her target utterly speechless.

"Lady Barbara," he said smoothly, taking her hand lightly in his, "you are most elegant this evening. It is so pleasant to return to England and all the charming English beauties."

Juliana had wondered if Lord Barry would avoid the usual stunned reaction of a gentleman when exposed to Barbara in her prime. He had, and she could forgive him a great deal for being above Barbara's wiles. He had turned his compliment into a general one. How neatly he avoided her snare. Evidently he wished to look the current crop of beauties over before rushing into matrimony and his English bride. She wished him luck. He'd need it.

Lady Hamilton entered the room shortly, followed by the Marquess of Titchfield and Lady Titchfield with their daughter, Lady Rosamund Purcell. Juliana knew that they fully expected their precious Rosamund to capture the hand of a duke at the very least or perhaps a marquess. Lord Barry, as a mere viscount, was somewhat beneath their consideration. However, there was always the matter of his wealth. Juliana had observed that money quite often compensated for a lot of things. And, as well, available dukes were a bit thin on the ground just now.

Lady Titchfield boomed her good evening to one and all, looking down her most imposing nose at Lord Barry with the attitude of one who is inspecting a possible purchase.

"Lady Titchfield, Lord Titchfield," Lord Barry said in his most polished manner, "charming to meet some of my new neighbors, for I feel it will not be long before I am able to reside in my new home." This remark was made with a glance at Juliana.

"True," she agreed. "All that remains is to complete the details."

"My, what a clever girl," Lady Titchfield blared forth. "How fortunate one of your children was able to step in and take over when your husband went aloft," she concluded with a pat on Lady Hamilton's arm. "It is a pity that so many men do not appreciate a clever woman. I suppose they find them too masculine." It was clear that in her eyes any woman who was clever had intruded on male territory.

Edmund frowned a trifle, then drawled, "Far better a clever woman than one who is without any wit at all." He wasn't sure why he had come to Lady Juliana's aid. He hadn't liked the way she was treated; to have snide remarks made about her capabilities irked him. He might not appreciate all she did for him, but he well knew the value of her knowledge—even if he chose to pretend otherwise.

Sir Phineas entered at that point with his eldest son, Peregrine, in tow, followed by the charming and fashionably gowned Lady Cowell, widow of Sir Jonas, and Lord and Lady Plunket. The baron was a thin, angular man, whereas his lady wife was a dumpling, beaming smiles at all and immediately chatting with Juliana in the most friendly fashion. Algernon Plunket was right behind them, eyeing the London elegance sported by Lord Barry with envious eyes. Kitty slipped into the room like a soft gray shadow.

At some point Henry Scott had drifted into the room, remaining in the background. Edmund noted that Henry kept his gaze mostly fastened on Juliana. Precisely what was the relationship between those two? She appeared to treat him with casual affection, relying upon him for support. However, it seemed to Edmund that Henry felt different.

They all went in to dinner in strict precedence: George Teynham, as host for his widowed sister, escorted the marchioness while Lady Hamilton accepted the arm of Lord Titchfield. Lord Barry smiled at Lady Rosamund, who accepted his attention as her due. Juliana gratefully joined the genial Lord Plunket. Unfortunately, Barbara had to be paired with Sir Phineas and his smug grin. Algernon politely did honors for Kitty—looking fine in her simple blue gown, while Peregrine Forsythe offered his arm to Lady Plunket. Henry escorted Lady Cowell with a gracious smile and comfortable conversation. Everyone liked the baronet's young widow, and she was everywhere invited. If Lady Hamilton hoped to encourage a friendship between Henry and Lady Cowell, the lady appeared most willing.

The dinner was much as Juliana had anticipated. Lady Titchfield dominated the conversation by sheer volume. Her comments on the food were such as must please any hostess. As long as she contained her remarks to menus she had known and food she had enjoyed, all was well. Juliana could forgive much as long as Lady Titchfield left her alone, not making sly little digs at Juliana's lack of a London Season and her *masculine* interest in building.

Once the ladies withdrew from the table, Juliana found herself led to the pianoforte by her mother and quietly urged to play something lively.

Lively, it was. A rondel was followed by a country air that melded into another such tune. Lady Titchfield tapped her toe for a bit, then launched into the latest gossip with Lady Cowell and their hostess.

Lady Rosamund stood by the harp, as though contemplating whether or not she ought to volunteer her talent for the evening's entertainment.

Lady Plunket chatted comfortably with Barbara, leading her over to where Juliana obediently played. "I know you have a pretty voice. Do sing for us, Lady Barbara," Lady Plunket begged. Kitty trailed along, watching silently.

Since Barbara was not loath to perform when she suspected the men would be soon joining them, she quickly agreed. The sisters briefly discussed possible songs, then settled on one about a country girl and her sailor lad. This was followed by a French tune, for Barbara did rather well at those.

Algernon Plunket was the first of the men to enter the drawing room, pausing at the sight of Lady Barbara warbling by the pianoforte. He was closely followed by Peregrine, Henry, and Lord Barry. They also seemed to appreciate the vision of grace and charm who also managed to sing rather well. Uncle George, Sir Phineas, and Lord Plunket, along with Lord Titchfield, chose to dawdle in the dining room, perhaps because Titchfield liked to escape his wife's company whenever possible.

The younger men clustered about the pianoforte, praising Barbara for her lovely songs. Edmund noted that the others totally ignored Juliana and discovered that it annoyed him.

She played extremely well, and she certainly accompanied her sister's charming, if erratic, renditions with spirit and understanding. It could not be easy to anticipate just when Lady Barbara would choose to hurry or to hold a note longer than its due.

"You play well, Lady Juliana," Edmund offered in a break during all the chatter.

"Juliana does everything well," Henry said quietly.

"In a somewhat *masculine* manner, you must admit," Lady Rosamund inserted. An angelic smile on her rosebud mouth, she looked exceedingly feminine in her rose sarcenet trimmed lavishly with blond lace and tiny rosebuds.

"Is capability and practicality totally a *masculine* trait, Lady Rosamund?" Edmund inquired lazily. "I have met any number of fribbles who are capable only of gazing in their looking glasses—unable to manage the smallest estate, and men who are frivolous—looking only to their own amusement. It seems to me that any woman should require both those assets—in order to run a household, for example."

He was pleased to see her toss him a vexed look. He suspected that the daughter of the quiet marquess was accustomed to being the leader of the younger group in this area. She did not like having a stranger—even if he was an eligible viscount and had wealth to boot—cross her. It was also becoming clear that Lady Rosamund enjoyed making not so subtle slurs at Lady Juliana.

Juliana rose from the stool upon which she had uneasily perched the last few minutes and said, "Shall we join in a game?"

Kitty had heard Edmund's defense of her sister. She bestowed a grateful smile in his direction, then said, "We might do charades."

"You always want to do charades—merely because you do not choose to hear what we say when playing other games," Lady Rosamund said with a flicker of annoyance.

"But you do so charmingly at charades, Lady Rosamund," Algernon inserted, quickly seconded by Peregrine Forsythe. Both Algernon and Peregrine knew they hadn't the slightest chance of winning the hand of the neighborhood beauty. This did not prevent them from worshiping at her feet.

Rosamund was not proof against these pleasing words. While she might not consider either of the young men as a husband, they were all very well to practice upon.

Edmund graciously joined the group, even if he felt ages older than the Forsythe and Plunket heirs. These were to be his neighbors. Joining with them in a bit of entertainment would be useful in understanding them as well as acquiring a better acquaintanceship with them. Both were important. He'd not want to be thought high in the instep by any of them.

Kitty ignored the cattish remark by Lady Rosamund, quite accustomed, it seemed, to her little digs. Kitty quickly suggested that they play hidden proverbs instead of the despised charades. Rosamund was elected to be the first victim.

While she was out of the room, Peregrine offered, "A rose by any other name would smell as sweet."

"Capital!" Algernon chimed in, not surprisingly in view of his admiration of the fair Rosamund.

Edmund watched as the victim returned and tried to guess the proverb. Each word was stressed in turn in a sentence that was supposedly to give a clue. Rosamund pretended not to be clever, but she reached the correct resolution in an amazingly short time.

When it came to be Edmund's turn, he was amused to find his proverb turned out to be "A barking dog never bites." He was not certain what that meant, but suspected—from the twinkle in Lady Juliana's eyes—that she had suggested it.

When Juliana gracefully accepted her turn, Edmund was quick to offer, "Every man is the architect of his own fortune."

"You read Sallust?" Peregrine inquired in surprise.

"I came across the quote somewhere," Edmund said by way of denial. "It is a common enough saying."

"True." It was clear that Edmund had slid a trifle in the estimation of the evidently bookish Peregrine.

"*Every* person will be pleased when you guess this one," Kitty said once Juliana had returned.

"Each *man* is supreme in his chosen task," Rosamund followed, smug she could stress the masculine with Juliana.

"It *is* always time to be prudent," Henry inserted with a frowning look at Lady Rosamund.

"*The* rose is known for its thorns," Barbara said, looking annoyed with Rosamund, not for the first time.

"The fate of an *architect* is the strangest of all. How often he expends his whole soul, his whole heart and passion, to produce buildings into which he may never enter," Edmund said, offering far more than he ought for the solution of the proverb. But the words had come to him, something he had read somewhere, sometime, and he thought them fitting.

Juliana quickly completed the proverb and then suggested they try a bit of dancing, begging Lady Plunket to play for them as she often did. Juliana's pale face did not reveal what she thought of Lord Barry's clue.

Henry quickly came to solicit Juliana's hand. "That seemed a trifle harsh, I must say."

"He certainly made it evident that I shall not be on his guest list, at any rate," she concluded with a faint bitterness to her tone. "But you must admit, he has the right to select his guests, and quite often the feelings between architect and patron become strained by the completion of the structure. I have heard of situations in which they refuse to speak at all."

This did not appear to distress Henry in the least.

Well, Juliana thought as she accepted Henry's hand, once she completed the house, she would take herself off to southern England—after allowing herself the luxury of that trip to the mantuamaker. She would patronize the premier mantuamaker of London. She had earned it.

Lady Plunket played a tune for a country dance, a sprightly thing that kept the younger people bobbing and spinning about. Juliana skipped down the line with Henry, carefully averting her gaze from Lord Barry. It seemed to her that he was more than a little displeased with her, and she did not look forward to their next clash, for clash it would be.

Rosamund was clearly in her element. At first Algernon and Peregrine had vied for her hand. Lord Barry had swept them aside and claimed right to partner her by way of being the guest of honor this evening. Lady Rosamund decreed he had the right of it.

Lady Barbara soothed Algernon's sensibilities with her pretty charm. It must be admitted that with her sweet nature Lady Barbara was the prettier of the two girls—if one considered behavior as well as looks when measuring.

Kitty welcomed Peregrine as a partner, cheerfully ignoring his lack of enthusiasm. It had been understood by the family that Kitty would not be given a Season; they felt that her difficulty in hearing would be too great a detriment to overcome. Kitty had accepted this, but she dearly loved music and dancing and grasped any chance that came her way to participate in such. Soon her ability brought a smile to Peregrine's face.

A second dance brought about a change of partners. Juliana found her hand being removed from Henry's light clasp and taken by none other than Lord Barry. Henry looked as though he would gladly punch Lord Barry in the nose for his remark about architects. Juliana gave him a warning look, then went off with his lordship.

"I have the oddest feeling that your Henry does not care overmuch for me," Edmund murmured most discreetly to his partner in a barely heard aside.

Juliana did not quibble at Henry being called hers, for he belonged to the family, albeit the extended family. "Pay no attention, my lord," she admonished when she faced Lord Barry in the opening steps. "*Henry* is inclined to be a trifle protective of me." It would be clear that she quite understood his little quote on architects not entering the buildings they complete.

"Scott looks gloomy, as though worried about something." If he caught her meaning, he gave no sign.

"He has many responsibilities, and he elects to be very conscientious in his duties." They were separated in the pattern of the dance, and Juliana had no further opportunity of defending Henry, not that he truly needed it. Henry was quite capable of defending himself if needs be.

Lady Titchfield watched the dancers with a sharp gaze, checking to see who solicited her daughter's hand and noting that Lord Barry had cut the others out for the first dance. A viscount was not to be considered as a husband for her precious girl, even one who had wealth. But she was pleased to see that Rosamund had first claim on the highest-ranking of the younger gentlemen, as was only proper.

When the dance concluded, her ladyship rose from the chair where she had dominated the conversation. "It is time that we return home, my dear."

Lady Rosamund, who was ever conscious of what her mother had taught her regarding her position in life, quickly assented.

That effectively broke up the party. Lady Cowell would share a carriage with the Plunkets. She glanced coyly at the widowed Sir Phineas, then accepted with wry resignation.

Sir Phineas had no opportunity to put forth his notions regarding the Gothic style—much to his annoyance. Thus Lord Barry and those around him were spared a lecture on the advancements in the development of the fashionable Gothic.

"Next time, Rosamund can play the harp for you," Lady Titchfield boomed, to her daughter's slight discomfiture. "She is doing better every day and bodes well to becoming most gifted at it."

Lord Titchfield said nothing, but from the expression on his face, Juliana guessed that he was not in total agreement with his wife.

When all were departed and Lady Hamilton had gone upstairs, chatting with Barbara about the evening, Juliana strolled back into the drawing room with Henry.

"Where is his elegant lordship?" Henry quietly demanded.

"I suppose he has gone to his rooms. I care not about him at the moment. I should like very much to know what is troubling you. All evening you have looked as though you were on your way to your own hanging. What is it, my friend?" Juliana picked up a fan that Barbara had left behind and toyed with it while she waited for Henry to offer an explanation for his behavior.

"You will not like what I say," he prophesied.

"Do not spare me the bad news, for I can see that something has happened."

"Just before I left the house, I found out that the carpenters are not returning tomorrow."

Juliana groped for a chair, then slowly sank down in a complete daze. "All of them?"

"Most," Henry replied. "I shan't even ask you to guess who has hired them away by offering more generous wages to work at his building site."

"Sir Phineas. I wondered about that smirk he wore this evening when he took Barbara into dinner. That man!" she fumed. "How does he have the effrontery to attend a dinner at our home after doing such a dastardly thing? I do not understand."

"If you were a man, he would not dare commit such acts. Because you are a woman, anything is possible in his eyes. You rate no consideration." Henry took one of Juliana's hands in his and offered comfort. "Cheer up; I shall be off come morning to find other carpenters—even if I have to go as far as Oxford."

"His lordship will not like this," Juliana said, exchanging a worried look with Henry.

"How charming," Lord Barry drawled from the doorway, a book in his hand testifying to a pause in the library. "Who will not like this? Your brother, Lady Juliana?"

With a worried glance at Henry, Juliana freed her hand, then rose to face her patron. "There has been some bad news, my lord."

His expression altered immediately, and he crossed the room to join them. "Regarding the house?"

Juliana nodded silently.

Henry spoke, his words bitter. "The carpenters have been lured away by another builder who has offered them higher wages."

"What shall you do?"

There was not a flicker of reaction on Lord Barry's face, which surprised Juliana greatly. She had fully expected him to issue a cutting diatribe on the folly of having a woman in charge of anything like a building.

"Come first light I shall be off to a hiring hall. I may have to go as far as Oxford to find good carpenters."

"And most likely offer a higher wage?"

"Possibly." Henry gave his lordship a steady look.

"I suppose you will attempt to blame this on Sir Phineas." Lord Barry's gaze was icy, his voice utter frost.

"I have no need." Juliana thought she was prepared for anything, but she found herself ill-prepared for his look of disdain. "I know."

Lord Barry gazed at her for a moment, then turned to leave the room, pausing at the door to look back at the pair, who stared after him. "I expect my house to be completed with all possible speed. See that it is done, no matter what is necessary! Oh, and Scott, I suggest you confine yourself to business. I very much doubt if Lady Juliana's brother would appreciate your sentiments toward her."

Chapter Six

"Kitty, that man is not a monster; he is far worse than that," Juliana declared upon entering her sister's room. Advancing across the room to where her sister was curled up in her bed, apparently reluctant to rise and greet the day, Juliana declared, "He defends me at one moment, then out of the blue accuses me of dalliance with Henry, of all people. It is the outside of enough, I tell you. Saying that my brother would not appreciate Henry's sentiments toward me! The very idea. I scarce slept a wink last night for thinking about how unjust his accusations are." Juliana paced back and forth beyond the end of the bed, looking utterly furious. To accuse her of such a thing with her cousin, who seemed more like her brother was not only an insult, it was ridiculous.

"Goodness! What happened after I went upstairs?" Kitty sat up in bed, wrapping her arms about her knees while watching her eldest sister with shrewd eyes.

"Henry revealed that the carpenters have been lured away by another builder and other men must be found. He will most likely have to go as far as Oxford before he can hire sufficiently skilled carpenters. Someday I shall do violence to Sir Phineas, I swear it, for we know he is responsible for this. It is *his* project that took *our* men."

"Oh, dear," Kitty murmured, quite sympathetic.

"Then, Lord Barry—in a perfectly odious manner—came into the room and near as like accused Henry of . . . oh, I can scarce believe he truly said that. He said, in a rather snide way, that he supposed I would place the blame for this on Sir Phineas—which, of course, I will. We know the men have gone to work on that Gothic monstrosity Sir Phineas is in charge of building several miles from here." Juliana sank down on the edge of the bed, looking vastly discouraged at the turn of events.

"I was chatting with Peregrine last evening while the rest of you were talking. He is very concerned about his father. He thinks that Sir Phineas is using materials that are not all they ought to be. And from what else he said, I suspect Sir Phineas has been charging for higher quality goods and pocketing the difference."

"Peregrine has always been taken with you," Juliana said musingly. "It is not surprising he confides such dangerous information to your sympathetic ears."

Kitty blushed and said, "Well, he never is annoyed if I do not hear precisely what he says, and he does try to speak slowly and clearly. I appreciate that."

"Best not repeat what he said to anyone else. I may not like Sir Phineas, but I would not repeat unproved tales about the man."

"Your problem is that you are too fair and honest." Kitty grinned at the face her sister made at that remark.

"I do not see that as a problem," Juliana said with a laugh, then added, "besides, what about Lord Barry? I fear he would not agree with you. I have concealed a number of things from him, remember?"

"All for good cause. And you must admit, it was to prevent that pernicious Sir Phineas from purloining your building."

"Pernicious Sir Phineas purloining? You must have been dipping into a Minerva novel," Juliana teased, again laughing at Kitty. "Oh, you are good for me, for you can always make me laugh."

"That is what Peregrine says, too," Kitty confessed with another blush. "I like to see the happier side of things."

"He is so serious, so very unlike his father, that it is hard to see they are related." Juliana watched her sister carefully to see what reaction this remark might bring.

"He adores Rosamund, you know. She is like a shining star for him." Kitty exchanged a look with Juliana that revealed how aware she was of this and more.

"And just as unattainable. Never fear, I am a great believer that things work out for the best if we give them half a chance." Juliana rose from where she had perched on the bed and strolled to the window.

"So what will you do regarding the carpenters?"

"Hope that Henry will find a goodly crew of men. He will probably find them in Oxford. It means housing the men when they arrive here. I had best consult with Dalston; he is knowledgeable about so many things." She turned and walked to the door. There, she paused and looked back at her sister. "You are all right this morning, are you not? No ailments, or anything amiss?"

"Nothing you need worry about," Kitty said quietly.

"I see," Juliana said, leaving the room and thoughtfully walking down the stairs in her hunt for Dalston the butler who had served the family for so many years. Poor Kitty, to be attracted to one who was so beneath her. Yet what did that truly matter? If she was not to have a Season in London and their mother refused to allow Kitty to go about in Society, how was she to meet a man who would suit her—and their mother's exalted sense of what was proper? Of course, to have the man you liked infatuated with the local reigning beauty was a bit of a problem.

"Lady Juliana, may I have a word with you?" Dalston said in an unusually quiet voice, stepping forward from near the bottom of the stairs where it appeared he had been waiting for her.

"Of course. I was just coming to seek you out, for I need your help," she said in an equally soft undertone.

"Mr. Henry said you would be needing housing for some carpenters, my lady," Dalston said, casting a wary eye around the hallway.

"Precisely. How like Henry to forewarn you. Have you anything in mind, for that is what I wished to discuss with you." She drew him along down the hall into the morning room, where they would not be disturbed or overheard.

"There is a building that has been used in the past when needed for extra harvesting help or other men your father used from time to time. With a bit of work, I venture to say it could be made most habitable. I doubt the men will bring their families along." He stood most correctly at Juliana's side, hesitantly offering his help, yet not being the least officious. It was something she had always liked in the elderly man, his precise balance of attitude.

"Splendid. That appears to be just the thing. When Smithers returns, pass along that request from me, will you? I imagine I will be long gone by then." She shared a look with the butler, for they were both well aware how Smithers, the estate manager, tended to dawdle in the morning. However, he knew his job well and compensated for his late start in the day by working twice as fast once there.

The butler murmured his assurances and left the room, leaving the door open behind him.

"So there you are," Lord Barry said, strolling into the morning room without so much as a by-your-leave.

"Indeed, sir." Juliana clasped her hands behind her, unwilling that he see how nervous he made her. She gave him a look of dislike, then dropped her gaze, wishing to appear demure. "Is there anything I might do for you?"

"Yes. Join me on a ride to my house. I still have questions that remain unanswered. Your works supervisor, the esteemed Scott, left very early this morning."

"I trust he did not disturb you?" Juliana flashed a curious look at his lordship. Why had *he* risen so early?

"I was unable to sleep," he said as though in reply to her unasked question. "I noted that he rode out at an early hour after pausing here a few moments."

"He had a message to leave for me regarding the carpenters," she reluctantly revealed.

"Housing, I expect." He remained by the door, looking at Juliana expectantly. "Shall we go? You are dressed for a ride, I see."

Juliana had hoped to have a brisk canter before attacking the problems of the day. That apparently was not to be.

She passed him, compelled to brush against him as she went through the narrow door into the hall. Drat the man, his very proximity gave her nervous palpitations. What an excellent thing it was that he couldn't know it! Or perhaps he did and deliberately set out to disconcert her.

Beauty was waiting along with Lord Barry's horse, Firefly. Once mounted, Juliana led the way from the stables, heading in the general direction of Lord Barry's home.

The morning was exceptionally lovely. Juliana suspected that the day would be most tiresome, given Lord Barry's attitude toward her. Why shouldn't she enjoy a tearing ride— even if it was a short one? With an impish glance at his lofty lordship, she nudged Beauty, who needed no additional urging. In moments Juliana, seated securely on Beauty, was flying across the fields. She glanced back to see that Lord Barry followed right behind her. She had to give him full marks for swift response.

They dashed across the Hamilton lands until they reached the boundary that defined Lord Barry's property. The fences needed mending and the fields had a ragged look to them. Yet it was lovely land, good soil, with an excellent prospect from the high ground. She detected a look of satisfaction on his face when she glanced over at him. If only that gratification would remain with him for a time, long enough to cast a glow on what was going on in the house.

When she reined in before the building site, she was pink with pleasure and unable to refrain from a broad smile. No matter what followed, she'd had a bit of joy this day. Not even Sir Phineas could snatch this from her.

She slid from her mount and faced his lordship, her sparkling eyes having not a little mischief in them. "That will dismiss any fidgets," she said.

"Are you given to fidgets?" Edmund inquired of the girl who faced him quite fearlessly. Any other woman he could think of would have been trembling with apprehension for doing such a bird-witted thing.

"Not really," she replied with a tilt of her chin.

"That was not well done of you," he began. He fully intended to give her a piece of his mind.

"I know," she admitted. "It was simply too beautiful to plod along at a sedate pace. Come—confess, did you not enjoy the race over the fields?"

She had him there, for he had enjoyed the run, especially across his own land. He could see that it needed work, and the challenge that faced him made him long to be settled in his home instead of a mere visitor.

"I would have my home completed so I might ride my lands at will," he stated.

The light went out in her eyes, and she turned away to hand over her horse to a young fellow who had come dashing to assist her. Edmund observed, not for the first time, how the men all jumped to do her bidding. He could see from the look in their eyes that they admired her—perhaps more than admired her. She seemed quite unconscious of the emotions she stirred.

"Thank you, Bert. Are there any workers around at all?" She knew the carpenters were gone, but sure Sir Phineas had not managed to hire everyone away.

"The pipe fitters are here, and the painter-decorators are busy inside. Best be on your guard, milady, they be a messy sort." He took Beauty and Firefly, intending to lead them off to a spot of grass and trees nearby.

Lady Juliana graciously—if somewhat absently—acknowledged the information, then made her way to the house. Edmund followed her closely, for he had seen that expression on her face before. She was about to try to cozen him into something. He could tell by that evasive shift of her eyes, that tilt to her chin. She would not wrap him around her pretty finger. He might have yielded on the matter of the shower bath, but only because he became convinced of the practicality. The same could be said regarding the hot and cold running water.

As he had admitted to himself, he liked his creature comforts. But he strongly resented having a woman best him in an argument. And it seemed to him that Lady Juliana managed to do that more than he liked.

Juliana cautiously stepped over a pile of lumber that had been stacked just outside the entrance to the building, then marched along to the rear of the house where she suspected the pipe fitters would be at work. The confrontation over the shower bath had been settled yesterday. The matter of hot-air heating had not. As to the hot and cold running water, he had seemed bemused by it, perhaps a trifle annoyed at not having been consulted over it, but did not appear to deny it. The final test would come today.

"Lord Barry, it is as well you were not here when the house was nothing but a carcase, before the floors were laid, the lath and plastering work done. Now you have a far better notion of how the finished place will look." She gestured to the walls that had acquired a coat of primer, the first coloring of the plaster. Pausing by what was to be the breakfast room, she added, "This room is to have India paper on the walls in a cheerful green and white print."

"I do not recall approving India paper for any walls," Lord Barry said, returning to his familiar ominous tone of voice, one that she was coming to recognize all too well.

"All the best houses have India paper in some of the rooms," she argued. "The hand-painting is charming, and the Oriental designs lend themselves to traditional furniture extremely well, you know." That ought to please him, as old-fashioned he seemed to be in his tastes.

He halted, touching her arm lightly. Juliana turned to face him, willing herself to be reasonable and calm.

"I was unaware that your duties extended to decorating the house." He wore that superior look again, the one with raised brows and a cool mien. How Juliana disliked it.

She gave him an exceedingly cautious look. "It is customary for the architect to design, not only the building, but the interior scheme, furniture, and in some instances, to work on the garden plans."

"That is something I want to set in motion as soon as possible. Grass, and a great deal of it," he concluded with a sweep of his arm. "But as to the other, what assurance do I have that I will like your ideas? Will they also be revolutionary—the latest thing?"

"Indeed, I hope not," she denied, even as guilt nudged the back of her mind regarding the Etruscan room. He'd probably hate it, no matter how exquisite it proved to be. And then there was the Chinese dairy as well. One of these days she would have to admit to the existence of the place when he checked over the outbuildings.

"Where did you order the paper?" he said, quite out of the blue.

"The finest is Robson Hale and Company. They do—"

"All the best houses," he concluded with a wry grimace. "Is that your criteria? That the article or whatever must also be found in the best houses?"

"It does settle a goodly number of arguments," she replied, that impish gleam returning to her eyes for a few moments.

"I believe we were going to consult with the pipe fitters," he prompted. "I hear noises."

Something crashed with a loud bang, and Juliana jumped. Her nerves were not strong today. She blamed all her troubles on the man at her side—at least the nerve-related ones. All else could be laid at the feet of Sir Phineas, who sought to undermine her authority by any means he could. Between the two men it would be small wonder if she didn't develop palpitations!

She led the way again, skirting a bucket of paint and a ladder with ease. This was her element—the smell of wood and plaster, paint and all the other associated odors that came with building. She especially loved the smell of freshly cut lumber.

"G'day, milady," the older of the pipe fitters said, doffing his cap. "We have about finished installing the boiler. All else is 'bout ready."

"Lovely," Juliana said, not quite comprehending all that had been done or had yet to be accomplished. Henry had promised to handle Lord Barry regarding this matter of the hot-air heating, and now he was gone. Another complication that could be laid at the feet of Sir Phineas.

"Milady," said a man wearing the garb of a painter-decorator. "If I might have your ear for a few minutes?"

"Excuse me, Lord Barry, there is something that needs my attention. Perhaps you could discuss the matter of the heating with this gentleman?" She gestured to the pipe fitter, who looked dumbfounded at the very idea of explaining anything to a peer of the realm.

"Indeed. At least I might receive some straight answers." He bestowed that raised-brow, somewhat supercilious look on her again, and she hoped that the pipe fitter would be able to satisfy all those questions.

Juliana tossed a pleading look at the pipe fitter, then followed the painter-decorator down the hall, up the stairs, and along to where the Etruscan room had been planned.

Stepping inside, Juliana drew in a delighted breath. It was utterly magnificent—even if half completed.

"I cannot see a problem. I think this is utterly lovely."

"Thank you, milady." The man relaxed a trifle. "I wished to know where the torchères are to be placed, for I can work the design so it will appear to include them."

Juliana surveyed the room, then consulted her set of plans. "Here," she said to the man who now peered over her shoulder. "I intend to place them here on this east wall." The door opened, and one of the workmen stuck his head inside, disappeared, then in short order came in again, this time as the first of two carrying the Etruscan fireplace mantel.

"Oh, I am pleased," Juliana said with delight. Now if Lord Barry would agree, she could face anything else.

The men set the large piece of marble into place, inching it back and forth before fixing it to the wall. The painter-decorator studied it, then gave it his nod of approval. He went back to work, leaving Juliana free to go.

Hearing steps in the hall, she scurried around the door and along to the central area where the stairs were located.

"Lord Barry! Did the pipe fitter satisfy your queries?" Juliana advanced on his lordship, willing herself not to look back at the Etruscan room, and hoping that the workmen would not make too much noise. One thing about painters, they were usually quiet.

"Indeed," he said absently, "and I suspect the thing will actually work as he claims, oddly enough." He looked down the hall to the room from whence the pounding came and raised his brows in silent questions.

Juliana decided she hated that look. "Installing a fireplace mantel. The painter is busy in there as well. It is a messy room at the moment. I expect you would rather see it when they are done and gone. Come with me to see the India paper that has come for your future wife's bedchamber?" As Juliana uttered these last words, a blush crept across her cheeks, annoying her greatly.

"You are taking a surprising amount of interest in my future wife," he said with a wry note in his voice.

"It is part of the duty of an architect to try to please every person who must live in a house. Since you have not chosen your wife, I can only guess at what she might like."

"You like it, then?"

"Indeed, I do," Juliana replied with enthusiasm.

She found the rolls of paper that had been carefully placed in a fabric sack. Pulling one forth, she unrolled it and gasped in dismay. Puce and lime green flowers splashed across an orange background. It was quite hideous.

"And you *like* this paper? Lady Juliana, if this is a sample of your taste, I should prefer to hire a specialist to do the house," Lord Barry said firmly, without thought of tact or diplomacy in the least.

"No! That is, I have never seen this pattern before! There has been a mistake, I tell you. How could this happen!" Juliana took one last look at the loathsome paper and swiftly rolled it up, stuffing it into the bag before examining the remaining rolls.

"Well?"

"They are all the same. I will have to return them. I have never heard of a problem with orders to Robson Hale before. Why, they do paperhanging to the Prince of Wales!" she checked the paperwork, then slumped against the wall, thinking furiously.

Lord Barry reached over to pull the invoice from her unresisting hands. "This is not the same design?"

"Not in the least—wrong number. Your India paper was paper-napped!" She smiled wryly at her attempt at humor.

"Do not tell me you ascribe *this* to Sir Phineas; I'll not believe it," his lordship said with a scornful look at Juliana.

"I'd never say anything of the sort—to you," she added under her breath.

"Well now, there seems to be a problem," Uncle George said in greeting, only to see Juliana in the doldrums.

"Uncle George," she said with relief, knowing her uncle would sympathize with her. "Would you believe that the order of India paper from Robson Hale is the wrong pattern?" She pulled out the first roll, exposing it so her uncle could see how vastly unlike the original this was.

"Goodness me!" he exclaimed. "I believe that must have been printed by someone who had not the least taste."

"The invoice indicates the correct pattern was shipped, not this. Robson Hale is not given to making errors. I believe this dreadful paper was substituted for the one I ordered."

"You think someone waylaid the parcel and made the exchange?"

"She called it paper-napping," Lord Barry drawled, his expression indicating how little he thought of the notion.

"One may smile and smile and be a villain," her dear uncle said with a knowing look. "I believe the man we have in mind is about to pay us a visit, for I noticed his carriage coming this way just before I entered the house. Hide your February face, my dear. Do not allow him to know all we suspect."

"I cannot believe what I hear," Lord Barry began.

"Then keep quiet," George retorted quietly as the echo of footsteps on the stairs drew nearer.

"The tartness of his face sours ripe grapes," Juliana murmured just as Sir Phineas strolled into the room.

"What wind blew you hither?" Uncle George said, using one of his many favorite quotes from the bard.

"Well, well, is there a problem?" Sir Phineas asked, his lean face lighting up with a devious look that might pass for a smile. He managed to ignore George's greeting.

"Why should you think so?" Juliana said with what she hoped was an innocent gaze.

"Discussion here of all places?" He looked about the room, then turned his rascally gaze back to Juliana. "Place is oddly quiet today."

"We were not pleased with the carpenters who had been working here, so we let them go," she said with a cool stare at the interloper. "Stupid mistakes are costly and untenable, would you not agree, Sir Phineas? As well, I feared that one of them would drink too much—for they seemed to like their ale more and more as the days went on—and kill himself through sheer carelessness. I hope they perform better for their next employer—poor man. I do not envy him," Juliana concluded sweetly.

Sir Phineas gave her a narrow look. "I thought you were satisfied with their work."

"At first, perhaps," she admitted. "But they developed a problem with reading a plan that I could not tolerate." She did not reveal the matter of the too-short stable walls, not wanting to give Sir Phineas the satisfaction of knowing how much trouble he had caused, nor did she want Lord Barry to hear of the matter, either. He had quite enough on his plate for the moment.

"Hello, where is everyone?" Within minutes Barbara appeared, followed by Lady Rosamund. Both girls were dressed in delicate sprigged muslin and looked like flowers from a summer garden.

Juliana turned aside from the sight of her lovely neighbor simpering at Lord Barry.

"We have the most famous idea," Barbara said with a delightful laugh. It had the effect of cascading water on a hot day. She fluttered a pretty fan, one of her collection. She always carried one with her wherever she went.

"Lady Hamilton has graciously consented to allow us to have a ball," Lady Rosamund said, slightly breathless from the exertion of climbing the stairs.

"And we are to have the pleasure of the planning of it," Barbara cried with glee.

"I trust I shall be invited," Sir Phineas said.

"Oh, of course," Barbara said with no enthusiasm whatsoever. However, she was proper in her regard for their neighbor, in spite of his insinuating ways.

"And I trust Peregrine will attend as well," Juliana added, knowing that it would please Kitty.

"I doubt if anyone will wish to miss the entertainment of the season," Uncle George said, giving Sir Phineas a look that should have curdled his blood.

"Summer is so often dull here in the country. Nothing but crops growing, and gardens needing tending, berries picking, all that sort of thing," Barbara said artlessly, although if she had ever picked a berry or tended a garden, Juliana didn't know of it.

"Indeed," Lord Barry said, offering his arms to both girls to escort them to the ground floor. "Why do we not go outside? I would seek your opinion of the garden I plan."

Since both girls detested the smell of paint, they leaped at the opportunity to leave. As well, they thought the idea of putting a stamp of approval on any plan the viscount nurtured would be an excellent notion.

Once alone with the man, Juliana faced Sir Phineas, permitting the loathing she felt for him to be revealed in her face. "I wonder, do you know about a shipment of India paper from London? Oddly enough, it appears to have gone astray." Juliana crossed her fingers behind her back and added, "The courier who brought my order also had one for you, Sir Phineas. I believe I shall take this one over to where you build and check yours—if you do not mind? It is possible the lad did not read well and confused the two."

"Now, see here," he blustered.

"Cut line, Phineas," Uncle George said, his voice sharp and cold. Turning to Juliana he added, "I'll carry this package for you. You are done here?"

"For the moment. Join me, Sir Phineas?" she commanded, not trusting the man for one second. She shuddered to think what he might do if left alone, considering his macabre sense of humor. "We will ride to your construction immediately." She guessed he would not have bothered to destroy her order as yet. At least she hoped it would still be around. From the unhappy look on his face, she supposed she guessed rightly.

The trio marched from the house, ignoring Lord Barry and the girls where they laughed and chattered about gardens and views.

Uncle George and Juliana mounted their horses, then left Sir Phineas in the dust as they galloped off in the direction of his building site. They would beat him, and with cunning, would find the correct paper before he could prevent it.

Juliana smiled as she thought of the look of frustration and anger that had settled on his face. Then she sobered as she considered how Lord Barry had taken to Barbara and Lady Rosamund when they arrived. Never had he looked at Juliana in that manner. And, she confessed, she was greatly attracted to the man—when he wasn't criticizing her. It seemed her attraction was as doomed as Kitty's.

Chapter Seven

 uliana slid down from Beauty just as George Teynham tethered his mount to a post. He glanced at Juliana as they half ran to the Gothic manor house under construction.

"I vow, it is the most overornamented monstrosity in the country, if not the world," Juliana muttered, looking up at the design Sir Phineas had created.

"Hurry, Sir Phineas cannot be seen as yet, but we do not know just where the India paper might be. It may take us some time to find where he has concealed it." George motioned her to precede him into the house.

Juliana nodded and ran lightly up the stone steps to the front entrance. Once inside, she glanced about for help when she chanced to espy Peregrine studying the plans for the house.

"Peregrine! Where might I find a parcel of India paper that was misdirected here in gross error?" She glanced at her uncle, who produced the package that held the puce, lime, and orange print wallpaper that had been brought to Lord Barry's home. Peregrine flinched when he saw the colors, then exchanged a look with Juliana that revealed a great deal.

"This is what we received, and as Robson Hale rarely makes an error, we suspected that perhaps the two parcels were switched?" Juliana said tactfully, not wanting to place Peregrine in the position where he felt he had to defend his conniving father. "Is there one here, perchance?"

Peregrine gave Juliana a grim look, then walked across to one of the workmen. They spoke briefly. Peregrine exited the entry room, reappearing in short order with a parcel that looked much the same as the one George Teynham held.

"Perhaps this is the one you seek?" Peregrine said, offering the parcel to Juliana.

She tore open the wrapper to uncover the first of the rolls of India paper inside and breathed a sigh of relief. "Oh, thank goodness. We will not have to reorder after all. This is the pattern I selected from London." She gave the delicate pink brocade design a fond look, then smiled at Peregrine. "I am much obliged to you, sir."

She turned to leave the house to find Sir Phineas advancing upon them, a fierce scowl on his unlovely face.

"How dare you abscond with material I ordered from London! If you have a problem with delivery, perhaps you need a competent man in charge of construction." He gave Juliana a scathing look, transferring his fulminating gaze to George and the parcel in his arms.

Juliana was dismayed to see Lord Barry immediately behind Sir Phineas. How he had managed to arrive so quickly puzzled her—when last seen he was absorbed in the description of his garden-to-be with Barbara and Lady Rosamund.

"He will lie, sir, with such volubility that you would think the truth were a fool," George muttered in an aside that must have been heard by both Sir Phineas and Lord Barry.

Peregrine surveyed all with a watchful gaze. He edged closer to Juliana, still holding the puce, lime, and orange print wallpaper he'd accepted from George Teynham.

"*This* is the India paper I ordered some months ago from Robson Hale, Sir Phineas," Juliana declared, tilting her chin in a defiant manner. "It matches the fabric ordered for a chaise longue. I find it difficult to believe that you also ordered this same design as I and not what is in the other package." Juliana gestured to the large parcel in her uncle's arms. "Mine would not be at all the thing to have with Gothic."

"What if I did order the same paper?" he said with a cunning smile. "Simply because a house is Gothic on the exterior does not mean the interior *necessarily* follows suit. It is my paper. Put it down, George." He bestowed a sneering look on Juliana's uncle that was full of derision.

"I think not," George calmly replied. "Juliana, show Lord Barry and Peregrine the paperwork you brought along. The

correct number of rolls are here. Can *you* produce an invoice
that has the proper information, Sir Phineas?"

"I, er, do not have such paperwork here," Sir Phineas sputtered. "I leave such details at home in my library."

"Then we shall lay claim to this India paper until you can
prove to our satisfaction that it is indeed yours, instead of
Lord Barry's. Good day, Sir Phineas, Peregrine." George motioned to Juliana to go ahead of him.

They left the house, carefully minding their steps over the
piles of sawdust and bits of lumber, George hanging on to the
parcel with grim determination.

"You were a trifle hard on the old man," Lord Barry said at
Juliana's side, having caught up with her.

"However did you manage to arrive here so quickly, my
lord?" Juliana said, pausing beside Beauty while awaiting her
answer. "And no, we were not hard on that scheming old fool.
He is as considerate as a stone."

"I decided to follow you and find out what was involved. I
am glad I did."

Juliana did not wish to hear him tell her that he thought her
full of nonsense. She accepted his assistance onto her saddle,
then gathered the reins in her gloved hands. "I suspect our discussion could wait until later. I must return to the house and
instruct the painter-decorator about this paper." She glanced
at the Gothic pile under construction and smiled wryly. "I intend to have that paper hung on short order. Let's see Sir
Phineas try to remove it from your walls!"

With that she nudged Beauty slightly, and the mare obediently took off in the wake of George Teynham.

Edmund stared after Lady Juliana with a bemused gaze.
What a fiery little thing she was, full of passion and righteous
contempt for her neighbor and competitor. He swung himself
up on Firefly and set a course after this most amazing young
woman.

It had been interesting to watch the son, Peregrine. He had
not leapt to his father's defense. Rather, he had most likely
been assisting Juliana in obtaining the India paper before his
father arrived on the scene. Was this another male who was
smitten with the lovely Juliana? Henry, and now Peregrine? It

seemed that Lady Juliana had hearts strewn from one end of the countryside to the other.

However, the matter of the paper had given him much food for thought. There was little doubt in his mind that the old man had been up to something and snaffled that paper for reasons of his own. If he had ordered the monstrously dreadful stuff that had first been brought to view, Edmund could well appreciate his wanting to switch.

Somehow, he suspected this was not the case. In fact, he reluctantly came to the conclusion that Sir Phineas wanted to throw an obstacle in Juliana's path. Perhaps it was truly as Juliana had said, that the old chap wished to wrest the commission from her control and take it upon himself. If he hadn't known about this particular incident, Edmund could well have assumed that Juliana did indeed need to relinquish control of the project—and that he required a new architect.

As to Lady Barbara and Lady Rosamund, who had voiced such interest in his garden-to-be,—well, they represented the finest flower of English young womanhood. He would do well to observe them, for such was the sort of woman he wanted to marry. Certainly, he had no wish to tie himself to a daring, lively, passionate woman like Lady Juliana. It occurred to him that while Juliana possessed that fiery, determined nature, she most likely would not be a conformable woman—the sort he desired for a wife. No, Lady Barbara or Lady Rosamund was the type who would fit that description nicely. He would most definitely hunt for a woman like them. The notion that Juliana might be the better choice in the long run was pushed to the back of his mind.

When he arrived at the house, he saw a curious stack of crates being unloaded from a dray wagon. Empty crates gave evidence that some items had already been taken inside the house. After looping the reins around a post, he sauntered over to watch.

Juliana appeared absorbed in the unloading process. She checked some paperwork against the number of crates and smiled.

"Everything accounted for?" Edmund asked and was rewarded with a flashing smile that could blind a man not accustomed to bright sun.

"Indeed. All properly labeled and present. This is one order Sir Phineas either did not expect to come or simply did not bother with—not knowing what to do with it."

"There have been other orders that have disappeared?"

"Yes, although I cannot prove that Sir Phineas was at fault. Just the other day a shipment of marble was ruined because of rocks on the road that the driver did not notice. That road has always been reasonably well-maintained, yet I cannot accuse a man of dumping rocks on the road just to cause me problems. But I can suspect him of such a dastardly deed," she concluded with a snap.

Edmund studied her flushed face, those sparkling eyes, and wondered if he had ever seen a woman so truly alive. Not for her the languid smile, the gentle pace, the hours at the embroidery frame. She sizzled, snapped, simmered with vitality.

Yet, he could honestly say she was not improper in her conduct otherwise. While at dinner—and afterward—she exhibited every evidence of a well-bred lady. He suspected this house had become a passion with her. And he distrusted passion in a lady.

"What is in these crates that is so important?" he ventured to inquire when the last had been unloaded from the dray.

"The water-closets," she admitted. Lady Juliana looked at him with a wary gaze, as well she might.

"You agreed that they were acceptable, sir," she reminded. There was a dull red flush beneath her skin, a sort of quiet blush. It was not easy for her to discuss so personal a topic with a gentleman, yet she held her ground. He rather admired her for that. Yet, as Lady Rosamund might have said, it was such a *masculine* thing of her to do. Unladylike. However, *he* found nothing masculine about Lady Juliana Hamilton. Not in the very least.

Why did he enjoy baiting her? he wondered. It was not at all gentlemanly of him. Yet it proved irresistible. She always rose to that bait with such fire and unwomanly logic. Women were not supposed to have the brains to match wits with men, yet she disproved that notion. She possessed sharp wits and a clever mind. Not to mention a highly desirable body, came a thought from the back of his observant mind.

"I shall reserve my final judgment until I have seen one of these contraptions in operation. You said the plumbing is complete?" If she wanted to assume the role of her father, she would be put to the blush in this instance.

"Indeed," she agreed, walking along at Edmund's side into the house to the small room where the first of the water-closets was being positioned.

Once the water-closet had been set in place, the elegant mahogany seat was put over it.

One of the workmen glanced at Lady Juliana, then Lord Barry, and ventured to explain, "The water supply comes in here, sir, then this here trap that holds the water is released by the flap valve that's operated by this cranked arm here. Quite simple, actually."

Edmund inspected the clever device and agreed that in theory it seemed as though it should work. He watched as final connections were made, then stepped forward and, at a motion from the installer, cranked the arm to the side of the water-closet. Water came down in a loud rush, the trap opened, and the water disappeared down the pipe.

"Most efficient," Edmund commented to the installer. He turned to Juliana and said, "I see no reason why the rest cannot be installed as planned. I only hope there is no problem with them later," he concluded skeptically.

"As you wish, Lord Barry." She gave a patently relieved nod to the installer. He disappeared to the rear of the house, no doubt in search of the next water-closet and the location for same.

Edmund crossed the entry, approving the soft gray of the Portland stone underfoot. The painting here had been completed, and he liked the colors—palest gray picked out with white. It was pleasant and not the sort of thing one would tire of easily.

"You selected the colors here?" he said to Juliana while studying one of the several niches in the wall, speculating on what statuary he would like to place there.

"I did. Papa died before he could reach that point. I felt this to be masculine in tone, and I think an entry should set the character for the entire house."

"The dining room?"

"It ought to be masculine as well, for men spend such an inordinate amount of time at the table," she said with a flash of those magnificent eyes.

Edmund smiled and failed to argue with her as she apparently expected of him. He strode across the entry into the dining room to study the walls. The painters had finished their work here. The room was a soft celadon with an ivory ceiling and trim. A discreet touch of gilt was just enough to satisfy a woman, perhaps a man as well. He liked it. It looked elegant, refined, and far better than what he had seen at the Gothic pile Sir Phineas was constructing.

"Nicely done," he said, allowing his approval to sound in his voice as well as in his words. "I have a large painting by Stubbs that would look well against that green color. There is another one I bought of a hunt scene by George Morland. I am of a mind to have it here rather than in the library."

"Oh, that will look fine," she said with unfeigned enthusiasm. One thing he admired about her—when she liked something, there was no false admiration. She allowed her excitement to show. It might be unladylike, but it was definitely gratifying.

"The drawing room is completed as well," she reported, changing the topic. "The new carpenters will have to finish two rooms on the first floor, then complete the partitions in the attics. Of course there are a number of outbuildings to construct." Juliana turned aside and stared out of the window. She was beginning to like this man, and she had better keep her distance for the nonce. He was too close for comfort, and there still was the Etruscan room and the Chinese dairy to hurdle.

All at once there was a roar of a noise. Startled, Juliana whirled about to find herself against his chest. His arms came up to steady her, and for a few moments she knew the comfort of being held safely in a gentleman's embrace. Oh, he smelled so masculine, all lavender mixed with a dash of horse and something spicy. There were so many times when she longed for such consolation.

"What was that?" She edged away from him and looked about her in confusion.

"Perhaps we had better find out?" But he failed to move, nor did Juliana take another step.

She looked at him, wondering how it would be to have him kiss her. She had been kissed once or twice, depending on how one considered those things. Both were snatched, hurriedly done, and highly unsatisfactory. What *would* it be like to be kissed at leisure by a man of experience—a man among men, widely traveled and finely polished. Dare he?

Edmund stared at her. As he had noted before, she was a delicious, fiery bit of womanhood. Somehow, he knew that kissing her would be a vastly different experience from the cold salute he might expect from Lady Barbara or Lady Rosamund. More dangerous, as well. What a pity Juliana was a lady. He'd have enjoyed exploring the subject with her.

She stepped back, breaking the spell that seemed to bind them. "We shan't find it in here," she said, her voice husky with some emotion.

He followed her out of the dining room to the entry. They came to a halt, listening for the expected babble of voices. Nothing.

They exchanged a questioning look, then marched along to the rear of the house. There, some distance beyond the main building, stood a shed that held the steam engine.

"That is one of the Trevithick steam engines," Juliana murmured to her patron. "It will be used to pump the water to the house. Perhaps what we heard was some malfunction?"

"Perhaps," Edmund allowed. "Let us hope that it is not often repeated. Tell me, where is the fire for this hot-air heating you promised me?"

"The furnace is under the house in the ground level, my lord." Juliana, very conscious of her attraction to this man and fighting it every moment she was near him, led the way down to the lower level of the house to the large brick chamber with an opening into which coal could be shoveled.

"The servant places coal into this chamber. When burned, it produces heat. The heat rises through all those pipes that you cannot see now because they are covered by walls and floors.

When you walk through the rooms, you will perhaps note small registers through which the heat can escape. The cold air returns to the furnace to be heated again. It is very simple," she concluded, thankful that Henry had taken the time to equip her with an easy explanation to a subject she did not thoroughly understand.

"Indeed," Edmund said in a reply to what was foreign to him. However, he would never admit it to her. "I wonder if it is practical. Seems most unorthodox to me."

"But, sir, think of the comfort."

"What if there is a fire? Should think the pipes would get overly hot. What then?" He rubbed his chin with an immaculately gloved hand, one that made Juliana very conscious of her own grubby gloves.

"One is careful to keep the fire just so," she said, crossing her fingers behind her, for she wasn't sure just how this matter was handled.

"Hmm."

Juliana watched her patron walk around the furnace, inspecting the brickwork, peering into the interior, tapping on one of the pipes that was exposed. "We shall see."

She wouldn't have put it past the man to have had her tear the bricks down. Odd, when she had taken over, she had anticipated a venturesome young man, one who would appreciate the very latest in design and invention, one who would embrace the new and unusual. Instead, she found this conventional man, rooted in the past, and holding somewhat fixed notions of what might be acceptable. She was thankful she had persuaded him—by fair means or foul—to agree to retain the new-fashioned ideas. He would thank her come some snowy evening and he was cozy in his well-heated house.

Relieved that he didn't expect her to rip the brick furnace out, Juliana led the way up the stairs to the living area. They found Henry entering the house as they came into the entry way.

"What luck did you have?" Juliana eagerly inquired, hurriedly crossing the room to greet her dear cousin who also happened to be her assistant in this project.

"Very good luck, as a matter of fact," Henry said, smiling at Juliana with his usual charm. "While in Oxford I found all the men we need, and as well, met a carver who was out of work. He is of the York school and from a sample I saw, most gifted."

"Oh, wonderful. He can begin immediately on the library carvings." She turned to face Edmund, a wary look creeping into her eyes. "Would you like to see the drawings I have done for that room, my lord? I doubt if the copies I sent reached you before you sailed."

At his nod Juliana found her roll of plans and drawings, to extract the delicate and most clever depictions of the muses and each art she governed. Clio sat with her laurel wreath slightly askew on her head, scroll in hand. Euterpe played on her flute. Erato strummed her lyre, a wistful expression on her face, and Urania stood with a hand placed on a globe, looking most militant. The remaining members of the nine muses were equally well done and truly clever. There was a hint of playfulness about most of them, a touch of amusement in the faces that he could only hope the carver might duplicate.

"Very nice," he said with unfeigned pleasure. He glanced up to see Juliana standing close to Henry, and all of a sudden he felt the most intense surge of what could only be envy. She obviously liked her works supervisor. They seemed far closer than was called for under the circumstances. He would that she had the same liking for him, yet he knew this was impossible, given his position in relationship to hers.

"The plasterers are wanting to begin work on the dairy," Henry Scott said, intruding into Edmund's mental meanderings.

"The dairy?" he said, full of curiosity. Was this the ordinary plasterers? Or was it that team of Italians who still littered the place with their bottles of red wine and scampering children?

"Very well," Lady Juliana said, withdrawing from both men. "Excuse me and I will see to matters."

Henry marched off in the opposite direction, intent upon directing the carpenters when they arrived, particularly the carver.

Edmund wandered along the hall to the morning room and over to the window to look down on the grounds at the rear of the house. He stood there, hands behind him and feet planted firmly apart. He had an excellent view from here.

Juliana hurried along, only to be accosted by that fellow they had seen earlier—Peregrine Forsythe. He had left a carriage some distance away, approaching Juliana with hat in hand and a hesitant smile on his face. Whatever did the chap want now, Edmund wondered, and again felt a stab of envy that she should smile so broadly in greeting to the son of her avowed enemy.

Out in the yard Juliana greeted Peregrine with heartfelt gratitude. He had truly saved her bacon, as her brother would have said. "We meet again, Mr. Forsythe."

"Lady Juliana, I had to come over as soon as may be to tell you how sorry I am that the paper was taken, the substitution made."

She nodded her acceptance of his apology. "It was not your fault, you know, but I appreciate your kind words all the same. It might have been worse," she allowed with a mischievous look. "Imagine that other paper hung on the walls!"

They shared a few moments of comfortable laughter.

Juliana studied Peregrine. She could see why Kitty admired him. He was better-looking than his father. No doubt he inherited his looks from his mother's side of the family.

It was interesting that he confided in Kitty about his concerns for his father and his integrity. All the more to promote Kitty and hope that Peregrine would forget all about Lady Rosamund.

"You are coming to our ball, are you not?" she inquired while walking with him toward his carriage. A dog raced past her followed by one of the Italian children. The child yelled at the animal, laughing and uninhibited as an English child would never have been before strangers.

"Indeed. Kitty saw that I received an invitation." When he observed Juliana's raised brows at his familiarity, he continued, "Now do not pucker up when I call her Kitty. We have known each other all our lives. Do not forget I helped her learn to toddle her first steps."

"I suspect nurse never forgave you. Kitty was always a favorite of hers. It made it difficult for us all when we discov-

ered that Kitty finds hearing difficult." Juliana thought of her
mother's rejection of the child who was less than perfect.

"I know that none of you ever mention it. Is there nothing
to be done for her?"

"Not at the present. Perhaps someday a man will think of
something brilliant. When she is older, no doubt she'll resort
to an ear trumpet. Now, she merely requires someone to speak
distinctly to her." Juliana placed a timid hand on his arm, then
withdrew it when he looked down at her. "She told me that
she much appreciates your kindness to her. Perhaps you know
that mother refuses a Season for her. Barbara will go to London next spring. I imagine Kitty and I will trundle along to
enjoy life on the fringes."

"Kitty is not to have a Season!" he exclaimed.

Juliana did not remind him that she was denied one as well.
"Our lovely Barbara pays for dressing. I am too old and Kitty
impaired."

"There is nothing wrong with Kitty," he said in a fierce undertone. "Your mother—" and he halted, perhaps realizing
that he had almost overstepped the bounds even friends were
allowed.

"Well, I have persuaded Kitty to join us at the ball. You
may console her there," Juliana said lightly.

"I'd like to return to explore the house—sometime when
his lordship isn't around. He is a trifle intimidating."

"Patrons tend to be that way," Juliana agreed. "Come
whenever you are able."

When he had driven off, Juliana glanced off at the nearly
completed Chinese dairy, then returned to the house once
again. She would have to give instructions to the plasterers,
then go back to Beechwood Hall for a late nuncheon. Small
wonder she had lost weight; she forgot to eat half the time.

"That was Peregrine Forsythe," Lord Barry said when he
stepped from the morning room to join her.

"Yes. He wished to apologize for his father's behavior." Juliana knew an urge to confide the story Kitty had told her
about Sir Phineas and his less than excellent work, yet she
knew she had best remain silent on that score. It was not fair
to Peregrine, never mind that toad, Sir Phineas.

"You chatted for some time," his lordship observed, looking somewhat hostile to Juliana's worried gaze.

Annoyed, she blurted out what she would never have uttered normally. "He sympathized that Kitty and I will not be given a Season when Barbara and Mother go to London next spring. I am too old and Kitty impaired—she does not hear well, you know."

"You? Too old? But you are scarcely into your twenties, are you? A mere babe!"

"Inform my mother, sir. She thinks me ancient, despairs of ever finding me an eligible husband. I would not be surprised were she to put me in caps and send me to my Aunt Tibble, who must be all of fifty."

"This will never do," he murmured, ushering Juliana from the house and to her horse. He assisted her into the saddle and stood there with an inquiring gaze, studying Juliana like a strange and unfamiliar object with which he scarce knew what to do.

Juliana agreed with him, but was mortified to think she had been betrayed into voicing her litany of complaints.

"Forgive me, sir. I am not usually given to lamentations. Do you join me on the ride home? I suspect there will be something to eat if you desire."

Edmund looked at the shuttered expression on the girl at his side. Too old for marriage? Lady Hamilton was shatter-brained. He ignored his desires, which had more to do with kissing Lady Juliana than food.

They rode in complete silence, neither willing to give voice to thoughts.

Chapter Eight

Juliana attempted to remain out of Lord Barry's path for the next two weeks. In this she was, for the most part successful. If he saw her at dinner, she disappeared immediately after with Kitty happily in tow. Since Lady Hamilton did not expect her eldest daughter to strike anything other than curiosity in the heart of their guest, she seemed not to mind in the least.

Barbara most gladly entertained, playing the harp and looking angelic. If Lord Barry suffered a surfeit of harp playing during his time, he was far too polite to say a word about it.

Barbara was also deeply involved in the plans for the coming ball. Lady Hamilton decided it would be excellent practice for her come-out the following spring. Invitations had been sent and, although it was to be but a modest country house ball, acceptances were most gratifying in numbers.

Lady Rosamund had urged that every eligible earl, marquess, and duke within reasonable distance be invited. In this Lady Hamilton agreed, for if one could fire off a daughter without the expense of a London Season, it was most desirable. Yet, few of these indicated they would attend.

"Kitty, I have heard quite enough!" Juliana declared, after a week of listening to Barbara wax eloquent over everything from the table arrangements for a light repast, to the musicians who had been located, to the elegance of her gown. "I should think that you have heard quite enough of this coming ball, as well. How I wish—not for the first time—that Lord Barry was still in Jamaica."

"I thought you said he had not been a problem these past two weeks?" Kitty said from where she was curled up on the window seat in the morning room, catching the best light for reading a book on botany.

"Only because I have managed to avoid him at every turn," Juliana explained. "What a clever notion I had to suggest that Barbara and Lady Rosamund take his nosy lordship on various tours of the countryside—to show him the many beauties of our area. I vow he has been royally entertained."

"Indeed," Kitty murmured with a smile. "He seeks his room at first possible chance come evening as of late. Do you suppose he is tiring of those two beauties as well as the countryside? Not to mention the harp?"

"It would serve him right. He desires to marry a typical Englishwoman, and they are both splendid examples. Today's lady is a far cry from the ladies of old. They were a sturdier sort, I believe. Papa told me the story of Bess of Hardwick—who also liked to build houses. Now *there* was a woman who knew her mind and dared to do as she pleased. She even," Juliana said with emphasis, "defied her queen. I think the story is rather romantic, urging two young people to marry when she knew Elizabeth would be furious."

"Sounds quite stupid to me," Kitty observed.

"Today we have bland and affable women who do their husbands' bidding, remaining in the country—breeding, for the most part—while he has a smashing time in London."

"What has put you in such a frightful mood?" Kitty inquired, seeing to the heart of her sister's roundaboutations.

"The work on the Etruscan room is completed," Juliana said with an expressive grimace at her sister. "I cannot put off the day of reckoning any longer. The windows are completely installed everywhere, and it is time to test the hot-air heating system—all we need is a cool, dampish day for that and it is misting today. The stair railings ought to be finished this coming week. I wonder if he will like them?" She sighed and confessed, "Were it anyone other than Sir Phineas who offers to take over this construction, I believe I would yield to him. It is a monstrous job, and I am growing weary of all the little, plaguey problems."

"What now?" Kitty patted the seat beside her, inviting her eldest sister to confide her woes.

"If it is not one thing, it is another." Juliana plumped herself down on the seat, leaning against the satin smoothness of the wainscoting to close her eyes for a moment. She opened them to fix a tired gaze on her sister. "The carver whom Henry found in Oxford is a wizard at his craft, but we have had problems obtaining just the right sort of wood. Mr. Maine wishes lime wood—the proper lime will speed his work immensely. Henry finally obtained it, but at some expense."

"Well, that is a relief for you," Kitty observed.

"True. 'Tis amazing how fast Mr. Maine works. Of course, no one dares bother him. He sits in one of the back rooms, a fire burning nicely to remove any chill, and creates my drawings to scale in wood with incredible accuracy and detail. He adds flowers and leaves that you swear are real."

"What else?" Kitty asked.

"The Etruscan room. What if Lord Barry detests it? I ought to have shown him the detailed drawings for the decor once he arrived here. But after I saw what sort of man he is—*such* a conventional man—I feared he would reject the room without seeing how magnificent it would be."

"You do realize that Lord Barry is to live in this house, and not you? I should think you would wish to consider his feelings first," Kitty said, eyeing her sister with a frown.

"I do. Only . . . this is such a beautiful room. You will quite fall in love with it when you walk into it. The colors are so fresh and vibrant. It is very well done," Juliana assured her sister with a smile and nod.

"You had best show him the room before he discovers it on his own. There is no point in postponing the inevitable." Kitty shook her head in sympathy.

"I know." Juliana rose with a sigh, then chuckled. "Besides, I believe Barbara and Lady Rosamund have run out of beauty spots they think will please him. He is too polite to tell them to jump off a bridge, or something equally terminal. I know I must do my duty. But I won't like it, I promise." She marched to the door as one going to her doom, glancing back at Kitty with a wistful gaze.

In the hallway she espied Lord Barry, who wore the hunted expression of a fox who seeks to escape the hounds.

"My lord, would you care to join me at the house today? I believe there are several things you might wish to view. As well, the heating ought to be tested, and I suspect you would wish to be present."

He strode down the hall with long steps, clasping Juliana's upper arm and urging her along to the front door. "By all means," he said in a low voice, as though fearing to be overheard. Once outside, he suddenly released her arm, perhaps realizing it was highly improper to touch her so.

"I have tried to ride over to my house for this past week without success. I would see how things go on there." There was a hint of exasperation in his voice, but Juliana was far too wise to inquire as to his difficulties.

"Of course," Juliana replied, trying to put a note of sympathy into her voice. Never would she admit she had aided and abetted in keeping him away by suggesting to her sister that it would be a kindness to show his lordship about. That Barbara was not averse to capturing an admittedly handsome viscount might have contributed to her enthusiasm.

Juliana rode Beauty in silence, quite ignoring the falling mist, mulling over what she intended to say to his lordship when they reached the house. She did *not* plan to reveal the problem that had occurred with some of the plasterwork. It seemed that a portion of the gypsum had been improperly burned—or not burned at all. When it was combined with the sand and water, plus the animal hair to give strength, the whole had fallen apart within a brief time, to the dismay of the plasterers.

Fortunately, the work had been the very last to be completed in a bedroom and not of great amount. It had been hastily remedied, and the bedchamber was now finished to everyone's satisfaction.

The plasterers had moved out to the Chinese dairy where they were busy creating an Oriental fantasy it was hoped all—even the dairymaids—would appreciate. She well knew that many noblemen who had such elaborate outbuildings invited one and all to see them. This particular "dairy" would be a work of art, though of course not truly a dairy.

But Juliana was quite sure that no other building project had been so plagued with disasters great and small. Henry made certain that no more bad lime made its way to the plasterers. But what would be the next dilemma to be faced?

"You are rather silent this morning. Any problems?" Lord Barry inquired in a casual, almost lazy manner as they approached the house.

"Nothing serious," she admitted, as close as she'd come to confessing all.

Someone had cleaned and swept the entry. The stairs winged upward in elegant style—the hand railing completed on the one side and the other in the process of being installed.

She gave the work a critical look, hoping that Henry had scrutinized it. At the bottom of each wing of the stairs stood beautifully designed standards, the product of the first carver who had been here. They had been executed in wood and painted to look like stone and would have exquisite oil lamps on top of them.

Lord Barry walked up to them and stopped. Juliana held her breath, for this was the first of the things she must show him this day. It was difficult to gauge his reaction, for he was most adept in keeping a closed countenance.

"Very nice," he finally commented, glancing to see the workmen watching him from midpoint on the stairway.

Without waiting for additional remarks, Juliana whisked him up the stairs to the first floor, then along the hall to the door that led to the Etruscan dressing room. She turned to face him, her hand resting on the doorknob.

His encounter with the standards—which she privately thought most fine—had brought faint praise. What his reaction to the Etruscan room might bring was beyond her imagination.

"Well?" he said with that familiar raise of his brows. "Do we enter?"

Juliana swallowed with care, then slowly opened the door, motioning him to go in first.

Edmund strolled into the room and could immediately see why Juliana had shown such a hesitant look. He didn't know what he'd expected—some great disaster, perhaps. But this? Never.

"The painter-decorator is famous for his work," Juliana said in a beguiling manner.

"The wainscoting is plain, at any rate," he commented, watching her face without seeming to. She looked so disappointed, he felt bad—almost—but not quite. The chit ought to have discussed this with him first. This was no simple decorative scheme; it was a plan of the first magnitude. He honestly did not know if he liked it or not.

"Note that each of the little medallions is a different scene," she quietly said. "And I would have you know that you may buy vases and other objects in the Etruscan style from Wedgwood."

"Well," he drawled, "it seems elegant, if cold. I am not convinced that this is what I wish." Juliana deserved to be placed on tenterhooks for a time while he mulled over the matter of this room he supposed was called the Etruscan style. The colors were black, red, ochre, and white—a somewhat limited palette, yet effective, nevertheless.

She watched him with an intent gaze as he wandered about the room, studying the various classical designs. He had heard of this sort of decoration, that many had adopted it in one form or another. It was much admired, or so he'd read. He was not certain he wished to be among the throng.

The sun cast a path across the floor, lending its warmth to the otherwise cool room. It was not chilly, merely that the strange formality in the rather bizarre antique designs chilled him. The smell of the oil paint still hung in the dampish air of the room, adding to the unpleasantness he felt.

"Somehow I cannot imagine someone caring to enter this room—you said it is to be a dressing room?—and see sphinxes and ancient dancing ladies cavorting around some odd type of urn. Wherever would you place any furniture? An armoire, for instance? Or chairs? Or is the room intended to be an expensive show and not for sensible use?"

He looked at the ceiling, observing that the center medallion had some mythological characters portraying an unfamiliar scene. But the general lines were pleasing, and he truly did not hate the designs. Quite simply, he had not been prepared for this. And he had *not* ordered it done.

He studied the fireplace surround that stood in the center of one wall. There were palm leaves at the top of the sides and a laurel wreath complete with ribands directly in the center. He supposed he ought to be thankful that this was all there was to it, and no fancy chimneypiece to add to the costs. Even if simple, this was not something that came from the catalog of a supplier of fireplaces.

"What *did* all this magnificence cost?" he wondered aloud.

"I have not seen the final reckoning, but I have a fair idea what it will be," she said hastily. "You must understand that the account lists every color of paint used in the room, how much, and the cost. The painter-decorator cites nut oil, white lead, lamp black, and red lead, among others, not to mention a dozen brushes. His charge is fair for the work executed," she assured him.

"How much," he insisted.

He blinked at the price she mentioned in her small, yet firm, voice. Painting half-nude women and bosomy sphinxes did not come cheap.

"I see," he said thoughtfully. "Which means that I had best learn to live with this." He gestured to the delicately and elaborately painted walls, the dancing females with floating draperies, and the solemn sphinxes who stared off into space.

"You hate it," she said quietly, so dejected he braced himself to withstand her appeal.

"No, I do not hate it—precisely." He watched her face light up and again thought what a pity it was that she would not make a proper wife. She had such charm at moments like this. "I shall reserve judgment for the nonce. But may I suggest that in the future you consult me before haring off like this?" If his voice sounded as though iced, it only reflected his annoyance with her. He took another last look about the room, then strode into the adjacent bedroom and stood there with a frown.

"I know it is plain," she said with determination, "but it is to have fabric shirred on the upper walls, above the wainscoting. The stuccoists did a very pretty border at the top, do you not agree?"

He had to smile at her then, for she was so eager to find something for him to approve. "The flooring is to be oak planks, I would hope?" He did not intend to ease her path.

"Indeed, sir. Nothing but the finest will do," she assured him. "It is to be installed before long."

"I seem to hear that phrase quite frequently." He suspected the wry note in his voice would put her on guard.

"Sometimes the supplies are long in coming. We order and wait." She made an expressive shrug worthy of one of the Italians he had noticed around the house.

"Then wait some more?" he suggested.

"How true," she said with what was almost a grin.

"What else have you to show me?"

She backed to the door that led to the hall and gave him one of those wary looks again. "The heating system. That is all."

"What is wrong with that?" he inquired with what he thought was remarkable patience.

"Nothing in the least—as far as I know," she admitted. "It has not been tested as yet, but since today is a perfect test day—what with being dampish and a trifle chilly—I asked Henry to see about the test."

"I have the notion that not a one of you has actually seen a system such as this in operation," Edmund said, not concealing his displeasure at yet another bit of evidence of this young woman's unseemly daring.

"Well, you might say that," she confessed, leading the way back down the stairs to the main floor. "It will be better than depending on fireplaces," she declared.

"What is wrong with our good English fireplaces!" he demanded.

"For one, you may freeze on one side while you roast on the other, unless you chance to be on the far side of the room, when the temperature is likely to be but fifty degrees. You would not believe the number of women who die of inflammation of the lungs." Juliana gave him a look that defied him to disagree with what she'd said.

"They might try dressing more warmly," he snapped in a perfectly odious manner while eyeing the low neck and generous bosom she refused to conceal.

A workman was cleaning windows on the outside. Another was tidying the floor, sweeping the sawdust into ragged piles. Edmund sneezed, one of those royal sneezes that startles everyone within hearing range.

Juliana bustled over to the workman, quietly suggesting he dampen his broom and finish the cleaning with all possible speed.

She gave his lordship a cautious look. How she hoped he would find Lady Rosamund fascinating, or better yet, become enamored of some young English miss during the coming ball. If only she could send him off on holiday. Of course it was his house they were building, but she found it utterly nerve-racking to be near him.

And then she hit upon the perfect plan! She would so involve him in the day-to-day decisions that he would become tired of it all and leave her alone. As Kitty had reminded her, Lord Barry was the one who would live in this house. It would be a good thing for him to become more involved, Juliana thought with glee.

"Follow me, and we shall find Henry and the man who will tend the furnace," she said with what she hoped was a sincere smile.

Henry and a soberly garbed man stood by the furnace. A heap of coal had been dumped into a brick bin off to one side. The servant held his shovel most militantly.

At a murmured order from Henry, coal was shoveled into the furnace. The lighting took some time to accomplish, and Juliana grew more nervous by the minute. Yet had she not determined that Lord Barry would best be served if he were to be involved in every detail from now on?

Once the fire took hold and was burning nicely, the servant closed the steel door with a bang.

"It will take a bit of time for the heat to rise upward, I expect," Henry said. "Why do we not go upstairs to see how long it takes for the heat to reach the rooms on the ground floor." He motioned the others to go ahead of him, giving Juliana a quizzical look when she passed.

"I have a plan," she whispered, not able to say more than that. She would talk with Henry before the ball. He would be sure to be there and she wanted to be certain that she had two dances with him before all the local belles sought his hand. He might not be of the peerage, but he was well liked and had a tidy income.

By the time they entered the breakfast room, a gentle warmth issued forth from the brass register. Juliana felt that at this moment she might retire with glory. If that furnace worked with any degree of efficiency, the house would never be as bone-chilling as most homes she entered on rainy or winter days.

Lord Barry placed his hands behind his back and strolled to and fro before the window. Then, without a word, he led the way to the morning room, that place so traditionally reserved for the use of the women of the household. Juliana followed after grabbing a thin book that lay on a stand near the door.

Here as well, a gentle heat radiated from the shining brass that was punctuated by a delicate scrollwork in a design quite Grecian in concept.

Juliana moistened her lips, then boldly stepped forward. "I would consult you about the lighting, my lord. I have with me a pattern book with many designs for fixtures. I should think you would prefer the colza-burning Argand lamp. It is so much superior to any other work of lighting—other than gas, which you indicated you did not wish?"

He gave her a startled look, then walked over to peer at the slim volume she offered him. "Indeed," he murmured after another, rather searching, look at Juliana that quite made her wish to squirm.

"Here are a number of splendid examples of the Argand lamp. I particularly like this one with a Roman influence, simple and elegant."

"You do like the elegant, don't you," he muttered. However, he did not reject that design, and Juliana hoped he might be led in the direction she thought the interior ought to take.

Henry lounged against the far wall of the morning room, studying Juliana and Lord Barry with what could only be considered a questioning frown. She ignored him, turning a page in the pattern book to where a number of quite lovely chandeliers were illustrated.

"I had thought this one for the dining room, the one below for the drawing room. And here is one that is indicated for hallways. Since you will not have gas, the multiple spout oil lamp seems a good choice." She strolled away from him, congratulating herself on her beginning.

"Do you have any other pattern books?"

Alarmed, she shook her head. This was the best supplier, her father had told her. Henry had agreed. It would not do for his lordship, inexperienced—and impressionable, perhaps—to view drawings of an inferior sort.

"I selected this company because it is known for quality workmanship."

That appeared to satisfy him—at least on that score.

"I will study this and give you my final judgment in the morning."

"Excellent," Juliana said briskly, enjoying the gentle warmth that had begun to filter through the room. "If you will go with me to the room where we keep the remainder of the pattern books, you can make a decision regarding the metalwork for the front of the house."

She did not wait for him, but led the way to the room she and Henry had taken to use during construction. Much had changed in the past week. With the walls painted and the floor about to come in, the clutter had disappeared and all that remained were the pattern books, the plans, and stacks of drawings that Juliana and her father had made for the interior decoration of the mansion.

"Oh"—Juliana paused in the hallway to half turn back with an added thought—"should you wish to see the carvings that are to grace your library? Mr. Maine is just down the hall and could show them to you."

Edmund looked at the retreating and exceedingly pretty back belonging to Lady Juliana and glanced at Henry Scott to see how he was reacting to the total changeabout. He was rewarded with a noncommittal shrug as the gentleman in question followed him along the hall.

In the room down the hall Edmund found a neat table loaded with papers and pattern books, a smiling Juliana beside it. Did he distrust that smile? Perhaps not, but he would be on his guard. He had learned over the years to be wary of the leopard who changed his—or her—spots.

They spent over an hour debating the design of the exterior lamp standards until Edmund decided on the style he thought would go best with the front elevation on his house. From the expression on her face, it seemed Juliana concurred with him.

"Excellent choice, I believe," she said, confirming his impression. "Do you not agree, Henry?" She smiled at her supervisor of works, who was far more than that if Edmund had any guess.

"Indeed." He picked up a pad and pencil. "I shall make note of the selections."

Edmund took notice of the pleased look on Juliana's pert face and wondered what would come next.

"Now to the wall coverings," she said with enthusiasm. "You seemed satisfied with the India paper for the breakfast room, and it *is* very pretty. I wondered if you would like to have a landscape paper for the drawing room? The Chinese ones with birds and flowers are quite nice for a bedchamber, particularly one for a lady," she said, offering him a pattern book from Robson Hale.

Edmund accepted the book, confused and wondering if every gentleman who built a house was confronted with so many little decisions.

"Had you a wife, I expect she would have done this for you. However . . ." and she shrugged most eloquently. She had lovely shoulders, Edmund noted absently. In fact, as he must have observed a good many times by this point, it certainly was a pity that she would not do for a wife. Too managing by half, however. He turned his attention to the pattern book and put aside that image of Lady Juliana, her dark hair tumbling about her head while ensconced in the very large bed he intended to have in the master bedroom.

"Here is a panoramic view that might do well in the drawing room," he said after turning a number of pages. "I noticed that it has not been painted as yet." He held out the book for her inspection and was pleased at her reaction.

"Why, sir, I wish I'd had you at my side while designing all of the house," she crowed with apparent delight. "I vow, you have excellent taste. Henry, after you take the measurements for each panel, send an express order for this paper, and I shall have the walls prepared for the hanging." To Edmund she added, "The paper is not actually hung on the wall; it is affixed to a frame that is then attached to the wall. This way, you could make changes if you so pleased, with little problem. Oh, this is lovely," she said, looking again at the selection in the book.

He had to believe she was sincere. He even found he wanted to believe that.

"You know," she continued after a few moments, "you might even wish to have window blinds continue this look—they can be painted with the same sort of romantic landscape. Truly lovely," she concluded with a wistful smile.

"I believe this will be quite enough," Edmund said, thinking that it was all well and good to have wallpaper, but it was too much to go into window blinds that were painted to match!

"The chandelier you chose will look well with this paper," Juliana declared. "Come, I believe we have accomplished a great deal for one day. It is time we head for Beechwood Hall and a well-earned rest. Tomorrow is the ball, and I have not even given a thought about a gown to wear." Her laugh sounded a trifle false to his ears.

Lady Rosamund and Lady Barbara had talked of little else, and Edmund wondered if it was indeed the case that Juliana did not have a new gown for the occasion. He found the subject interested him more than might be expected.

"I would think you have ordered some pretty confection from the local mantuamaker," Edmund ventured to say.

Henry muttered something that sounded very much like "A likely story," but Edmund wasn't sure.

"I shan't disgrace my family, you may be certain," was all the reply he received from Juliana.

They left the house and, after parting from Henry, rode home in a more amiable silence than in the past weeks.

"Your supervisor of works lives close by?" Edmund chanced to inquire, wondering for the first time what sort of life the chap lived.

"Yes," Juliana replied with enthusiasm. "He inherited a

lovely small manor house from his grandfather. It is quite charming and cozy, just the sort of place a lady would like for raising a family."

Edmund was suddenly sorry he had asked about Henry's place of living.

Chapter Nine

"What are we to do about gowns for tomorrow evening, Kitty?" Juliana asked of her pretty little sister.

"Mama's pleasure with the idea of a ball did not extend to us, did it?" Kitty said with a rueful smile. "I do not mind, for who *ever* looks at me?"

"They ought to, for you are such a delightful thing—except when you have your nose in a book," Juliana teased, looking directly at her sister and speaking quite clearly.

"Well, this does not solve our problem. I asked Mama's maid to help us, but she turned her nose up in the air—as usual." Kitty exchanged a knowing, amused look with her sister.

"And that puts paid to Barbara's maid as well. Those two always stick together. Oh, I had hoped that the gowns I ordered from London would arrive in time. Unless they come in the morning, we shall present ourselves in our shifts or last year's ball gown."

"I vote for the shifts. I have no doubt but we would become the center of attention then," Kitty said with an infectious giggle.

"What a shocking miss you are," Juliana said, her eyes lighting up with fondness for her confidante. "Say a prayer tonight and perhaps it will be answered." She rose from the window seat where Kitty spent all too much of her time and strolled to the door. "I shall go to bed early so tomorrow will come that much faster. Do remind Dalston that we await a package from London; make sure no one overhears you. I would dearly love to surprise Mama. And then, too, they may not fit or be a disappointment."

"Well, anything would be better than my old gown," Kitty declared with a nod of her head. "I wish . . ."

Juliana paused at the door, her hand resting on the knob. "What do you wish?"

"Peregrine will be there. I wish he might notice me and ignore Rosamund—just this once. Is that too much to ask? What do you wish, Juliana?" The hopeful look in Kitty's eyes was almost Juliana's undoing.

"I wish that for once we might both shine—modestly, of course. I would not like us to be thought *coming*. But I confess that as much as I like Barbara, she annoys me at times. I truly understand Mama's reasoning. *But* I know that were Papa still alive things would be different."

"I agree." Kitty rose to stroll toward her bed.

"Well, let us comfort ourselves that we are good people and that is what counts, I imagine," Juliana replied in light accents.

"It is *small* comfort, Juliana," Kitty said as her sister left the room.

Juliana walked along the hall to her room, holding her lit night candle high. What Kitty had said was true. It was small and rather cold comfort that they were obedient daughters, proper young ladies, and did not cause an outcry with their pleas. No tantrums from them, ever. Juliana was forgiven for her inclination to building, for most—if not all—suspected she sought to complete her father's work. That was showing respect for the dead and reverence for his creative genius—most commendable.

But once in her bed, she considered anew. She had not said anything to Kitty about one wish she had. After a surprisingly agreeable day spent with Lord Barry, she wished she might have a pretty gown to impress him. It was wicked of her, vain, as well, most likely. But there it was. He might be conventional and rooted in the past, but he seemed a little more open to change now. Certainly more so than when he had arrived, or so it seemed to her.

And she wished to have him think of her as other than a managing female, one who had perhaps hoaxed him just a trifle. He had as yet not given his final pronouncement on the

Etruscan room, but from what he'd said, she thought he would let it be. So she sighed with a small contentment and went to sleep with that modest comfort.

"Good morning, Teynham," Lord Barry said upon entering the breakfast room. He made no comment on the previous day's harmony, nor did he allude to the ball, in spite of the hustle and bustle of the servants as they went through the final preparations for the company that was to come.

"Off early, I see," George observed from over his third cup of coffee.

"I would not wish to be in the way," his lordship replied in a very soft voice, with a glance to the door, beyond which could be seen the redistribution of furniture. Chairs were being taken to the drawing room to be lined against the wall, and the drawing room sofa had been placed in the hallway where someone might find rest and retreat.

"Is Lady Juliana about?"

"I am here behind you—hiding, I fear, more's the pity," she whispered.

He grinned at her, and Juliana sank down on her chair, thinking it was vastly unfair of him to have such a beguiling grin. Just when she had discovered how to handle him, he had to show a nicer side of himself. It simply was not fair.

"What do we decide on today?" he said in a conspiratorial undertone.

"Goodness, let me think," Juliana whispered back. "Flooring and carpeting, for one thing. Do you wish to have fitted carpets in any of the rooms? They are becoming more and more popular, you know."

"Let me consider the matter. You are ready for the ball this evening?" He held his coffee cup in one hand, a slice of toast in the other, watching her with a narrow gaze that was a bit too penetrating for her comfort. She suspected he saw more than she would like.

"I suppose so." Juliana glanced at her uncle and detected an angry glimmer in his eyes.

"Never say that my dear sister did not order new gowns for you and Kitty?" When all Juliana could do was toss an anguished glance at his lordship and give a tiny shrug, her uncle snorted in disgust.

"I trust you did something on your own?" George said, remembering to keep his irate voice low.

"I sent to London for two gowns made to our measurements, describing ones we had seen in Barbara's copy of *Ackermann's*. They have not come as yet," she concluded in a resigned manner. It was fated to be; there was no use in bewailing her lot. Her mother would never understand that Juliana yearned for a home and family just as much, perhaps more, than Barbara did. If Juliana did not help herself, she would remain on the shelf.

Henry entered the room and walked quietly to Juliana's side. "Did they come?"

"Not yet," she admitted.

"Best get out of here before your mother decides to put you to work at something Barbara does not wish to do."

They all hastily left the table, taking pains to depart from the house with far more than customary care.

Edmund watched Henry Scott assist Lady Juliana onto her saddle with a twinge of resentment. There was no doubting that those two were close. What sort of closeness he still could not determine. But she had confided her predicament to him, and Edmund could easily see that Henry had sympathized with her plight. Troubles were never shared by enemies and frequently not even by friends.

"You'll be pleased to know I took those measurements and have sent off the order to Robson Hale for the landscape paper," Henry said.

He had addressed no one in particular, so Edmund took it upon himself to reply. "Good. The sooner the house is completed, the better."

Juliana nudged her horse into a canter and set off ahead of them. Edmund wondered what was in his remark that made her take umbrage. Perhaps she felt he criticized her for the slowness of completion. Well, so be it. Her father's death combined with the many delays could not be helped, but Edmund still believed she might have turned the project over to another.

"From fairest creatures we desire increase, that thereby beauty's rose might never die," George intoned in an absent manner, while gazing off into the distance. When he caught Edmund's look, he said, "I do not always use Shakespeare for insulting another, you know. It only seems like that."

"You think about your niece—her lack of a gown?" Edmund asked, moderating the sympathy he felt, lest it be considered intrusive.

"I intend to have a few words with my thoughtless sister, you may be sure. It is a pity you must be thrust into a household such as this—fatherless, like a ship without a rudder."

"It does reveal the importance of a father as the backbone of a family. That is an apt analogy, the rudderless ship. I perceive a good father steers his family on a true and worthy course. Am I right?" Edmund glanced over at George, hopeful that he was making a favorable impression on the unusual man.

"Don't ask me, I never married," George said, then dashed off after his niece, leaving Edmund to ride along with Henry—an odder assorted pair he couldn't imagine.

"Uncle George is in a mood," Henry observed.

"You call him uncle?" Edmund wondered. That seemed rather familiar. Too familiar for Edmund's liking.

"I hear the girls refer to him that way all the time," Henry replied with a grimace. "He doesn't appear to mind my usage. Distant family connection, and all that."

Edmund would have liked to inquire just how distant this distant family connection might be, but they had arrived at his house and the conversation came to an end.

When they entered the house, it hit them—the most utterly foul smell one could imagine! Juliana came running to them, clearly upset. Or was she merely furious?

"Oh, I shall truly do something wicked to that man, I swear it." She planted her fists on her hips and faced Henry, looking more angry than a wet hen.

Henry sniffed and made a face. "What on earth is it?"

"Some appalling cheese, I think. Someone—who shall remain nameless because we do not know for certain who he is—came early and put something into the furnace. When our man came to stoke the fire, this perfectly frightful smell came wafting throughout the house. The carpenters fled to the stables, to work there until the smell is gone."

"Best open the windows to air out." Edmund swiftly opened the closest window, then the next, and thought all the while that the smell reminded him very much of old socks much in need of a wash.

"I hope it will not linger long," Juliana cried as she ran to the next room, opening the windows there, then hurried up the stairs.

Edmund left Henry to open the remaining ground-floor windows and followed Juliana up and into the Etruscan room.

"I am so angry I can scarce think," she muttered while flinging open the first of three windows.

" 'Tis the aroma of something evil, perhaps," he misquoted slightly from the bard.

Juliana looked at him, an arrested expression on her face. "A very ancient and fishlike smell," she also quoted, somewhat out of context.

He thought for a moment, then his eyes gleamed with his thoughts. "It smells far worse than weeds. It smells to heaven."

"Gracious," she said with a chuckle. Then she raised a finger in the air, as though she had thought of an apt conclusion. "I begin to smell a rat."

"You indicated you thought you knew the perpetrator of this dastardly crime." He sought to make light of the situation, for it wasn't dangerous or permanent, just annoying.

"This is truly *not* the least bit funny," Juliana said with a sniff. The effect of supposed ire was quite spoiled by a silly grin that crept over her face, a look she tried to suppress in vain.

"Indeed?" Edmund dared her to deny the humor of the situation, and the first thing they both knew they were laughing quite helplessly.

"Oh, dear," she said at last, holding her sides and leaning against the wall. She gave him an adorable grin and shook her head, unable to speak anymore.

Edmund moved to use his handkerchief to wipe a lone tear of laughter from one of her lovely eyes. "The humor is there, even if it smells."

"Odious creature," she riposted, and they both began to laugh again.

"We shan't be able to open a single window if we don't cease this," she said. Then she took a breath, wrinkling her pretty nose at the lingering odor.

"Come. I shall help." Edmund held out a hand to her, and she looked at it for a long moment, then at him and slowly extended her hand until it was neatly tucked in his.

"There," he said with quiet satisfaction, although why it should be so important to him, he couldn't have said.

"Once we are able to breathe without fear of asphyxiation, I shall show you the materials from the carpet manufacturers. The widths are fairly standard. If you want to have peace and quiet in the house, a fitted carpet is a lovely thing to have." They entered the next bedchamber. She tugged her hand from his, then went to work.

Edmund followed her about, opening windows, noticing all the while that the odor was diminishing.

By the time they had reached the last of the rooms, one could hardly detect that wretched odor much like unwashed socks.

"Well," she declared, leaning against the wall once again, resting after her frantic rush through the rooms.

"Indeed." Edmund put his hands behind him lest he do something he ought not.

She turned her head to look out of the window, then around at the room. "This is a pretty bedchamber. It needs a nice carpet, a figured one from Turkey." She moved away from the wall, obviously warming to the decoration of the room. "And a lovely little four-poster bed with pretty draperies at each corner and with brass finials atop the posts. Something cozy a young girl would enjoy."

"You would have liked something like that?" Edmund queried, coming to stand quite close to her.

She glanced at him, nodding. "Yes, I think I would."

Edmund said, "And I should like something more like a grand state bed, with all the fringes and furbelows and embroideries that are customary."

"Goodness," she whispered.

He dared to place a finger under her chin, tilting that pretty face so he could see her eyes better. They flashed like a turbulent sea, a rich blue from the tropics. It proved his undoing. He lightly touched her lips, then found it was a heady experience, one he could not end immediately. It did not help matters that she melted against him, so sweet and dear in his arms, for he had quickly wrapped his arms around her.

Then his conscience prompted him, and he drew away. "Excuse me. I forgot myself."

Juliana touched her lips with her fingers, then turned away from him.

"I will leave you now if you wish."

"No, no," she said, her voice muffled. She turned slightly, to look back at him over her shoulder. "I did not expect that."

"Nor did I," he responded truthfully—not but what he hadn't desired this for what seemed like an age.

"This must not happen again," she said, recalling his quote about the architect who would not enter the finished house. "We are like patron and architect, or in my case, patron and the one who concludes this project. I would not presume to classify myself as an architect, for although I have trained with my father, I did not study abroad."

She turned away again, composing herself. Footsteps echoed in the hall, and Lord Barry moved to another window, placing a greater distance between them.

"The smell seems to be dissipating," Henry declared upon joining them in the bedroom. "I cannot help wondering who would do such a thing." If he noticed a constraint between Lord Barry and Juliana, he gave no evidence of it.

"The old toad, of course. Or ought I say a rat, for I certainly smelled one," Juliana concluded.

"You have not one shred of proof," Lord Barry reminded her.

"It is the sort of petty, disgusting thing he would do. How good it is that Peregrine is not the least like his father." Juliana turned away from the window, then walked to Henry's side. "I expect we had better go back downstairs and discuss those carpetings. Will you come, my lord?"

He had to admire her calm, her amazing resolution. The thought occurred to him that Lady Rosamund or Lady Barbara would have had the vapors at the very least if he had taken such liberties with one of them. He was glad it had been Juliana, for a good number of reasons.

The horrid aroma that had flowed through the house had now faded. He wondered if that fragile bond that had been reached for so brief a time was also fading into the mist.

She led the way to the ground floor, and once in the little room that had been used for their work, she produced the pattern books.

"I suppose," he mused after paging through the first book, "that I had not realized there was such a profusion of designs. I believe I should like to see them firsthand before deciding on them."

Wordlessly, Juliana handed him another pattern book, this containing designs for mosaic flooring. He found it interesting, if one liked things that appeared to have come straight from Pompeii.

"Perhaps you would like to have the *SALVE* one in your entry, that is, if you welcome one and all to the house."

Whatever did she mean by that remark, he wondered. "Of course I should. I cannot think who would be unwelcome in my home—other than the villain of the piece, naturally."

Juliana smiled and wondered if he considered her a villain—for he had no opinion of architects, it seemed.

"The *SALVE* it is, then," Henry declared. He made notes on that pad he carried about with him, his pencil scurrying over the paper with great speed.

Juliana unrolled a set of floor plans, spreading it out on the table before them. "How about a fitted carpet in the drawing room, perhaps one with a border? And in the dining room, I should think a deal floor, or should you prefer one of the new carpets with a lovely woven design in it? You ought to be able to have a table that will seat at least twenty-eight with not the least trouble. Either a wooden floor or one of those patterned carpets would present little problem beneath a table—although it is a trifle easier to clean a wooden floor. Should someone spill wine on the carpet, it is difficult to remove," she mused.

"Wooden flooring, by all means. But deal, not oak?"

Juliana repressed a smile. "You have frequently questioned costs, my lord. Oak is ruinously expensive. I planned to change all floors from oak to deal."

"I see. I shall have to think about that."

"It is past time to order the wood, my lord," Henry said with an impatient look at Juliana, as though questioning her including his lordship in such discussion. He ran his fingers through his unruly sandy hair.

"After all, Henry"—Juliana sought to give her assistant a reminder of what she had heard before—"Lord Barry is to live in this house, not to mention pay the bills. I believe it only right and just he be involved in all the details of finishing." She bestowed a sharp look on her old friend and cousin.

She could see the words sinking in. After a moment Henry looked at Lord Barry and smiled a trifle ruefully. "She is correct, of course. How could I have been so remiss as to not think of this myself?"

His lordship nodded most gallantly in reply, then gave a thoughtful look off into the distance before making an observation that shook Juliana to her toes.

"I want to travel down to London to explore the warehouses for myself. There is nothing like seeing the color for the carpet and comparing fabrics for the furnishings. I would have harmony, and no clashing as I have seen in a few homes."

"You would not go alone on this mission, surely?" Juliana queried, aghast at the possibilities that flooded her mind at the mere notion of a man let loose in a warehouse without someone to guide him in his purchases.

He gave her a bland look, only for a few moments revealing a hint of a gleam in his eyes. "Of course not. I would that you come with me. At my expense, of course. I believe we ought to allow several weeks for the trip, although I know we can drive to London in a day."

"I see," was the most of a reply that Juliana could manage. He desired her to travel with him to London? Alone? Heaven help her, she would go in a minute!

"It is growing late," Henry reminded with a look at his pocket watch. "If Juliana is to prepare for the ball, she had best return to Beechwood presently." If Henry had any opinions regarding the propriety of Juliana haring off to London with Lord Barry, he gave not the least indication.

"I would like to know if the parcel arrived from London," she murmured to her cousin. She gathered the pattern books together, stacking them neatly in a pile.

Edmund heard that little comment and vowed that when he whirled Juliana off to London, there would be several visits to a top mantuamaker included. He was highly incensed with Lady Hamilton, that she could so ignore the needs of her eldest daughter to concentrate on the one who, as Juliana had put it, paid for dressing merely because of great beauty.

Within short order they had left the construction behind them and were headed in the direction of Beechwood Hall. Impatient to learn her fate for the evening, Juliana dashed ahead of the others, hurrying into the house.

Dalston met her in the entry hall, a faint smile crossing his face as he caught sight of her.

"They came!" she whispered, for she so wished to surprise her mother and Barbara.

"Indeed, Lady Juliana. I had the parcel taken to your room. I believe Lady Katherine awaits you there."

Not pausing for an instant, regardless of any seeming lack of courtesy to Lord Barry, Juliana rushed up the stairs and along to her room with all dispatch.

Kitty sat on the window seat as smug as a cat with a fat mouse beneath its paws. "They are here! I fear we need not attend in our shifts. I hope this does not disappoint you?"

"Silly girl." Juliana undid the parcel with trembling hands. "However could you wait for me?"

"Well, they arrived but a short time ago, and had I to wait much longer, the parcel would not have remained wrapped."

A gown of shimmering rose, enhanced with a white gauze

overlay and trimmed with silver rosettes, was the first to come to view. Then Juliana shook out a pretty delicate blue gown in the finest muslin imaginable from its folds.

"I vow, I cannot decide which is the prettiest," Kitty declared with great reverence.

"We shall bloom this evening, dearest sister. Do you think that Mama will notice?" There was no hint of bitterness in Juliana's voice, just acceptance of their lot.

"Maybe not, but I fancy Barbara will. Most definitely Lady Rosamund, for you will be wearing rose, and she thinks that is her color exclusively." Kitty giggled at the notion of what Lady Rosamund's face would look like at the sight of Juliana in her London elegance.

The gowns were immediately tried on and needed only minor alterations, which Kitty insisted she could do, as she was far better with a needle and thread than Juliana. The maid they shared would press the gowns.

The afternoon wore on with the usual bustle before a large gathering. Juliana and Kitty kept out of their mother's way as much as possible. Barbara gave a delighted description of the gown the local dressmaker had created for her. Kitty giggled, but didn't spill the news.

At last the hour arrived when the girls donned their pretty gowns. They fixed one another's hair, entwining silk rosebuds in Juliana's dark hair and silk forget-me-nots through Kitty's golden locks.

Juliana touched the dainty strand of pearls at her neck and gave her sister a wistful look. "I would that Papa had given you your pearls."

"Never mind. I sewed a riband with hooks and eyes and will attach this cameo pin to it." She followed suit and Juliana shook her head in admiration.

"We are as fine as fivepence. Shall we go belowstairs?" She put out her hand to her sister.

"Oh, let's do," Kitty replied with another of her infectious giggles.

They both felt self-conscious while descending the stairs to the main floor of the house. Exchanging frequent looks, they joined their mother and Barbara in what would be the receiving line. Uncle George ran down the stairs behind them, giving Juliana a pat on her shoulder.

"You both look exceedingly well. I see the parcel arrived on time," he whispered and gave his dear sister a smug look.

Juliana grinned at him. "I vow everyone around but Mama and Barbara knew about it." She glanced at her mother, then surreptitiously spun about so he might have full appreciation of the gown.

Then Lord Barry descended the stairs, and Juliana looked at him in mild alarm. What would he think? Might he consider her a vain creature, wanting a lovely gown so much that she would go over her mother's head to order one herself?

"Lady Hamilton, I find myself overwhelmed by the beauty before me and the evening has yet to begin," he exclaimed, bowing correctly before his hostess before turning to admire Barbara.

Lady Hamilton preened slightly at the gentle compliment and beamed a smile of approval at her guest, then at her middle daughter, who—it must be confessed—did pay for dressing.

Juliana exchanged a look with Kitty, a wry one, for she truly had hoped for more, yet knew she ought not.

The other guests began arriving at that point. Juliana and Kitty found themselves marshaled by Uncle George into the receiving line. It earned a vexed but resigned look from their mother. She paused a moment, staring at the two girls with a faintly puzzled look, then had her attention claimed by Lady Plunket, who had just entered.

The ball was given in Lord Barry's honor, requiring him to remain in line, greeting his new neighbors with curiosity and politeness that must charm all.

"Here comes the odious toad," Juliana murmured.

"And Peregrine with him," Kitty whispered back.

When the tall and gentle Peregrine came to where Kitty stood last in the line, he held her hand, casting an appraising look at her glory.

"Well, sir?" she said pertly.

"You will do admirably, sprite," he said clearly, winking at her with surprising charm.

"Oh, my," Kitty whispered to Juliana when he had moved on. "I believe he actually saw me."

Which was more than Lord Barry had done of her, Juliana thought gloomily. The evening did not begin with great promise—at least for her.

Chapter Ten

*A*ll went as it ought until Rosamund came into the entry. Lady Hamilton greeted her with polite charm. The Titchfields deigned to speak to Lady Hamilton, but were far more effusive when greeting Lord Barry. Lady Titchfield boomed her greeting with ardent fervor. It would seem that while his title was no more than viscount, they had developed an appreciation for his wealth.

Rosamund smiled serenely at Barbara. And she in turn preened a little, quite obviously believing her gown to be superior to Rosamund's confection in rose sarcenet.

It was then that Rosamund cast her gaze upon Juliana and Kitty where they stood to the far side of Uncle George.

In a way, Kitty said to Juliana some time later, it was really more like a mouse squeak than a cry of outrage. But whatever it was, it was clear that Rosamund was not best pleased when she saw the pair, prettily gowned and looking fine as fivepence, as Juliana had declared.

"Good evening, Lady Rosamund," Juliana said to the younger girl, who had turned an unappealing shade of blotchy pink.

"Wherever did you find those gowns?" she hissed in a reply that was louder than it ought to have been, given the circumstances and somewhat like a rather minor explosion.

"From London," Kitty said happily. "I am quite delighted with mine. Pale blue has always been a favorite color."

Rosamund ignored Kitty, concentrating on Juliana. "How *dare* you wear my shade of rose?" she demanded, apparently unaware she was making a cake of herself, fortunately to very few. She failed to take note of Peregrine's presence.

"*Your* shade?" Juliana queried, finding herself extremely annoyed at the presumptuous vanity of this pampered young lady. "I am unaware of an edict passed to that effect. I saw this design, liked it, found the color pleased me, and ordered it from a mantuamaker we know in London. Uncle George thinks it charming. But I must say, the local woman does wonders, all things considered." She gave Lady Rosamund a level stare that would have put any other woman into a taking. Never again would Juliana permit this very snobbish and spoiled girl to treat her and Kitty less than they deserved.

Peregrine had been standing behind Lady Rosamund, waiting to speak with his paragon. Upon hearing this interchange—for he was close enough to overhear it—he frowned and left the entry without speaking to anyone, least of all, to Lady Rosamund.

Lady Rosamund sniffed and pranced away to join the others in the drawing room.

Kitty and Juliana exchanged eloquent looks.

"Perhaps . . . ," Juliana mouthed, then smiled wisely with a raise of her brows, for she suspected that Kitty would not hear a word she said if spoken in muted tones given the amount of background noise.

Lady Titchfield gave Juliana a narrow look through her quizzing glass, then said, "London, did you say? Second-rate, if you ask me."

"But then, no one did, did they?" Juliana replied sweetly, figuring that she was doomed to a scold so she might as well say what she wished to her prosy ladyship.

The press of newcomers prevented additional comments. Her ladyship went off to soothe her daughter's wounded sensibilities, muttering words about young women who were overstepping their places.

There was a pause in the flow of guests, and Juliana found her dear mother marching up the line to look at her.

"Those gowns!" She gave an appraising look that did not so much as miss a well-sewn thread. "When? How?" Then she caught sight of Lord Barry's watching eyes and concluded, "We shall speak about this matter later."

"Yes, Mother," Juliana said, then reached out to give Kitty's hand a comforting squeeze.

Minutes later, Peregrine again presented himself to Kitty and smiled in a most encouraging manner. "I would like to have a dance if you have one left to spare."

Since Kitty was rendered speechless by the incredible happening—so like her wish—Juliana had to give her a sharp nudge, saying, "Kitty would be delighted, I feel sure. Kitty, why do you not show Mr. Forsythe the new plant in the conservatory until it is time for the dancing to begin?"

Still in a daze, Kitty went along with Peregrine. Juliana hoped that he would be able to make Kitty feel comfortable. His altered sentiments were not really a surprise. He was far too intelligent to be taken in by Lady Rosamund for long. But how lovely that it happened this evening, so Kitty could enjoy her first ball.

Lady Rosamund had not endeared herself to one of her adoring admirers. In fact, Rosamund may have terminated that particular source of admiration permanently. Juliana smiled, feeling rather like a hen whose chick has outshown all others.

With nearly all invited guests present, Lady Hamilton swept off with Lord Barry on one side of her and Barbara on the other. The ball would begin with Lord Barry leading out the most beautiful and worthy daughter of the house.

Juliana decided to follow, wondering what the very traditional and orthodox Lord Barry would do now.

"I wish you to lead out the first dance, Lord Barry," Lady Hamilton said graciously with a pointed glance at Barbara.

"With the daughter of the house, naturally," he replied smoothly. "Although, if I were to suggest the most lovely lady, it would have to be you, Lady Hamilton." He bowed again, while her ladyship preened slightly at this unexpected and charming bit of flattery.

Barbara stood in her pretty gown, bright eyes expectant, waiting. Her blond curls had been pulled to the top of her head, cascading in a pretty array to one side. The gown she wore was pretty as well—quite suitable for a miss of eighteen about to make a come-out in London. Delicate white muslin

with rows of tucks and tiers of white lace with dainty rosebuds nestled here and there flattered her slender figure nicely.

His lordship, however, turned slightly to find Juliana standing sedately behind her mother. He smiled at her, the look
bordering on intimate, for they had exchanged so much this
day. "Lady Juliana, your mother has requested that I lead out
the first dance with you. Shall we?"

Without looking at Barbara—whom she suspected would
be ready to throw a tantrum—or her mother—who would be
astounded that anyone should choose Juliana over Barbara,
regardless of what was proper—Juliana accepted his hand and
proceeded to the center of the room.

The musicians had been playing quietly—a minuet if she
was not mistaken. When they saw the couple obviously waiting for them to begin, they did so immediately, without waiting for Lady Hamilton's signal.

Juliana had not been mistaken. The very traditional Lord
Barry would not dream of overlooking the eldest daughter
when leading out the first dance. It would have been against
his sense of what was proper. The lovely part of it was that
her mother really could not say a thing, for Lord Barry was
correct. Barbara might have a second dance, take a second
partner to enter, but it was Juliana's right to be with Lord
Barry since Lady Hamilton did not dance. And heaven help
her, Juliana was not yielding to her indulged sister this time.
And, she thought as she accepted his hand in the pattern of the
dance, she did not intend to do so ever again. Tonight marked
the beginning of a number of changes in her life.

"I see Lady Katherine has acquired Peregrine Forsythe for
a partner." He glanced over to where Kitty held Peregrine's
hand in a delighted haze.

"Indeed. He usually dangles after Lady Rosamund," Juliana
murmured when she drew close enough so her words would
not be overheard by others.

"I seem to sense a few undercurrents about this evening."
He glanced at Lady Hamilton, who was deep in an agitated
conversation with Lady Titchfield. Then he looked at Juliana
and smiled. "May I compliment you on that lovely gown you
ordered. It equals anything I saw while in London. I am re-

lieved and very pleased the parcel arrived in time. It would have been a shame for you to appear in anything less fashionable."

"That is a most handsome compliment, sir. I will admit I was pleased as well. The gowns certainly exceeded our expectations." Juliana twirled about in the pattern of the dance, advancing and retreating with utmost grace. That her mother failed to provide gowns suddenly ceased to vex her.

"It is not only the gown; it is the lovely and gracious lady in that gown." His eyes held that gleam she was coming to recognize. It appeared when he was pleased about something.

"There is an odor of nonsense about that, sir," Juliana said with a twinkle in her fine eyes, almost gray-green in the delicate light of the candles. A wayward curl tickled her neck, and she wished she might brush it away, but he firmly clasped her one hand, while her other hand clutched her fan, a slender confection of ivory and parchment.

"Fragrance, please!" he riposted.

"Absurd man," she quietly replied, gracefully dipping a curtsy at the conclusion of the dance. She glanced over to see an incensed sister Barbara and a mother who looked as though she could cheerfully scold Juliana clear into next Tuesday and said, "Would you be so kind as to deposit me by Kitty? She may need me, what with the crush of people. It is difficult for her to hear, especially in such noise."

"How severe is her hearing loss?" Lord Barry asked, having looked in the same direction and reached the identical conclusion. He skillfully guided Juliana along to where her youngest sister stood by young Forsythe.

"It is most peculiar. There are times when Kitty can hear well enough. Other times, as in crowds, she hears only a part of a word. She does not hear the consonants and, I fear, makes amusing mistakes."

"And you worry about her," he stated, giving Juliana a warm look.

"Well, that is what a sister is for, to worry about and care about, and help if possible. She is the dearest girl imaginable, and I would do most anything for her."

Lord Barry looked across the room to where Barbara and Lady Hamilton stood in polite discussion. "Indeed?"

"May I suggest it would be a kindness were you to seek Barbara's hand for the next dance," Juliana whispered.

"If you insist," he said. "Although it smells of a plot."

"A rose by any other name," Juliana said, then covered her mouth lest she begin giggling.

"I shall spend the next minutes trying to think of something to top that," he promised before bowing most correctly, then crossing the room to seek Barbara's hand.

Rather than watch that painful exercise, Juliana searched the room for Henry. She had not seen him while in the receiving line, but as a member of the family he was free to enter from the rear of the house and quietly merge into the assembled guests without a fuss.

Kitty and Peregrine drew closer to where she stood. Peregrine said, "You hope to find someone in this crush?"

"Are you in a hurry?" Kitty asked, a confused look on her face.

"Crush, not rush," Juliana said distinctly. "I was searching for Henry. Have you seen him?"

"No, come to think on it," Kitty replied, looking about her as she spoke.

"Perhaps he was detained?" Peregrine said.

"What have we here?" Lady Rosamund said, glancing about the group when she abruptly appeared at their sides. "Everyone looks far too serious for a ball." She gave Peregrine an expectant look that turned into a frown when he remained standing close to Kitty and gave Rosamund the merest nod.

"Nothing much." Juliana knew that as a daughter of the house she must be polite to a guest. Not that she would have said anything nasty to Lady Rosamund. But she might have ignored her. How lovely it would be to give the cut direct to that spoiled girl.

Then Juliana relented, her own sweet nature forbidding such disgraceful behavior. "We were merely chatting. I trust you have a surfeit of partners, as usual?"

"Of course. I must say, your London gowns are quite plain—for London. Did your mother order them?"

"But Lady Rosamund," Peregrine said, "have you not seen that the latest in fashion are truly plain? It is far more elegant than the overly elaborate. The simple, pure lines are most flattering to young ladies. At least, most young ladies." He did not, to his credit, give her flounced and lace-bedecked gown that made her look just a trifle plump a glance when he spoke. "I think Kitty looks lovely in that blue dress she's wearing." He spoke directly to Kitty, so missed the flash of anger that crossed Lady Rosamund's beautiful face.

Rosamund was in a miff. No duke or marquess, not even an eligible earl attended; three viscounts and four barons were the best to be found. She turned to the nearest of her court and smiled in a beckoning manner. Within moments, she drifted off across the room on Algernon Plunket's arm.

"Well, this is a jolly group," Uncle George exclaimed as he joined the three. "Did someone pop off when I was not looking?"

"Have you been keeping an eye on . . ." Juliana almost said the toad, but realized in time that it would be a horrible error, what with Peregrine standing right there. Instead, she lamely chose another word—"things?"

No slow top, George merely looked knowing and said, "Indeed. Your mother depends on me to see that all goes well. Although what I would do if things went amiss, I confess I do not know."

"Be a tower of strength," Juliana replied promptly.

The conversation was abruptly terminated when Sir Phineas strolled over to join them.

Juliana longed to flee and escape his odious presence, but good manners prevented her from doing as she pleased.

"Good evening, one and all. I trust you are enjoying your little ball, my dear ladies?" He looked at Juliana, then at Kitty with that oily smile of his that was falser than promises made while tipsy. Juliana was saved from any sort of reply when Lord Barry appeared at her side. "I come to claim my second dance," he said with his customary smoothness.

Peregrine swept Kitty away, leaving Sir Phineas to jaw with George.

"You are a knight-errant this evening?" Juliana said softly to her partner.

"Did you need rescuing? I am sorry, I can but say that I wished to dance with you, not rescue." He twirled her about as they proceeded down the line of the country dance.

This explanation pleased Juliana enormously; she could not help the smile that spread across her face. When he was not complaining about the house under construction, Lord Barry was vastly delightful.

When she came close to him again, she looked back at Sir Phineas and said, "I was in a difficult position, not wishing to remain, yet unable to walk away. There's small choice in rotten apples, you know," resorting to one of Uncle George's many quotes.

"Ah, that reminds me. I was going to tell you that comparisons are odious." His face remained impassive, but his eyes gleamed for a moment when he looked down at her.

Juliana just barely refrained from giggling. "Indeed." She thought a few moments, then retorted, "He is as stale as mouse-eaten dry cheese?" Really, Lord Barry tempted one into indiscretions.

"We progress from scent to taste? That ought to provide a wider selection of quotes from which to choose. I must admit it is a progression I enjoy," his lordship said with that gleam flickering in his eyes again.

Juliana wondered at that remark all the while she stood watching him across from her in the line. He was undoubtedly the most distinguished of all the gentlemen present, his London togs outstanding, yet not appearing flagrantly obvious. It was only when Henry came around that Lord Barry seemed to alter his admittedly pleasant character. Juliana could not fathom why, unless he felt that Henry was greatly beneath him, or perhaps that Henry took liberties not entitled.

At the conclusion of the dance Lord Barry led Juliana to where her mother awaited her. He murmured, "How about a Banbury cheese?"

"Odious creature," she muttered just before they joined her mother. "Blasts and fogs upon thee." Uncle George would be delighted with the insults Juliana was able to produce this evening.

"Only if I am deprived of your most stimulating company, my dear girl," he said so quietly that not even Barbara could have heard him.

Juliana turned to face her mother, thinking that as yet, Lord Barry knew nothing about the Chinese dairy.

"Well," Lady Hamilton exploded in an undertone, "what do you have to say for yourself, my girl? Not a word to me about your order from London."

"You might have commissioned a gown for Barbara had you wished. You preferred to wait until she went to London for her come-out. Since I had no such treat in store for me, and you have repeatedly declared that Kitty will not go out into Society when you go to London, I decided that we deserved to shine just a little. I sent the order in as soon as the date was fixed."

Lady Hamilton, for once in her life, was speechless. "You surely do not think I shall give you a come-out at your advanced age, do you?"

"You? No, I doubt you would," Juliana replied quietly, then accepted the hand of the Marsh eldest when he solicited her for the next Scots reel. She expected that her mother had given her nod of approval, but she would have gone regardless. Was that another example of what Lord Barry called her radical behavior? She did not feel she was a radical, rather a young woman awakening to the possible world around her. Across the room George Teynham chatted with his old adversary, Sir Phineas. "You seem extraordinarily pleased with yourself this evening, Sir Phineas," George said with more bonhomie than he felt.

"Indeed, indeed," Sir Phineas said with a frown directed at his son, which seemed to belie his mood, but didn't, for he immediately returned to that incredibly smug expression when he looked at George once again.

"Work on your project going well, is it?" George said.

"Why, yes, it is, although I am surprised you ask."

"Oh, I am an odd sort of fellow; I have an interest in a great many things. Like Kitty's happiness, for instance. I would take a very dim view of anyone who spoiled things for her." George gave Sir Phineas a narrow look.

"I cannot imagine who might be inclined to do such a thing," Sir Phineas said with a trace of pomposity.

"She's a sweet child. Stands to inherit my share of the Teynham estate, you know. Nothing entailed there, just money and a tidy estate in Kent."

"I had no idea you were fixed so well," Sir Phineas said, quite clearly surprised.

"I remain with my sister to keep an eye on things, and to prevent her from moving in with her son and his wife. The present Lord Hamilton does not need any interference—few young folks do, if you ask me."

"Radical lot, most of them," Sir Phineas countered. "Cannot understand why they do not respect the past more than they do." He looked to where his son walked along the far edge of the room, escorting Kitty to refreshments.

"I take it you refer to Gothic design. If I want to be surrounded by a church, I'll go to one. Don't want to live in one," George grumbled. "Gloomy places, most of 'em. Can't think how they manage a drapery at those windows."

Sir Phineas took umbrage at that remark and fired a parting shot at his old adversary. "Well, I shall complete my house long before your niece manages to finish that bland classical thing she works away at. Heard rumors about it. True that the carpenters all left?" He smirked and took a step from George, seeming intent upon the refreshment table.

George placed a firm hand on his foe's sleeve. "If anyone should know about it, you should. We are more aware of things than you might expect," he said with a hint of menace in his voice. "Smell something unpleasant, Phineas?"

Sir Phineas had worn—most briefly—a startled look, his nostrils flaring in just such a manner as to believe he did, indeed, detect an offensive odor. "Rubbish," he replied before stalking off in the direction of his son.

"Rubbish? Well, that might be it," George said reflectively to the ceiling.

"Talking to yourself, Uncle George? Is that not a sign of old age? Heavens, do not allow that to be nosed about!" Juliana crowed with delight, for she and her uncle enjoyed baiting one another. "Is there a disagreeable odor? I thought you said something about rubbish." Juliana looked about, sniffing the air.

"Just something that antiquarian said before he left. I do not trust that fellow. He's a villain with a smiling cheek," he said, borrowing a line from Shakespeare.

"We know," Juliana murmured. "I have not told Lord Barry about that Chinese dairy as yet. I begin to think he might just approve the design. 'Tis a pity I am such a coward, for I quail at the thought of presenting it to him. I imagine I might be cast as just such a villain for not revealing the whole of it to him."

"It is forbidden to be so serious at a ball. I have it on excellent authority," Lord Barry said as he joined them.

"We discuss a man over whom lingers an ominous aroma of something rotten," George said with a final look to see if Sir Phineas had intruded upon his son and Kitty. He hadn't.

"I can see that you two are related," Barry said with an amused glance at Juliana.

"I said nothing," she said defensively. "Indeed, this is the silliest stuff ever I heard," she concluded, borrowing yet another of her uncle's lines.

"Come along and show me which of the delicacies on the table are most apt to please me," Lord Barry insisted, taking Juliana by the hand as he spoke.

She found his touch irresistible. Even through her gloves, and his, she could feel the firm warmth of his hand, the almost comforting sensation, when comfort ought to be the last thing associated with the man who could send her into tingly shivers without half trying.

"You are certainly a determined sort of fellow," she complained in jest.

"However"—he turned to look down into her eyes with that gleam in residence again—"do you know, I usually obtain precisely what I wish."

"Of that I have little doubt," she confessed with a rush. "You strike me as quite capable of anything."

"I shall remember that at some future and advantageous moment," he murmured.

"The lobster patties," she said after clearing an unexpected obstruction in her throat. "And try the melange of fruit. Cook has a sherry sauce for it that is delicious."

"Delicious," he repeated.

Juliana would have sworn he was deliberately trying to disconcert her. If truth be known, he was doing an excellent job of it. To divert his attention from her, she said, "I wonder what has happened to Henry this evening? He promised to come, yet he is not here."

Edmund glanced about him. He had observed that Scott hadn't attended the ball and been perversely pleased at the absence of the man he could not quite like.

"Foul play, perhaps?" He cursed himself as thoughtless when he saw the alarm that leaped into her eyes. Their color deepened to a stormy blue, and she touched his arm with a trembling hand.

"Do you think that likely?"

"Of course not. Perhaps he was waylaid by something important. It must be to keep him from here." His defense of his rival earned him a tremulous smile, most heartfelt, it seemed. Drat the fellow, how could Scott hope to claim the lovely Juliana when she was so far above him? Then Edmund realized that if Juliana truly cared for this chap, she would never permit a thing like rank to come between her and the one she loved. It was a most lowering thought.

There was a stir across the room by the door as someone came in to greet Lady Hamilton.

At Edmund's side Lady Juliana peered around a stout lady with a plumed headdress to see who it was. She leaned against Edmund until she identified the newcomer.

"Henry is come at long last. Now we shall find out what was so important." The relief in her voice was unmistakable as she took a step away.

Edmund found for the first time in his life that he would

delight in punching out a chap just because he pleased a lady. It was a distinctly odd feeling.

Henry wound his way around the room, searching all the while as he went. Edmund had little doubt who was sought. Obstinately, he detained her at his side with a flow of small talk, even though she answered absently.

"There you are," she declared with relief when Henry drew near. "I worried about you. I see I need not have, for you—" Then she noticed what Edmund had seen as soon as Scott drew close; the man looked gray and haggard.

"What is it?" Her voice was not sharp, but it might have been, for her concern was clear.

"There has been an accident at the house," Henry said, oblivious to Edmund's presence.

Juliana was not to that point, and she shot Henry a warning look that Edmund did not miss.

Henry ignored it. "Someone tampered with the scaffolding. It collapsed late this afternoon."

"How bad is it?" Juliana asked, her hand going to her lips in a gesture of fear of what she might hear.

"One man was killed, two others badly injured."

It was a stark declaration, which made it all the more frightful.

"How terrible!" she whispered, looking across the room to where Sir Phineas complacently chatted with Lady Hamilton. "I think he has slipped over the edge to madness. Surely no sane man would do such things."

"He does advance his cunning more and more," Uncle George quoted. "Indeed, he is deep, hollow, treacherous, and full of guile."

"Surely you cannot mean a guest is behind the accident," Edmund said.

"I fear it was no accident, my lord," Henry Scott said in a low voice. "I went over the scaffolding later with one of the men, and we found decided evidence of tampering. It was deliberate."

Lady Juliana swiftly put a handkerchief to her face to muffle her cry of outrage and stem the tears that threatened to flow. "The black-hearted villain!"

"Indeed, he is that. But to prove it is another matter," Uncle George said with a narrow look at his foe.

"Aye, he is a clever devil," Henry Scott added.

"Are you discussing Sir Phineas?" Edmund asked, amazed that the three could blame a guest with such a dastardly deed.

"I think I told you he was up to no good," Lady Juliana said, her eyes troubled. "I hope this does not mean more serious setbacks."

"What else could happen?" Edmund demanded.

The others merely looked at him and shook their heads.

Chapter Eleven

"Perhaps we should discreetly move to another room?" Edmund suggested. "The library, perhaps?"

"If all of us go at once, there may be raised brows. They might jump to all manner of conclusions," Juliana declared with a dry tone.

"Now, Juliana," George admonished, shaking his head.

"I shall go with Mr. Scott first," Edmund said quietly. "That should cause no comment, for it is known he collaborates on my home. We can appear in deep conversation. Then Juliana and Mr. Teynham can leave shortly after we go and seem to go a different direction—at first."

"Hurry. Kitty and Peregrine approach. No matter what, I would not say anything against his father when he is present." Lady Juliana made shooing motions with her fan, then turned to greet her sister and Peregrine Forsythe.

Edmund led the way, although he suspected that Henry Scott was far more familiar with his house than he was. It was difficult not to like the chap, for he was an able, willing worker. He was also dashed clever, from everything Edmund had seen at the house. The last few days, when he had become more involved with the building, he had seen numerous instances when Henry had stepped in to solve a problem, displaying a sound knowledge of construction.

But Edmund found he could not like that attachment he detected between Lady Juliana and Henry Scott. Although, given her innocent response to that kiss, it was unlikely their relationship had gone far. Still, it was unsuitable—most unsuitable. Perhaps while he was in London with Juliana, Edmund might convince her to forget about her country swain.

He smiled wryly. It should not be so very difficult to accomplish. She needed to be reminded of her position as an earl's daughter and a member of Society. She owed it to her family to marry well. Perhaps he might even suggest some worthy gentleman—once he became more acquainted with Society—a peer who would not mind a progressive female.

"Here we are," Henry said, jogging Edmund from his preoccupation.

They entered the library where a low fire burned even on this mild evening. The masculine aroma of leather-bound books and very old sherry permeated the air. A comfortable-looking leather armchair sat behind the desk, and Edmund wondered if Juliana worked on the building plans in here. A branch of candles stood off to one side on the desk, ready for lighting.

Henry went about the business of bringing light to the room, finding another branch of candles on a table nearby. Soon the room glowed with a mellow light, striking glints on the gold tooling that graced the book bindings.

Within minutes, and before Edmund and Henry could have any meaningful conversation, Juliana peeped around the corner, then swiftly entered, followed by George Teynham, a grave expression on his face.

Not bothering with preliminaries, George plunged ahead. "When I spoke with Sir Phineas a short time ago, he indicated that he would have his Gothic pile completed long before Juliana had finished what he called her bland classical thing. He looked quite startled when I hinted that we knew who was responsible for the carpenters being lured away, not to mention all the other happenings at the house."

"You missed one," Juliana quietly inserted. "I have not had a chance to tell you about what happened earlier."

At George's inquiring look, Edmund said, "Someone placed some extremely pungent cheese atop the coal in the furnace, so when it was stoked, the nasty smell went throughout the house."

"We dashed madly about opening windows to air the place out," Juliana added. The brief look she flashed at Edmund was revealing—to him, for it was clear she recalled what oc-

curred in that last room as vividly as did he. The hint of pink
that suddenly bloomed on her cheeks gave her away.

If anyone had happened on them, it would have meant
marriage, for one did not trifle with the daughter of an earl—
even if she was a progressive chit. While she was not the sort
of wife he sought, he reminded himself, she was an extremely taking lass. Memory of how well she fit in his arms
and how ardently she had returned his kiss—yet with her innocence revealed—clung in his mind. He wished that memory would go away. He found it disconcerting to be close to
her. He kept wanting to repeat the experience, and that way
lay trouble.

"A smell might be annoying, but it ain't serious," George
said. "The scaffolding catastrophe is a far different matter. A
man was killed. We must find a way to implicate the person
we feel certain is behind all this—Sir Phineas. But how?"

"Is there some way we can lure him to the spot, so that one
of us can actually catch him at his foul deeds?" Edmund
asked.

"He always has contrived to have another do his dirty
work," Henry said with a wry look. "We have a fair idea as to
whom that might be, for he tends to use the same man—less
danger of detection that way. The fewer who know about it,
the better, is undoubtedly his motto."

"Unless . . ." Juliana mused.

"Unless what?" Edmund asked, wondering what had been
going on inside that lovely head. According to accepted ideas,
women were not supposed to be creative thinkers. Juliana
gave the lie to all such notions. A lesser man would be intimidated by her intelligence. Edmund thought it stimulating and
challenging—if annoying at times.

"Unless . . . we might contrive to have him think he has a
chance of taking over the house in the event there is one more
accident. And let him know that we *have* pegged the helper he
has used in the past. Then *he* will be forced to do whatever
wretched thing he intends." She looked to the others to gauge
their reaction to her suggestion.

Edmund spoke first. "It seems to have merit. Sir Phineas
strikes me as a vain man, one who would think he could dis-

pose of any evidence with no danger of being caught. And he will never yield on the notion that his Gothic designs are superior to the classical."

"True," George agreed, rubbing his jaw while he considered Juliana's proposal.

"I believe Juliana has the right of it," Henry said slowly. "There is no way we can hope to hush up the scaffolding disaster. Sir Phineas will soon learn of his success if he does not know now. I think a word casually slipped into his ear by Uncle George would be all that is required. For he must think that the scaffolding collapse would be the final straw for Lord Barry." Henry gave Edmund a cautious look, as though fearful he might have given him an idea he'd not had until now.

"If I did not know about his involvement, I would believe you guilty of gross negligence," Edmund inserted.

"Perhaps we ought to have Lord Barry be the one to drop the hint," Juliana suddenly declared. "It would be logical. He would certainly have reason to be angry with us if he believed us blameworthy."

George and Henry exchanged long looks, then slowly nodded agreement.

"True," Henry murmured.

"So be it," George said, moving toward the door. "The sooner, the better. I know his lordship wants to have his house completed, and we will be glad for it as well. It will go much quicker without all these demmed calamities."

Henry and Juliana nodded fervently, clearly recalling the delays and frustrations they had encountered.

"We are so close to completion now," Juliana said as they left the library. "Details and finishing like the flooring, trim, and the like are what remain. True, they do take time, but errors are costly both in time and materials, and lengthen the process. We are at least two months behind our schedule because of all of Sir Phineas's little schemes. Trying to regain lost time is not my favorite pastime. We want this project concluded."

Edmund found that while he was anxious to move into his home, he had mixed feelings about ending his association with Lady Juliana Hamilton. She might not be the most proper English lady around, but she was dashed desirable. What a quandary—to be attracted to a lady he didn't want for a wife, yet one he must not dally with.

He moved ahead of the others and down the hall, intent upon his quarry. When he spotted Peregrine where he chatted with Lady Katherine, he paused. "Do you know where your father is?"

"I last saw him speaking to Lady Hamilton, over there."

At Peregrine's gesture, Edmund immediately espied Sir Phineas conversing in apparent amiability with his hostess. He immediately strolled in that direction, pausing to chat with the Plunkets, admiring Lady Titchfield's plumed headdress, before at last facing the man who sought to gain his patronage in a most monstrous manner.

"Charming ball, Lady Hamilton. I have enjoyed meeting so many of my future neighbors," Edmund said, bowing low over her hand. Then he turned to the man at her side. "Good evening, Sir Phineas. I trust you are well?" He carefully drew his prey away from Lady Hamilton, for he did not wish to malign her daughter within her hearing. His ploy worked well, for Lady Plunket claimed her hostess's attention immediately.

"I am, but may I say you look a trifle downpin?" Sir Phineas replied, a gleam that could only be sparked by malice lighting his eyes.

"Well, the news has been dreadful. Perhaps you have heard that there was an accident at the house late today? After we left, a scaffolding collapsed."

"How so?" Sir Phineas said, although his attempt to look sympathetic fell short of the mark.

"They said it may have been put together incorrectly." Edmund exchanged a meaningful look with the older architect and noted the satisfaction that flashed in his eyes.

"What a pity," Sir Phineas said with false compassion.

"However, I heard Henry Scott tell Mr. Teynham that he had a good notion of the chap responsible. Should that fellow come near, he will be spotted immediately and dealt with, you may be sure."

"Indeed?" Sir Phineas looked alarmed for a moment, until that bland facade slipped over his face again.

"Still, a man was killed. I cannot tolerate such happenings. Should another accident—however small—occur again, I believe I shall seek a new architect to complete the house."

"Really?" Sir Phineas looked as though he was mentally rubbing his hands together with glee.

"Indeed," Edmund said in a grave manner. "Sad. I rather like that chap, Henry Scott. Lady Juliana seems most capable, as well."

"But a woman!" Sir Phineas declared in affront. "A woman has no business building a house—even completing one half finished. She should have called on someone else—like me—to finish the job."

"Quite so," Edmund said blandly. "Good evening to you, sir," he concluded, then strolled off across the room to seek Lady Barbara's hand for a country dance.

Sir Phineas left immediately.

Juliana stood with Uncle George and Henry on the far side of the room, just inside the door from the hall leading to the library. They looked at each other, wondering precisely what had been said to provoke such prompt action.

"Henry," Juliana said after a moment, "you have not danced with me this evening. May we?"

"I have no heart for dancing, what with the death of that fellow on my mind. He was a good man." Henry bestowed an angry look at Juliana that had her inwardly cringing.

"True, and you think just as you ought. But people will wonder if you remain propping up the wall. Do you wish gossip so soon?"

"Let them say what they please. If you want to dance, ask Lord Barry." Henry gave George a bitter look, then turned away and left the house.

"I must seem a frippery sort," Juliana said, much chastened by what Henry had said.

"How many balls have you attended in your young life? There is naught you can do about the death this evening," George counseled. "Tomorrow you can visit his family, offer assistance, do what is necessary. Nothing you do this evening can alter what has happened."

"Well," Juliana said, most subdued, "of course I shall do as you say on the morrow. Perhaps I had best retire?"

"That would give rise to gossip of the worst sort. Best put a brave face on and seek out his lordship. Maybe he will tell you precisely what he said to Sir Phineas. I vow I should like to know."

"Very well," Juliana said dutifully. Her heart was no longer happy with the thought of dancing, but she itched to know what had sent Sir Phineas off like a shot.

"La, Juliana, you look far too serious for a ball," Barbara chided when she found her sister at her side at the conclusion of the country dance. But then, Barbara was quite unaware of the bad news. She looked happily about her and at the gentleman who approached to take her hand for the next dance. "If this be a taste of what London has to offer, I cannot wait to go. Are you not sorry you went without a Season? I do not know how you could give it up, just to build a house." She ignored Lord Barry, apparently not recalling that it was his house that was the cause of the abandonment of Juliana's come-out plans.

"I need to speak with Lord Barry. Sir?" Juliana clutched her fan before her, ignoring her sister's anticipation for the Season to come and her remark about Juliana's lack of a Season. It was a sore point with her.

The rose of Juliana's gown reflected needed color to her face, for her worry could not be concealed and she was paler than normal.

"Perhaps we could sit out the next dance, a *boulanger*, if I make no mistake," Lord Barry concluded at the opening strains of the music.

"That is most agreeable," Juliana replied. Although she had longed to dance with him once again, she found herself quite content to merely talk.

They strolled along the edge of the room, Juliana pausing to exchange pleasantries with those who sought her attention. Obviously, word of the disaster had not reached these people. It soon would, and then what? People such as the Titchfields were inclined to view the loss of a workman as of no account. But others like Lord Plunket would be deeply concerned, for he was a good landowner, considerate of the men and women who worked on his property. Would he place the blame on Henry and Juliana? Ultimately, responsibility for safety rested on their shoulders.

Juliana found she did not wish to speculate anymore on that matter. As Uncle George had said, there was nothing she might do about it this evening.

"Do you care to view the newest plant Mother has placed in the conservatory?" she inquired, just loudly so the nearest person might hear what she said.

"Indeed, I would. Have you given thought to a conservatory for my home? It might be rather nice, come winter and the dreary landscape outside," he said, speculation clear in his voice.

They left the room and continued to stroll—most casually—in the direction of the conservatory.

"Are you serious? Or merely making conversation?" Juliana demanded.

"Perhaps it would be a good idea?" he replied thoughtfully.

Juliana paused before the door to the conservatory and gave him a puzzled look. "That would mean a change of plans, and it would increase the cost. Are you certain you want that?" The man had complained of costs at every turn. Surely he would not wish to increase them.

"However," he countered, "it would cost less to make the change now than to add it later on. I believe I fancy a bit of garden within the house." He reached around her to open the door.

They entered the humid room, walking a few steps before Juliana turned to face her patron. "Well, I must know how it went."

"I did just as we agreed. He took the bait as avidly as we hoped he might. In spite of George's hint, he seemed surprised that we had twigged to the identity of the man we suspected responsible for the deeds. I was careful not to implicate Sir Phineas in the least. I even intimated that were there another accident, no matter how small, I would seek another architect. When he suggested himself as replacement, I did not say nay."

"Would you?" Juliana had to know.

"Not now. Not when I have learned the truth of the matter. I confess I came close to making that change when I first arrived. But I felt it necessary to allow you to prove yourself." He stood close to her, for the aisle through the conservatory was not wide and the ferns cascading behind him gave him little space to move.

"I am glad you did, and that I did—Henry, too," she added. "He is an important part of my work, you know."

"Just how important is he to you?" his lordship quietly demanded, taking a step forward.

"Henry has been here for a long time, helped my father, and now me. I'd not know how to go along without his help." She wished she knew what was behind his urgent question.

He said nothing to give her a clue as to his thoughts on that matter. Rather, he placed his hands on her arms and drew her toward him, allowing her time to bolt if she would. But Juliana could not more flee than fly. Rather, her eyes drifted shut, closing out the world.

"Juliana," he whispered, and then she again knew the touch of his lips on hers. Either he was improving, or the conservatory lent a special atmosphere. The kiss was utterly delightful, and she had not the least desire to bring this to a stop as she supposed she ought.

Of course, reality struck her eventually. At the first hint of resistance, he freed her mouth. But he did not step away from her. His coat brushed against her, and she was aware of a myriad of sensations, feeling that touch acutely, as though every nerve in her body was aflame.

"Juliana," he said, his voice pleasantly husky.

"Yes," she said, although she had not the least idea to what she might be agreeing.

He frowned and shook his head, at last stepping away from her. "This will never do. I cannot take advantage of your innocence, no matter how desirable you may be."

She ignored the bit about her desirability, tucking it to the back of her mind for later examination. It occurred to Juliana at that very moment to recall that Lord Barry had declared that he wanted her to go to London with him. Did he have some underhanded, ulterior motive for her company?

"About London," she began.

He moved a few steps away, then turned to face her, looking somewhat startled. He did not look devious, she admitted to herself. Or was she merely trying to convince herself of his freedom from guilt because she wanted it that way?

"What about London? I said I wished to go into the city to prowl through the warehouses, see fabrics and styles of furniture for myself. It is not that I do not trust you," he said placatingly. "It is more a desire to place my own stamp on the interior. So much else is you."

The grin he flashed at her was enough to melt away any suspicions she harbored. He could, she mused, be very charming when he wished.

"Of course, you will need a chaperon," he added, looking pensive. "Do you have someone in mind? I doubt Lady Hamilton would care to traipse about London warehouses," he concluded dryly.

"Heavens, no," Juliana agreed. "What a shame Kitty would not do, for she would dearly love to visit London. She has never gone there," Juliana concluded with a frown. "I expect I could call on Aunt Tibbles to accompany me."

"Would it not be difficult for an older woman?"

Juliana smiled. "Wait until you meet my Aunt Tibbles."

The door opened, and Uncle George entered, looking from one to the other with a questioning face. Juliana was devoutly thankful that he had waited until now. She had no desire to be forced into marriage with Lord Barry over a mere kiss. Although, she considered, it could scarcely be described as "mere."

"Well, I decided you had time and enough to discuss everything."

Juliana prayed that she did not blush. "We did," she agreed.

"I spoke casually with Sir Phineas once I found him," Edmund said, retelling his conversation with resignation. Truth to tell, he'd rather have gone back to kissing Juliana. "He is now aware that you have a good idea as to who has perpetrated all those past foul deeds. All that needs doing now is to wait for him to make his next move."

"Fine. I think your mother wishes to speak with you, Juliana. I shall see you later, or in the morning."

"Good night, Uncle—Lord Barry," Juliana said, suddenly glad to be leaving this place that had become far too dangerous for her. She whisked around the door and along the hall, pausing at the door to the drawing room until she espied her mother not far away.

It was clear that people had begun to leave. A ball of this sort, being in the country, tended to end much earlier than one in London. No one had been invited to remain overnight—although had the weather turned suddenly bad, they would have—so all must needs travel through the dark to reach their homes. Outriders and well-lit coaches were the order of the evening.

"Yes, Mother?" Juliana queried as she joined her parent.

"You have spent little time dancing. I thought you would wish that," her mother began.

"Once I learned of the terrible accident that happened at the construction site, I lost heart of amusements," Juliana countered, hoping she might avoid a scold by that means.

"Accident? I had not heard." Lady Hamilton looked dubious and obviously wanted an explanation.

Juliana promptly gave her a slightly edited version of what had occurred as well as their intentions.

"Best head for bed, in that case. But Juliana, I am not pleased with regard to your gown. It was most improper of you not to consult me first." That the gown had outshone Barbara's was most likely an additional thorn.

"Yes, Mother." Juliana was grateful to scrape by with no more than that admonition. It could have been worse.

Come morning the plan appeared to have been set in motion. Uncle George and Henry Scott had taken off quite early for the building site, prepared to stand watch.

Juliana did as her uncle had suggested. She called upon the family of the man who'd been killed to offer her condolences and whatever help might be needed. They lived closer than most of the new men, a short drive to the south.

It was most difficult for her, for the wife was a good, kind woman with two little children in tow. She had not expected much and seemed embarrassingly grateful for what Juliana offered.

When Juliana drove back toward her home, she encountered Peregrine coming from the direction of the Gothic manor house that Sir Phineas designed and constructed. She drew the gig to a halt and gave him a questioning look. "Are you going my way?"

"I thought to see how Kitty does after all the excitement of the ball. My father does not want my help today. It seems he has something he wished to do." He studied Juliana with care to see how she accepted his company.

"Ride along beside me and we can chat." She felt horridly awkward; his father was her enemy, yet she knew nothing but admiration for Peregrine.

They chatted lightly about a great number of things while slowly proceeding toward Beechwood Hall.

"Kitty tells me you plan to go up to London with Lord Barry sometime soon." There was a question in Peregrine's voice and eyes.

"Indeed, he does not wish to delegate the selection of his furnishings to a mere woman."

"I thought you had designed a number of pieces to go with the decor of the house?" Peregrine sounded endearingly indignant upon her behalf.

"Well, as to that, I imagine we can locate something similar without too much effort. Those warehouses are known for containing just about anything one might wish."

They entered the avenue and shortly drew to a halt before the house. Juliana handed the reins to the young groom who came running up to the gig. Peregrine absently handed over his horse to another groom who had followed.

Peregrine paused on the steps, looking hesitant, then resolved. He said, "I have no right, other than as a good friend, to beg a favor of you, but I would that you buy some things for Kitty when you are in Town. She needs shawls, and dresses, and a new pelisse, and a goodly number of things like bonnets and gloves. Is it really true that your mother does not intend to give her a Season?"

"Kitty and I shall share the same fate, it seems. We shall have to find husbands on our own, without benefit of the marriage mart," Juliana said in a joking manner.

This remark put Peregrine into serious reflection, and he ushered Juliana into the house while quite obviously deep in thought.

"Juliana," he said when Dalston had informed them that Kitty was to be found in the morning room, "you must know I have high regard for your younger sister. What do you think my chances are with her?"

"Quite good," Juliana replied simply and directly. "She has considered you in the light of a hero for some time, you know."

"But your mother," he inserted before Juliana could add another word.

"She will not mind in the least, I suspect. It will allow her to concentrate on Barbara, you see." Juliana gave him a rueful grimace that revealed a great deal.

"I think I see all too clearly," Peregrine said with a wry smile.

When they joined Kitty in the morning room, Peregrine was greeted with shy enthusiasm and a warm smile, leaving little doubt in his mind that he was, indeed, well received.

They chatted over a generous tea until the time came for Peregrine to depart. Country ways might be a trifle more lenient because of distances involved, but even then, there was a limit on calling times.

He had risen to leave when Dalston hurried into the room, an anxious expression on his face. "There is a messenger here for you, Mr. Forsythe. He says 'tis urgent."

Peregrine glanced at the girls, then strode from the room to the entry, where he was greeted by his father's clerk of the works.

"What is it, man?" he demanded of the fellow, who truly looked as white as a sheet.

"Your father . . ." the chap began. "Something happened when he went to inspect the oriel window on the north side of the house." The man tightened his mouth a moment, then continued, "He had climbed up on the scaffolding to check the trim boards. As near as we can tell, the nails were not long enough, so did not hold well. He lost his balance and fell, the scaffolding caving in under him."

"He is alive?"

"I'm sorry to say he was killed outright." His blunt declaration left the entry in stark silence.

Kitty had followed, and at these words she crumpled to the floor.

Chapter Twelve

"**K**itty!" Juliana cried, kneeling at her sister's side.
"What's happened?" Lord Barry said as he ran down
to reach the two girls at the bottom of the stairs. He gave
Peregrine a curious glance, but he stood silent, quite as though
he'd been struck all of a heap by the news.

Juliana looked up, her expression stunned. "That man
came—" she gestured to the clerk of works—"to inform Peregrine that his father has been killed, and Kitty fainted." Belat-
edly, Juliana turned her gaze to Peregrine and added, "I am so
sorry. How tragic for you. How could it happen?"

Peregrine justifiably looked quite overwhelmed. "I just
came from there. He was going to check an oriel window, for
there was something amiss about the way the trim boards had
been applied."

"Nails too short, unless we miss our guess," the clerk of
works inserted quietly.

A grim expression crossed Peregrine's face at once. "I told
him he ought to have used longer nails. There's not a
ha'penny's difference in cost. He'd not listen to me." He exchanged a searching look with the clerk, then turned back to
Juliana.

Kitty stirred and sat up, ignoring the smelling salts that a
maid had rushed up with for her. "Peregrine? Is it true? You
poor man!" She brushed aside Juliana's murmured words and
offer of help, to scramble somewhat shakily to her feet. "Is
there anything I might do?"

"Thank you, no." He gazed down at her with a tender expression. "You are most kind, but I will have to take care of
matters myself—the lawyer, parson, all that needs doing."

"I have a smattering of law," Edmund said modestly, not revealing that he had once studied the subject with an eye to opening an office—before he inherited. He had found his knowledge quite useful in preventing others from swindling him. "Perhaps an extra hand, as it were?"

Peregrine studied him a moment, then nodded. "I believe you could help. Sorting through papers will be a time-consuming process."

"Henry and I are acquainted with the building end of things. Should you wish help with closing loose ends, you have but to ask and we will be there," Juliana offered.

"You are all too kind. I appreciate it." Peregrine turned and walked from the house as though in a daze, followed by his father's clerk of works and Edmund.

"Send word if we are needed," Juliana whispered to Edmund before he went from the house. "I feel so dreadful, for we have many times wished his father to perdition, and now he is there. No matter how I dislike him, I'd not wished this."

"I will do what I can to assist Forsythe. 'Tis a difficult task. I well remember what I found in similar circumstances after my uncle died." Edmund left the house then, marching down the steps to find his horse, which had been ordered earlier for a morning ride, now awaited him along with Forsythe's bay.

Kitty and Juliana followed them out and stood on the portico, watching as the men mounted their horses, preparing to return to the Gothic manor house that Peregrine would have to complete on his own now.

"We shall see you later . . . Sir Peregrine," Kitty called out shyly to the new baronet.

He shot her an anguished look, touched the brim of his hat, then dashed off down the lane.

"Poor Sir Peregrine," Kitty said to Juliana as they returned to the house.

"I'd not remembered he gained the title until you reminded me." Juliana, concerned for her younger sister, guided her along to the morning room, requesting a pot of tea and biscuits from Dalston along the way.

Once they were settled in the window seat looking out in

the direction the men rode, Kitty leaned against the wall and stared out over the pastures. "Do you think that will make him any more acceptable to Mama?"

Immediately grasping the direction of her sister's thoughts, Juliana considered their mother for a bit, then replied, "You would be Lady Forsythe instead of merely Mrs. Forsythe. I think that could well make the difference. And since he stands to inherit everything, she'd have no worry that you both would land back here underfoot and needful of a roof over your heads."

"He'd never do that, no matter what!" Kitty fiercely declared.

Juliana placed a comforting hand over Kitty's slim ones and sighed. "I trust Peregrine will offer for you."

"I believe there has always been something between us. He has forever been kind and understanding with me. His father presented an obstacle, you see, not to mention that temporary infatuation with Lady Rosamund. He saw her true colors at the ball. Was that only last night? It seems an age ago."

"Indeed, it does," Juliana agreed.

"I suppose you feel guilty, for so often we have wished Sir Phineas to his doom. Now he is dead, it is most frightening," Kitty murmured.

"Well, I do not believe you can wish someone ill and have it happen, just like that. Evil tends to find out those who commit evil," Juliana declared.

"And who is evil this morning?" Lady Hamilton said as she sailed into the morning room at an unusually early hour. "Gracious, such goings-on down here. I heard voices and doors slamming. Well?"

She seated herself just as Dalston returned with the tea tray. Juliana was grateful to see he had added two cups in the event her sister and mother joined them.

"Word came—just as Peregrine was about to take his leave after coming to see how Kitty fared this morning—that Sir Phineas had been killed." Juliana ignored her mother's horrified gasp to continue. "He fell while examining a window at the building site. He died instantly, so we were told."

"I spoke with Sir Phineas only last night," she cried in confounded disbelief. "Poor Peregrine, he will find his life turned upside down," Lady Hamilton said properly with a doleful shake of her head.

"He is now *Sir* Peregrine, Mama," Kitty reminded.

Her mother gave her an arrested look, then faced the tea table, a most considering expression on her face.

"Kitty fainted when she heard the news, so I ordered tea for her," Juliana said, pouring the restorative tea for her sister first before offering a cup to her mother.

"Fainted! But you never do," Lady Hamilton exclaimed.

"Never do what?" Barbara said crossly as she entered the morning room, her curls smooth perfection and her muslin uncrumpled. "You certainly make enough noise down here. I thought an army had marched into the hall." She gave Kitty a derisive look, wrinkling her nose at what she saw. "Really, dear little sister, you might try to do better. You look as though you slept in that dress. And you must do something about being so pale; you look like a ghost. I suggest a faint touch of rouge—the merest hint will have you looking more the thing."

"Sir Phineas is dead." Kitty said baldly.

"Oh." Barbara gave them a blank look, then carefully said, "That is a pity. Poor Peregrine will be all alone in that great big house. Mama, Peregrine is a baronet now, is he not?" There was no missing the calculating gleam in her eyes.

"Wouldn't do for you, missy," her mother reminded Barbara.

"But he would for me," Kitty said quietly.

"Oh?" Lady Hamilton took a sip of tea, studying her youngest child over the rim of the cup.

"That would certainly dispose of her neatly, Mama," Barbara said earnestly. "You'd not have to worry about her in London."

"Barbara!" Juliana said, shocked at her sister's callousness.

"Never mind, Juliana. Barbara means well." Kitty reached out to touch Juliana's hand, warning her to be silent.

Juliana knew that however generous Kitty might be, Barbara thought first of herself. It would suit her to a tee to have her mother's time and money for her alone. Barbara had never cared to share anything, not even a maid.

"Well," Lady Hamilton said at the conclusion of her cup of tea, "Sir Peregrine will be in mourning for six months. Time enough for you two to reach an understanding."

"Yes, Mama," Kitty replied. But there was a rebellious aspect in her pretty gray eyes, and her hands clenched briefly in her lap. Juliana suspected that her youngest sister yearned to be free of her mother and home. In the past it had been understood that the eldest girl would marry first. It was doubtful Mama would let that stand in the way of Barbara. Perhaps Mama intended Juliana to serve as a companion in her declining years?

It was likely that only Juliana noticed the defiant flush of most becoming pink that suffused Kitty's cheeks, or the mutinous glow that lit her eyes. She had met Peregrine's gaze while in the entryway and something had been exchanged between them. Juliana had looked away, unable to intrude. But she felt certain that come the end of those six months, Kitty would have her Peregrine and feel him well worth waiting for. Juliana wished she had as joyous a prospect ahead of her. A companion lived a pretty dull life.

"Ah, Mother," Juliana ventured, after recalling that she must bring the matter to her mother's attention, "Lord Barry has requested that I accompany him to the London warehouses to guide him in a search for furniture and the like for his house. He is so kind as to offer to pay not only for my way but for my chaperon as well. I suggested I might call upon Aunt Tibbles."

"London? *You* go to London?" She glanced at Barbara, then back to where Juliana perched next to Kitty. "Aunt Tibbles," she murmured with a hint of dread in her voice. "I suppose so. Goodness knows *I* would be worn to flinders in a moment were I to go with you. Warehouses!"

"Did our London house come all furnished, then?" Barbara asked, her nose wrinkling at the thought of anything not to do with her own pleasure.

"Mostly," her mother admitted. "Your father selected all

the bits and pieces to complement what was there. It was far preferable to consulting with those dreadful shop people."

"How fortunate you did not have to lift a finger." Barbara sipped her tea while studying the toe of her new slipper.

Juliana turned to Kitty, and both compressed their lips to keep from giggling. How wonderful that Mama and Barbara had each other—they were a perfect pair.

After a check of the clock, Juliana gathered her skirts and rose from the window seat. "It is time past when I should go over to the building site. Henry will think me a slugabed."

"Juliana, such words," her mother rebuked absently.

"I apologize, of course," Juliana replied as she slipped from the room, followed closely by Kitty.

"It is good that Mama does not mind that you go with his lordship to London. What would you have done had she objected?" Kitty whispered while they went up the central stairs.

"Sought Uncle George's help. Oh," she cried, exchanging a concerned glance with Kitty, "he does not know about Sir Phineas as yet, nor does Henry. I must hurry." Not explaining why it was so necessary, Juliana dashed up the remaining steps and along to her room. She hurriedly donned a pelisse and bonnet, and pulled on her gloves before heading out the back to the stables.

Fortunately, the gig had been brought out, her groom anticipating she would prefer it this morning. It took little time to have it ready for travel.

Juliana paced about the area, wondering how her uncle and Henry would react to the news.

She held the mare to a spanking trot all the way over to the building site. Once there, she tossed the reins to the boy who came running to greet her, then hurried to the house.

"Uncle George! Henry!" she called, looking about her as she almost ran through the house.

All was quite still. The oak flooring was expected today or tomorrow, and soon the rooms would be ready for furnishings. She marched on along the hall until she found a window that looked out on the rear view from the house. In a few minutes she espied her uncle and Henry some distance away near the Chinese dairy. Workmen had planted shrubs and begun to dress the lawn in a picturesque way. She hurriedly left the main house, and within minutes she marched up the slope to meet them.

"My, you look all flustered," her uncle teased.

"I have news for you both," she said, catching her breath after her rush.

"What could be so momentous?" Henry said, exchanging a cautious look with George.

"Sir Phineas fell early this morning while examining the trim around an oriel window. The scaffolding crumpled inward on him, and he was killed instantly."

The men stopped in their tracks, staring at Juliana quite as though she had spoken in a foreign language.

"Dead? Phineas dead?" Uncle George said wonderingly.

"Not mean to be disrespectful, but it will make things easier around here with him gone," Henry said.

"True, however callous that sounds. We will all sleep better now we do not have to worry about his next trick. But I had not wished him dead," Juliana declared.

"Wonder what will happen now?" George said.

"Never mind about that; I believe the dray with the delivery of oak planking is coming along the drive." Henry led the way and soon the men had left Juliana far behind.

Rather than follow, she walked along the path to the Chinese dairy to inspect the columns that flanked the entryway. They were close to the Doric style with a simple curve at the top, but with ornate Oriental diagonal supports from the pillars to the ceiling of the portico. The walls were also plain, with simple panels set into them. Only the roof had the characteristic slope with turned-up tips and Oriental symbols on the flat peak. Inside, the little garden building, which really had little to do with a dairy other than being idealized, held Oriental-style benches and low tables.

On the walls was the fantastic sculpting that the Italians had done. Exotic birds vied with leaves and flowers in great profusion around the niches and mirrors and above the doors. The contrast between the elegant simplicity of the outside and the exotic interior was utterly charming, Juliana decided. She only hoped Lord Barry would think so as well.

It was a touch of Chinese art that she hoped to increase by

the addition of a Chinese fountain. In fact, she mused, it might be interesting to design that conservatory Lord Barry had requested in a Chinese style. A number of books in the library contained lovely illustrations of Peking gardens and buildings. They had inspired this little building. There should be abundant inspiration for others.

Quite pleased with herself, Juliana turned back toward the house, admiring the view from this direction. As the late Sir Phineas had said, it was in the classical mode, but it was utterly lovely for all that.

It might be nice, she considered, to have one of those elegant garden seats that Mr. Papworth designed. She rather liked the ornate umbrellas that were pegged to the ground to prevent a wind from carrying them away. But then, she reminded herself, it was not to be hers to enjoy. It would be that very, very English wife whom Lord Barry selected to marry who would stroll about these grounds, delight in the wonder of the Chinese dairy, and, perhaps, take the shade on a fanciful bench beneath a Papworth umbrella.

"Well, your lordship, *I* am quite as English as any woman you are likely to meet," she said to the absent lord. But Juliana also acknowledged that Lord Barry was not likely to look in her direction for marriage. Although—and even he must admit this—he certainly seemed to enjoy kissing her.

Lord Barry was kept from inspecting the Chinese dairy for several days because he devoted a great deal of energy to assisting Peregrine in sorting out all the papers dealing with the estate.

It was fortunate that Sir Phineas had kept his estate in amazingly good order and that Peregrine found he was left with a well-run home and very few debts.

At the conclusion of the third day Edmund rose from the large and most ornate desk in the late baronet's library to exclaim, "I believe that is the last of the paperwork that required immediate attention. Have your man check the deed to that parcel of land your father purchased last year. It appears irregular, but perhaps things have altered since I last studied the matter."

"Indeed, I will, my friend. I cannot begin to thank you for all you have done. Now I may face the future with a more confident heart." Peregrine crossed to the window, then looked back at Edmund. His smile had a heartfelt quality that struck Edmund as being most genuine.

Immediately perceiving the directions of his thinking, Edmund hesitantly asked, "You have a young lady in mind to take for a wife?"

"I do, and what's more I know she'll have me, in spite of the fact I made a cake of myself over Lady Rosamund for a time. Kitty is not only forgiving, but understanding. She will make me a good and constant wife and a fine mother of our children. We are close to an understanding, I believe."

"She hears poorly." Edmund did not like to raise the topic, but he suspected no one else would attempt it, and Peregrine needed to be reminded.

The wide grin was an answer before a word was spoken. "I care not for that. She can understand me, and that is most important. I will train the servants so they will speak clearly and distinctly for her."

Edmund was impressed by the younger man's apparent concern and devotion for Lady Katherine. "Well, you will have six months' time to mull it over," he concluded.

That met with a frown quite as mutinous as the one Kitty had displayed had they but known it.

"At least she has never expected a Season in London, unlike Lady Juliana," Peregrine declared with a curious look at Edmund. "Did you know her work on your house kept her from her Season? Her mother did not forgive her that, you may be sure. And I feel bad, because I suspect that Lady Juliana feared to leave lest my father commit some dreadful deed while she was away. She was determined to see the project through to the end. She is a very loyal woman, demanding of others, but more so of herself," Peregrine concluded scrupulously.

"*That* was why she failed to have a Season in Town? I do not understand why her mother refuses to grant her one now." Edmund was incredulous that a mother could be so harsh.

"She prefers to lavish her attention on the daughter who is the most like herself. While Lady Juliana may enjoy pretty clothes, they are not the most important part of her life," he suggested.

Edmund looked at Sir Peregrine with increased respect. The young fellow revealed a perspicacity Edmund had not expected to find, particularly when Sir Peregrine had not spent all that much time about the house—at least not while Edmund had been around. Or, perhaps that was why he could see things so clearly; he kept his distance.

It was four days after the disaster that Edmund confronted Lady Juliana in the morning room. She was dressed to go to the site, drawing on gloves and about to leave.

"I will join you if I may. After we go over the house, I would like to take a tour of the grounds, inspect the stables and other outbuildings."

She paled at his words, but kept her chin up as she replied. Her gaze met his briefly before skittering off to stare out of the window before settling on her gloves.

"Of course, I have been waiting for you to have the time for this. It is long overdue, you know. There are still decisions you must make before going to London. And I have a number of questions I would have you answer as well."

Edmund strongly suspected that the day was going to be vastly revealing to him.

Rather than ride, he elected to join her in the gig this morning. That this clearly disconcerted her pleased him for some odd reason. He folded his arms before him and watched her handle the ribbons with surprising ease.

When they arrived following a drive during which they exchanged no more than mere pleasantries, he assisted her from the gig, then strolled along at her side. He admired the clean lines of his house. His, he thought with fierce pleasure. Soon he would move into this gracious country house and begin his hunt for a wife in earnest.

"The workmen have been clearing away the debris. You can see how the final appearance will be." She gestured with a broad sweep of her arm across the front aspect of the house. "Once some planting is done, the grass in place, and the gravel down for your drive, it will shine in all its glory."

"You paint a rosy picture."

"With all due respect to the dead, now that Sir Phineas is

no longer among us to plague us with delays and worse, you will note things move faster."

"The carpenters seem to have gone," he observed when they entered the house.

"The plasterers and painter-decorators as well," she added. "Mr. Maine has nearly completed the carvings for your library. Would you wish to see them now?"

Edmund debated. While he wanted to see those carvings, he wondered if it was a delaying tactic. Was there something she did not wish him to view? Or perhaps dreaded his seeing? Well, they had all day together, for Henry Scott had offered his services to Peregrine today, to help tie up loose ends at the other building site. And, Edmund admitted with an inward smile, he was supremely pleased to have Henry Scott far away from here.

"Let us see the carvings, if you please."

Her sigh of what sounded like relief almost made him smile before he wondered what it was that she had been hiding from him. He would relish putting her on pins and needles for a bit. She deserved it, he had no doubt.

Mr. Maine held up the last of the muses for Edmund to inspect. It was incredible artistry, with exquisite detailing. Urania gracefully posed with her globe to signify the science of astronomy she represented. On a nearby table were, among the other eight goddesses, Calliope with her tablet and stylus to represent epic poetry, and Thalia, the comic mask of comedy dangling from her dainty fingers. He particularly liked the representation of Terpsichore, for he thought he detected the likeness to Juliana in it. He glanced at her to see if she had caught it, but doubted if she did. She looked too calm.

He praised Mr. Maine, then guided Juliana from the little room where the carver had worked these past weeks.

"What next? I have seen the Etruscan room—and note that you will be required to help me find furniture and draperies suitable for there. Is there anything else in the house that I'm unaware of now?"

"We had best proceed to the stables, my lord," she said with what appeared to be stoic calm.

Edmund would have sworn she was girding herself for a battle, and he found he looked forward to exchanging barbs with her. Or whatever chanced to happen. He could not deny the feelings he knew while with her. It was dangerous to be alone with her, he knew that as well. Were she not so passionate in her innocent response, it would be otherwise, he supposed. But being close to Lady Juliana was like holding a burning candle near the fuse of a cannon.

"I recall there was a problem regarding the stables. It occurred about the time I arrived. I trust it was satisfactorily corrected? I have heard or seen nothing to give me to think otherwise."

"Sir Phineas hired a man who paid that first group of carpenters to build the stable walls a foot short. Fortunately, I chanced to catch them before the roof went on." She gave him a wry look while ushering him into the completed stable block. It was extremely large, but then, he intended to have a number of carriages and full complement of horseflesh.

Edmund suspected that other problems had been engendered by this event, but she was remaining silent on them. He approved of what had been accomplished.

"I can see your father's hand in this." He strolled along the length of the interior, examining the fine stone stall separations, the brickwork, and lastly the ceiling. It might be a trifle fancy, but good horses deserved a decent place.

Juliana smiled to herself at his almost pompous inspection of the interior. She would not quibble with anything he said, for indeed, her father had designed the stable block, and it had turned out most magnificently.

"Well," he said, rubbing his hands together with satisfaction, "lead me on to whatever is next to view."

Juliana's heart sank to her toes, but she refused to quail in the face of what was ahead of her. Surely he was in such a good mood he would not take umbrage at the rest of the buildings? "Come this way, my lord."

Acting as demure as could be, Juliana led the way from the stable block and along the path to where other garden buildings were eventually slated to be—if his lordship approved. She had been a trifle precipitate in building the Chinese dairy, but she had been so very proud of her design and longed to see the structure built. It had not been terribly costly, except for the plasterers. They had created the scagliola floor, which was most economical when one thought of the cost of marble.

"Here we are," she said as they walked up the winding path to the little rise to where the Chinese dairy sat in early morning splendor. The sun gently blessed the columns and enhanced the tile roof, causing it to gleam brightly.

"And what is this, pray tell?"

His voice was dangerously quiet. She couldn't tell a thing from his expression. How best to explain all this, she wondered.

"Well 'tis a Chinese dairy, my lord," she said patiently. "Actually, it is not a dairy, but a garden building where one may enjoy the sounds and scents of the garden about you. That it is called a dairy is but a silly conceit."

He marched up to the building, wordlessly studying the columns of which Juliana felt justifiably proud, then the interior with the delicate Chinese decorations around the mirrors and windows. It was an exquisite gem of architecture, and she could only hope he recognized it as such. And yet he said nothing.

Finally, after a silence that seemed to stretch forever, he turned to face her. His frown was not encouraging in the least.

"I ought to have been told about this long ago. Never say you intended this as a surprise for me? A gift, perhaps?"

Juliana thought of the cost involved and reckoned it would take her a while to pay off the expense of building this place.

"No, my lord, it was not intended as a gift. It is customary now to create garden structures such as this. I suppose I assumed you would wish to do as everyone else is doing nowadays. The Marquess of Titchfield has ordered an entire Chinese garden to be built on his land—a dairy such as this, a temple, a fountain, ever so many things. You would not want to be considered behind times—old-fashioned, would you?" She thought her argument most reasonable.

"And what is wrong with the past?" he growled, turning to face her. "I admire the past very much."

"Well, then, we will build you a nice Doric temple on that other little rise over there. It will be quite lovely." She came to stand before him, her hands clasped before her and chin tilted, not quite defying him, but allowing him to see that she would not be intimidated.

"You are humoring me, aren't you?" he said, the tone of his voice causing Juliana to take a step back from him.

She swallowed carefully, then shook her head. "No, that is not it in the least. I want to please you."

His expression changed, and she did not know what to make of it.

Of a sudden, she found herself swept into his arms and kissed with a thoroughness that put previous attempts in the pale. Worse yet, she made no effort to escape. She reveled in that kiss, more's the pity.

When he released her, he growled again, but more softly. "You do please me. Too much for my own good." Then he stepped away from her, but holding her gaze with his, his eyes blazing. "But let me tell you here and now that if you ever construct another bloody building on this land without my permission, I'll make you wish you had never thought of it."

His gaze seemed to sear her lips, and Juliana felt weak at the thought of what form his retribution might take.

Chapter Thirteen

T he remainder of the week was bustling with activity. First came the funeral for Sir Phineas. Juliana was grateful that she was not required to attend. The men of the house, together with Lord Barry, went to the little church in the village for the service.

"I cannot believe he is actually dead," Kitty said, curled up on her favorite window seat in the morning room.

"It does make a difference for all of us, but I suppose it affects you a great deal," Juliana said with sympathy, wondering just how patient her little sister would be in the coming months. It was evident that she felt little inclined to mourn Sir Phineas, for all that he had made life miserable for Juliana and ultimately been responsible for the death of a carpenter.

"Indeed," Kitty replied, a dreamy look creeping into her eyes. "Peregrine begs me to be resigned to the wait, but I can see he has no more patience than I."

Juliana had been called away at that point and had not since found the opportunity to remind Kitty that time passes faster than one would think. Her day would come soon enough.

The second event of the week was the arrival of Aunt Tibbles. She was without a doubt Juliana's favorite aunt, even if Lady Hamilton and Miss Tibbles heartily detested one another, in spite of the fact they were sisters. In this instance, the two would spend very little time together. It suited all involved to a tee.

The elegantly tall, thin, and most sprightly Miss Augusta Tibbles undoubtedly made softly round and somewhat indolent Susan, Lady Hamilton, feel frivolous, for Augusta could accomplish more in an hour than Susan could in a day.

They had never agreed on what was right for the girls. Augusta Tibbles insisted that regardless of her age, Juliana deserved a come-out. The subject reared its head again as soon as the two faced one another over the tea table.

"I do not understand how a sister of mine could be so remiss about her eldest daughter—one who has the intelligence of the Tibbles combined with the looks of the Gerards. Our mother was a famous beauty in her day," Augusta charged with more than a little belligerence.

"Brunettes are not in fashion now; blondes are," was Lady Hamilton's smug reply.

"Pish tush," Augusta said with a dismissing wave of a thin, elegant hand. "If you were half as clever as you think you are, you would have discovered a way to make Juliana all the rage." She buried her nose in her teacup, watching over the rim as her younger, and not as bright, and certainly more self-centered sister coped with that home truth.

"Augusta," Lady Hamilton at last declared, "you are a guest in my home, so I shan't tell you how utterly odious you have become in your old age. Instead, I shall tell you that I am pleased that it is you who will be shepherding Juliana and Lord Barry around London, to warehouses and linen drapers, and heaven knows where else. Even you will be worn to flinders unless I miss my guess."

"It sounds delightful," Augusta retorted. "Unless I am mistaken, I'll be treated to a view of the latest in decoration, furniture, and all matter of fascinating things. I shall enjoy seeing all that. 'Tis better than a raree show. What a pity you are such a stuffy, dreary creature, Susan. You miss so much life has to offer. I feel sure that not all countesses are as stodgy as you are."

With that final barb planted in her sister's hide, Augusta rose from her chair, set the delicate china teacup on the tray, and sailed from the room, her height lending a certain majesty to her exit.

"When do we leave for London?" Augusta demanded once she had found Juliana in the morning room.

Juliana looked up from a book of garden building designs and frowned. "Best seek out his lordship. He is the one planning the trip, and I imagine he will tell us when he is ready to depart."

"You have organized a list of the manufactories, warehouses, and linen drapers you intend to visit?"

"I had forgotten how you liked to make lists," Juliana said, smiling at her dearest aunt. "Indeed, yes, I have a list at the ready. I also have had one of the painters apply dabs of the various paints to a piece of wood, so we will have that for comparison when shopping."

"Most intelligent of you. I trust Lord Barry is anxious to move into his new home?" Aunt Tibbles settled onto a chair, looking out of the window to where Kitty strolled in the garden while having an earnest chat with Sir Peregrine.

"Now that old Phineas is gone, Barry will move in there a great deal quicker," George said, having caught the last sentence his sister had uttered while entering the room. "You are needed over at the site at once, Juliana. I ordered the gig readied for you to save time."

He didn't elaborate on why she was needed, but Juliana knew him too well to question his words. It must be something he wished to conceal from his sister Augusta.

"I shall go at once," Juliana said, closing the book and taking it along with her. She would show it to his lordship. Perhaps he might be reconciled to one of these designs.

"Don't lose a minute," he murmured as she passed him on her way out.

"Now see here, George," Augusta began, her voice fading as Juliana slipped along to the back door.

She thankfully escaped from the house and climbed into the waiting gig, anxious to be off. What could be so urgent that she must dash to the Barry mansion? On the way she mulled over the intriguing question from every angle, and short of some disaster that hadn't needed Sir Phineas to set it off, she couldn't fathom what it might be.

She handed the reins to the usual lad who cared for her carriage and horse when she was at the site, then walked to the house with a heart full of misgivings. There had not been a fire, for the house looked intact. There was no indication of an upset in the interior of the house.

Then she noticed a lovely chestnut mare off to one side, the groom in charge wearing the livery of the Marquess of Titchfield. Juliana quickened her steps.

Within the house voices could be heard, echoing through vacant rooms. The floors had been laid down and hand-rubbed with special oils, and now gleamed softly in the sunlight. No draperies, no furniture, no carpets were in place to soften noise. Along with the rise and fall of what was undoubtedly Lady Rosamund's dulcet tones came Lord Barry's deep replies, with a counterpoint of carpenters at work on one of the first-level floors.

On the first floor she found Lady Rosamund strolling along with Lord Barry on a languid tour of inspection. They had paused in the Etruscan room, where Lady Rosamund was giving vent to her feelings regarding such pagan display.

"I cannot think how any woman of sensibility will react when confronted with these paintings come morning and she enters this room," Lady Rosamund complained.

"Good morning, Lady Rosamund, Lord Barry. Is it not a blessing that you most likely will not be faced with such a dilemma in that event?" Juliana interposed sweetly.

Her greeting earned her a narrow-eyed glare from Lady Rosamund and an amused glance from his lordship. Evidently Rosamund's mother had decided a viscount in the hand is worth a duke and marquess in the bush.

"Did you really and truly commission this room for Lord Barry without telling him first?" Lady Rosamund inquired, her voice rising a few notes to indicate her amazement.

"Every now and again we, each of us, deserve a surprise," Juliana responded wryly.

"Well, supposing he did not care for it?" her ladyship said, leaning a trifle on Lord Barry's arm as she gazed coyly into his face, fluttering her lashes.

Juliana longed to give Rosamund a less than gentle pat on her posterior. "I would have crossed that bridge when I came to it," Juliana said tartly.

"My, how daring you are—so masculine." Lady Rosamund trilled a laugh that sounded quite as practiced as Barbara's. Juliana wondered what it sounded like when those two rehearsed their feminine wiles in private, with their respective mothers as mentors.

"I agree that Lady Juliana is quite out of the common way, but she is to be commended on her devotion to her father's memory and his talent," Lord Barry inserted, quite effectively bringing Lady Rosamund to a halt in her snide remarks about Juliana. "I find a woman with an opinion rather refreshing now and again."

Juliana clutched her book to her, then recalled why she had brought it along. She hoped to interest his lordship in a pretty little Grecian temple that would be perfect on a slight rise above and just beyond the small lake that had been created not far from the house. Once trees had been planted and shrubbery set in place, it would appear quite as ancient—and traditional—as anyone could desire.

But, the rub was, she did not want Lady Rosamund putting forth her thoughts on the subject. Juliana discovered that she did not want Rosamund inhabiting this house, nor even expressing a feeling about it.

"Aunt Tibbles and Uncle George send their greetings," Juliana said to Lord Barry, sure that had they thought about it, they would have done the polite. "Had they known that you were here, alone—" Juliana glanced pointedly around—"they would have sent greetings to you as well, Lady Rosamund."

Then Juliana wondered if Rosamund was trying to compromise his lordship. She'd put nothing past the girl, for she was quite accustomed to having her way in all things.

"La, Lady Juliana, my maid is never far from my side, I assure you. *I* am not so lost to propriety that I would ever consider walking with a gentleman without a chaperon." The elevated nose did not prevent her from giving Juliana a look full of suspicion.

Juliana wondered if she looked guilty and decided she really had not much to feel guilty about—unless one counted several passionate kisses. And not a soul knew about those, save herself and Lord Barry. Neither would divulge that.

The sound of hammering began at a room closer, thus became louder. Another carpenter must have joined the crew.

"I believe the noise is becoming objectionable. Perhaps we might go outside in the fresh air?" Lord Barry said, leading Lady Rosamund from the room and along to the top of the stairs.

Juliana followed, feeling quite as useless as a flea. Perhaps his lordship had decided the rich and beautiful young heiress of the Purcell family would be an acceptable wife. What a pity it would be were Rosamund to turn out like her mother. A shrewd study of Rosamund's face revealed an amazing similarity between the two, once one delved beneath the fat that covered the mother's face.

"You wished to discuss something with me this morning, Lady Juliana?" Lord Barry said at last as the three strolled down the perfectly proportioned steps to the gravel in front of the house.

"It is not urgent," Juliana denied. "I mainly came over," and she thought a second before continuing, "to check on the progress of the men who work on the flooring."

"Then check on them, by all means," Lady Rosamund said crossly.

Feeling that his lordship would make his own choices whatever she chanced to do, Juliana nodded pleasantly and left the two standing not far from Rosamund's pretty chestnut mare. So be it on his head if he made the wrong decision.

Once she returned to the upper floor, Juliana inspected the work being done with a careful eye to detail. This particular floor was being laid in a pretty pattern and required attention to wood grains and color to be effective. The man she had chosen from her father's list was proving to be a genius at his work. His assistant carried in another armful of exotic woods in various lengths for his use. In another room down the hall, more oak was being laid.

"You approve?" Lord Barry said from immediately behind her. It seemed that Lady Rosamund had been sent on her way—along with her ever-present maid and the groom.

"I should hope so," Juliana replied fervently, thus earning a smile of appreciation from the man at work. "Note how the colors of the various woods enhance the design. Once they have a coat of varnish, those colors will be even lovelier, particularly the ebony trim pieces."

"What was it you wished to show me from that book you clutch so fiercely?" he inquired, adroitly plucking the book from her arms and opening it to the page with the marker to the little Grecian temple she admired.

"See," she said, losing her feeling of constraint in the enthusiasm for the little temple. "Would this not be most fitting for the little knoll across the lake? Once you plant trees and shrubbery about it, you could think it had been there for ages. In the spring you could have pretty budding trees and daffodils on the bank. Come autumn you could have red oaks clustered behind to enhance the purity of the stone, with dianthus and bellflowers to bloom around the base of the building in wild profusion. It would be vastly appealing, my lord."

"You really care how the estate will appear, don't you?" He gazed down at her with a puzzled expression, as though trying to figure her out.

"Of course I do," Juliana said defensively.

"Even though you might never see the place again once you are done?"

The very thought was hard to bear. Never to see this architectural gem again? She would not make a good architect, she decided in an instant, for she grew too attached to her projects. "If I must never see it again, I must face that reality."

Edmund stared at the earnest young woman standing close to him. A shadow had crossed her face when he had posed his query. A husky quality had crept into her voice, and she had clasped her hands before her in a gesture of what seemed almost like anguish. She did not look forward to quitting his house. It pleased him, somehow.

Yet, no matter how attracted he was to her, she was not his ideal. Too aggressive, too bold and daring, she did not always observe the proprieties. He had seen no evidence of *her* maid lurking around a corner.

Or . . . did she consider him utterly harmless? No, he decided at once. There had been several instances when he had been unable to resist her charms. And, he thought with satisfaction, she had yielded for several long moments to the flare of passion that had ignited between them. Perhaps it was a part of her creative nature to be responsive, passionate in all she did.

He returned his gaze to the illustration in the book, then strolled to another room from which he might see better. Yes, he could envision a little Doric-columned temple nestled in a growing woods on the far side of the newly completed lake. How fortuitous that he'd been able to dam that creek without objections from those in the near countryside. Water continued to flow, and it would offer a reservoir in the event of a dry summer.

"I agree with you," he declared suddenly and almost smiled when she expelled a breath she'd been holding.

"Once you put in a pretty walk, and perhaps a picturesque bridge, and assuredly a fountain or two, you will be most pleased with your prospect, my lord."

She edged away from him, seeming intent on something she had observed from the window. Perhaps she was envisioning the scene as it might be. There were a goodly number of fine trees on site that would offer an excellent beginning for his planting.

Edmund found his enthusiasm rising with the image she painted for him, instilling a sense of excitement.

"I had no idea that you harbored such ambitions for my grounds." He offered her the book, which she accepted and clutched against her as though she wished a barrier.

"An architect does not stop his mind with the creation of a building. You imagine it softened by greenery to enhance the frame of the house—various shades of green, improved with blooming shrubs and beds of flowers." She stopped suddenly, looking a trifle embarrassed at her eagerness for a project that she would no longer guide.

"Hullo! Is anyone about? I would see my brother-in-law's final creation." Augusta's voice echoed from below, a warning of sorts.

Before Juliana walked more than a few steps, Aunt Tibbles entered the room, her face beaming with good-natured pleasure.

"Well, if it don't beat the Dutch," she said with great admiration evident in her voice. "And how much of this is your contribution, missy?" she said, turning to Juliana.

"Would you excuse us, my lord?" Juliana said with sudden formality. "I wish to show my aunt about the house—if you do not mind, that is."

"Be my guest," he replied, then left the room. His steps could be heard going down the stairs and fading away.

Juliana reflected that it would be the one time she might be counted a guest, if what he had said was true.

"You were here alone?" Aunt Tibbles observed, without any accusation in her manner.

"Lady Rosamund was here when I arrived. I suspect Uncle George wanted me to be present lest she contrive to compromise his lordship. After she left, we spent some time watching the man who is laying the floor in the next room. Hardly the stuff for compromise," Juliana concluded with a chuckle. Truth be told, she was beginning to believe she needed to be chaperoned by Aunt Tibbles!

"Good," her aunt said briskly. "Now, I wish to see one of those water-closets I have heard about, then after that the hot-air furnace. I declare, what's the world coming to with all these new-fashioned things!"

"You must see the range we installed in the kitchen. There is a nice tiled scullery as well, and a marvelous cellar for storage of fruits and vegetables, not to mention a perfectly splendid buffet in the dining room. And," Juliana added, "I believe you will like the Chinese dairy I designed."

"Whatever would you want with a Chinese dairy? Seems to me that a good English one is perfectly acceptable," Aunt Tibbles avowed, frowning in perplexity.

"It is not precisely a true dairy; more a pretty little garden building, a place to rest and relax away from the house, particularly on a summer day," Juliana explained while trying not to giggle. Her dearest aunt had a way of cutting to the heart of a matter. "It is the very latest thing. I admire innovation, you know." She cast a sidelong look at her aunt as she inspected the first of the water-closets, operating it with a touch of her fingers.

"My, oh, my," Aunt Tibbles said in wonderment. "Next?"

Juliana dutifully led her through the house from top to bottom and finally gave vent to mirth when Aunt Tibbles viewed the Etruscan room.

"I am not a prude, Juliana. You must know that. However, I would find all these undraped and scantily clad women right at eye level a trifle much first thing in the morning. 'Tis one thing to have them on the ceiling, and quite another to find them under your nose."

When Juliana recovered from her fit of giggles, she said, "Lady Rosamund said something similar. I cannot see a problem, unless Lord Barry marries Lady Rosamund. Perhaps he will have to hire a painter to cover the more imprudent ladies?" Then, the idea of a gentleman having to carefully paint drapery over every exposed bosom and thigh caused her to giggle anew. "One accepts a certain amount of revealed skin in paintings of antiquity, Auntie." This time, Juliana did not blush.

"I daresay your mother has not seen these, unless I miss my guess." Aunt Tibbles took Juliana by the arm and guided her along the hall and down the stairs to the entry. "It is a fine house, my dear, and you should rightly be proud of it. Is there no chance that you might grace these halls as a wife?" Aunt Tibbles toyed with her reticule while staring at the decorations on the ceiling.

"Not unless the man I might eventually marry buys it from Lord Barry," Juliana replied, honestly facing the reality of her situation.

"There are more fools in this world than can be counted," Aunt observed. "When do we leave for London?"

"Finished so soon?" Lord Barry said as he entered from a side room where it seemed he'd been looking at pattern books.

"Aunt was just inquiring as to when we will depart for London," Juliana said, disregarding the fluttering that arose in her stomach at the thought of traveling with this particular man all the way to the city.

"How soon could you be ready to leave?" he countered, looking from one to the other.

"I daresay we would be prepared in two days," Juliana said after exchanging a look with her aunt.

"Then in two days we shall be on our way to the city. I trust you have lists and names of manufactories and the like you wish to visit?" he inquired in an afterthought.

"Indeed, sir. Several pages, and samples of paint and marble as well. I have tried to think of everything."

He gave her a smile that excluded Aunt Tibbles completely. This was so brief that later she wondered if she had imagined it.

Her aunt seemed to notice nothing out of the ordinary, but accepted Lord Barry's arm to leave the building, chatting amiably while they walked down the steps.

"I shall drive back with you, Juliana," Aunt Tibbles announced. "I sent the carriage that brought me home again. No sense in having a groom lingering about here. We will no doubt see you later, my lord." She climbed into the gig and put up her parasol, ready to brave the drive back to Beechwood Hall with perfect aplomb.

"Until later, my lord," Juliana murmured politely. She had told him that she tried to think of everything. That was not quite true, however. She had not considered what it would be like to be in his company day in and day out, all day long. How could she arm herself against his charm, for she had grown to quite admire his sharp wit and suave appeal. Most likely they would be daggers drawn by the conclusion of their visit. It would make it far easier for her if it happened that way.

Perhaps, once in the city, he would chance to see a lady such as he desired to grace his home. The mere thought of such an event put Juliana into the doldrums all the way to Beechwood and into the house.

"I should like to visit a mantuamaker while in the City," Aunt Tibbles ventured to say, then studied her niece with a candid gaze. "It would not harm you to order a few things, for although I should not opine on your wardrobe, it is sadly lacking in style, my dear."

Juliana nodded her agreement. "Perhaps we can manage to

convince his lordship to visit a club while we conduct our pressing business?"

"Quite so," Aunt Tibbles agreed, then went off to her room to assist her maid in packing for London. Her help mostly consisted of contributing little things that were apt to be left behind. Juliana found Kitty in the stillroom, working at compounding a formula of rose essence. "Mrs. Dalston usually does this." She gave her sister a questioning look.

"I must learn to do these things if I am to assume control of Peregrine's household. Mrs. Dalston has agreed to tutor me in all things helpful. I would not waste a moment of time." Kitty peered at a measuring vial, then added its contents to a bowl.

"You have all of six months, my dear. When I return from London, perhaps I can go with you to your future home to help with inventory of the linens? I will be well up on the latest in furniture and draperies, so I could bring you up to date on the very latest thing."

Kitty flashed her an arrested look, then smiled. "Perhaps you could, at that. I should like to alter what I might, for I would remove as much of Sir Phineas from the house as possible." She stirred her compound, then glanced at Juliana again. "Where will you stay while in London? At the family residence? I trust our dear brother will not mind in the least. He is so busy in Kent, I believe he scarce recalls the house is there."

"That is our plan."

"And what about Lord Barry? Where will he stay?"

"I have not a clue," Juliana replied. "I expect he will stay at a hotel, perhaps Grillon's? It is fashionable, I understand."

"I had not thought him to be concerned with what is fashionable. He seems to prefer the solid and familiar."

Juliana accepted this remark, took note that her little sister did very well at her compounding, then left to head for her room. On the way she observed her trunk disappearing around the corner to her room. Aunt Tibbles had been busy on her behalf, it seemed.

Before she plunged into preparing to leave for London, Juliana paused to hope that her sister would continue in her excellent show of patience. Surely six months would not seem so very onerous. Why, were she to have the same to look forward to with regard to a certain gentleman, she would—and Juliana sank down on her bed, utterly dismayed. She would *not* have a great deal of patience were she to have to wait a long time to wed one she loved. Oh, dear.

Chapter Fourteen

W hat with one thing and another Juliana did not have another chance for that conversation with Kitty regarding the need for patience. Once Aunt Tibbles set things in motion, Juliana found herself swept up in her wake.

The third morning following the decision to leave discovered Juliana standing in the entryway with her aunt, checking over the list that had been handed to her and feeling slightly breathless.

"Patterns—in the event of rain—umbrellas and parasols—your books, my lists and samples, my books of designs, the sketches for furniture—everything is packed in the traveling coach," she assured Miss Tibbles at last.

"All we need now is his lordship," Aunt Tibbles said with a faint sniff in her tone. "I find it best to have an early start of a morning, then stop early in the day so one can have the best chambers available."

"Surely we will not need to stop overnight? I had not thought the journey so long."

"One must always be prepared," Aunt Tibbles said, turning to study the man who ran lightly down the stairs to join them. He was followed by George—at a much slower pace.

"Good morning," his lordship said with a bow to Aunt Tibbles. "I must apologize for keeping you waiting. I discovered that I had left some important papers in my room and could not leave until I found them."

He didn't explain what they were, nor would Juliana dream of prying, although she'd admit to being curious.

"Now you two," George inserted, "understand what to do about the bills you incur?" At Juliana's nod of assurance, he added, "Don't let that plaguey Hilsom raise those beetle brows of his at you," he admonished, referring to the butler who ruled the London town house. "You are to have first-rate care, and if you do not receive it, let me know."

He bestowed a handshake on his sister and accepted Juliana's fond hug with no more than a sniff and a gruff good-bye.

Naturally Lady Hamilton was not in sight, nor was Barbara. Both preferred to sleep as late as possible. Kitty stood by the front door, wrapped in a warm shawl against the early morning chill. Her forlorn little smile and wave cut Juliana to the quick.

"I worry about Kitty, Aunt," she said quietly once they settled on their forward-facing seat. "I do hope she will have the fortitude to wait patiently for what she desires." She leaned out of the window to wave at her sister and her uncle before the avenue curved and they were lost to view.

"You believe there is danger she might do something foolish?" Aunt said in an undertone as the coach turned off the avenue that led to Beechwood Hall and bowled along the road that went to the turnpike.

"I do not know, but she had a determined tilt to her chin when last I spoke with her about the matter."

"Oh, dear me," Aunt Tibbles murmured.

"Is there a problem?" Lord Barry said, glancing up from a sheaf of papers he checked over.

"No," Juliana hastened to assure him. "At least I hope not," she muttered in an aside to her aunt.

The carriage was remarkably well-sprung and the roads dry, with no deep ruts, so they made excellent time. Juliana ventured that his lordship's team of four matched grays were capable of at least ten miles an hour, and she relished the swiftness as they left the Hall far behind.

She found her gaze straying to the man who sat across from them far more than was likely proper. He made her heart beat that peculiar tattoo when he chanced to gaze at her. And as to those forbidden kisses he had taken without her permission, well, those would most assuredly not be repeated. She would make certain of it.

It was easy to understand why a chaperon was so necessary for a young lady of quality. A girl could be compromised—indeed, swept off her silly feet—far too readily with very little effort on the part of a man like Lord Barry. She gathered that was what seduction was all about, catching a girl off her guard and rendering her incapable of rational thought. She would be on *her* guard, no matter how dull that sounded. Dull had to be better than a broken heart, surely?

The pause at the first stage for a change of horses was accomplished with all due speed, as were the subsequent changes, until Lord Barry consulted his watch and declared, "I believe we had best stop soon for a light repast. Would that be agreeable? We will shortly be about halfway to London, and there is an excellent inn, I've been told, at High Wycombe where we can trust the food to be palatable."

"Lovely," Aunt Tibbles said, clearly impressed with his planning and foresight. As one who believed in sensible living, she could applaud his intelligence.

Juliana left the coach gratefully, for even a well-sprung vehicle grew most tiresome after a few hours. When Lord Barry offered his hand to assist her, she met his gaze and decided that she best write her sister a letter, begging her to have patience, for it was easier and easier to see how she might effortlessly be convinced to impropriety.

The meal was not leisurely, but not rushed, either. In an effort to be pleasant—for Lord Barry had studied his papers most of the way, leaving Juliana to converse with her aunt—she inquired as to what his precise plans were while in London.

"Why, my first order of business is to visit my tailor. I find I need particular items. I suppose you two will be off to the mantuamaker first thing?" He gave Aunt Tibbles a significant look that made Juliana wonder if he had schemed with that wily creature.

"Indeed, sir. I intend to have Juliana order as many pretty clothes as I am able, you may be certain." Her tone implied that she would do what her sister had failed to do—outfit Juliana in the latest styles.

"Sir Peregrine requested that I obtain a number of things for Kitty as well," Juliana added thoughtfully. "She tends to be neglected, being the youngest of us. My mother has been much occupied with the local dressmaker," she explained. "There has been no time to spare for Kitty, what with all of Barbara's clothes to make. Kitty has grown this past year, so really does need a fair number of things."

"You thought to buy for her and not yourself?" he said with an odd glint to those dark eyes.

"Oh, no," she replied with a vehement shake of her head. "I have intended for some time now to obtain a new wardrobe first chance I could. I am a vain creature, to be wishing the latest in fashion." She smiled wryly, then rose to leave the table, not waiting to see if he disapproved of her folly.

"We shall arrive in London in three hours. Amazing how the road has improved this past year. Ladies?" He gestured to the door.

Aunt Tibbles sailed forth first, in search of a necessary. Juliana quickly followed, convinced she dare not be missish about such a mundane thing.

While they had been at their meal, the coach had been cleaned on the outside. Now it gleamed. The mulberry color was a good background for his lordship's crest painted in gold on the door. His neatly maroon-liveried groom had joined the valet on the high seat that rose in the back of the coach. The coachman, his tall hat at a jaunty angle, stood by the leader, patting and talking to the horse. As soon as he caught sight of the women, he hastened to open the door for them.

Lord Barry stood off to one side, chatting with a gentleman who had just arrived for a change of horses. His gaze had followed the women while they entered the coach, but he'd not cut short his conversation as yet.

"This is a nice way to travel," Aunt Tibbles observed, smoothing her hand over the petit-point upholstery.

"Indeed," Juliana prosaically. Not that she was bored, but it would have been nice had Lord Barry conversed with them a trifle. She studied the vehicle with appreciation for the comfort wealth could buy. No doubt her mother would hire a nice post chaise when she took Barbara to London, sending all their belongings ahead by wagon.

"Well, we proceed," Lord Barry declared upon entering.

"The road ahead is in good repair, so I'm told, and we shall make our goal if nothing untoward occurs."

Juliana thought of all the disasters that had befallen her since taking over the management and responsibility of building Lord Barry's house, and grimaced. "That has a familiar ring to it, sir."

"I take it you refer to my house?" he said, instantly aware of her train of thought. "Well, since the most that might happen is behind us, surely the coming days will bring us a pleasant change." He placed his papers into a leather satchel he had brought along and proceeded to chat with Aunt Tibbles, utterly charming her.

He persuaded her to talk about times past until they reached Uxbridge, when she broke off to peer from the coach window. "I have a charming acquaintance who lives not far from here. Lady Jersey, daughter of an old friend of mine. I believe there are a few more Wednesdays at Almack's remaining to the Season. Why do I not request vouchers for us, Juliana? Would you enjoy that?"

Juliana nodded, but was unsure just how she would enjoy such a snobbish place. Perhaps it might be interesting to see what it was like and report to Barbara. Her sister would be utterly pea green to know that Juliana had attended the assembly before her.

The coach swept through Notting Hill Gate at a fresh pace with a goodly team before them, and before they knew it, they were on the street where the Hamilton house stood.

Aunt Tibbles reached the ground with a thankful expression on her face. She said all that was polite, inviting Lord Barry to join them for a late—by country standards—dinner, but not seeming surprised when he said he would take a meal at his hotel and see them on the morrow to discuss a schedule.

"Oh, I trust you have suitable attire for the opera as well as Almack's. I thought to purchase tickets. Have you attended the opera, Lady Juliana?"

"Neither the opera nor Almack's." How unsophisticated she felt to admit she'd not attended anything a fashionable young woman her age would accept as common.

"It seems this will be a notable trip for you in that event." He saw them into the house, glancing about to see that all was in readiness for them. Evidence that it might have been a hurried preparation could be seen, but that was to be expected, he supposed. He exchanged a cool look with Hilsom, then turned to leave. "On the morrow, ladies."

"We shall have a great deal to do tomorrow," Aunt Tibbles said loudly enough for the butler to overhear, her words echoing about the pleasant entry hall. "I propose we have a light repast and go straight to our beds." Then she turned to the rotund gentleman who had supervised the unloading with admirable dispatch and said, "We wish a meal in thirty minutes' time—something simple will do."

Assured that all would be as she wished—for the staff were well acquainted with Miss Tibbles from past visits—Aunt led the way up the stairs and along to Juliana's room.

"Thirty minutes, mind you," she admonished.

And so it was. They dined, then slept on excellent beds, managing to ignore the noise from beyond the windows.

Come morning, Aunt Tibbles, armed with list in hand, guided Juliana along to the finest mantuamaker in London, so Aunt proclaimed.

Juliana was awed at the discreet dove gray interior with trim painted white and detailed in gilt. Before long her aunt had commanded the amazing Madame Clotilde with her improbable red hair to do precisely as wished.

"I vow, I am vastly pleased that she had two perfectly lovely gowns for your immediate wear," Aunt said after they had left the salon. "How fortunate some other woman could not claim them because of a pinch in her pocket."

Pleased with her own orders, the things chosen for Kitty, and the prospect of the opera and Almack's, Juliana could only nod while succumbing to the lure of a splendid bonnet in a shop window. London was a far cry from the provincial store where she and Kitty shopped.

"Ladies, how fortuitous," Lord Barry declared, strolling up to greet them quite as though he had not traveled—mostly in silence—all the way to London with them the day before.

"Yes, is it not," Aunt agreed with a wry twist of her mouth. "Our gowns are ordered, and now we seek a selection of bonnets to go with them."

"Aunt Tibbles," Juliana whispered urgently, "I feel certain Lord Barry has pressing business to attend."

"My business for the morning is done. I suggest I oversee the purchase of a few bonnets, then join you for a nuncheon. Shopping is tiring work." His smile took any sting from his words.

"Particularly if you are with Aunt Tibbles," Juliana said with a chuckle. "She has a way about her that sees things are done, and promptly."

The splendid bonnet displayed in the window found favor, as did a satin straw that tied prettily under the chin and sported a small plume of ostrich feathers. An evening cap of lace and several other hats done in satin, twilled sarcenet, or fine straw also found favor in Lord Barry's sight. Needless to say, Aunt Tibbles agreed. Juliana accepted the bounty without a protest. Was this not what she had wished for when she came to London?

"I shall join you if that is agreeable," Lord Barry announced. "You may buy gloves, shoes, and the rest of the folderol tomorrow," he said to Juliana, then assisted them into the carriage he summoned, not waiting to see if Juliana had other ideas about her shopping.

"How fortunate we shan't go barefoot nor gloveless until then," Juliana riposted. Goodness, but the man was a dictator. He was ever worse than Aunt Tibbles! The thought of pining for a man like him faded rapidly. And—he seemed far too well acquainted with the shopping needs for a lady, to please Juliana.

Once they had reached the house again, Lord Barry strolled right inside as though he had been there a dozen times. Odious creature, Juliana thought. Just who did he think he was? Her patron, came the voice in the back of her head. One who was to pay her a goodly sum for overseeing the completion of his house, not to mention guide him through the pitfalls of furnishing the same.

"Now, we shall plan our attack. May I see the list you have compiled, Lady Juliana?"

She put her main list into his outstretched hand and waited for the expected explosion.

"What? This seems most excessive. There is a great deal of furniture and more on this list, my lady." He glared at her in the most disagreeable way possible.

"Unless you have furniture or carpets that I know nothing about stashed away somewhere, that is the basic shopping list for your house, my lord," she said, feeling quite breathless at her assertion. He had drawn close to her side, staring down at her with those dark and flirtatious eyes. Only there was no hint of flirting in them now. "And there are bed linens as well," she added for no good reason.

"We shall see." He stared down at her, then cleared his throat, resuming his study of the list.

"I brought a copy of the floor plan of your house and have sketched precisely where I would suggest the furniture be placed. Once you study it, perhaps you may have a better notion as to what actually is needed and what may be postponed, if you so wish."

That seemed to mollify him some. He perused the list again, then said, "Perhaps I could see what you have done?"

"Gladly, my lord," Juliana replied politely, reminding herself again that he was her patron. If she wished to pay for all her shopping without resorting to the solicitor who held the purse strings, she had better be on her best behavior.

She unrolled the sheet of paper that contained her drawing of the floor plans for the entire house.

"The kitchen table is being crafted by one of the carpenters," she explained, "as are the table and chairs for the servants' use, so there is no need to purchase anything for them, other than a few chests. Beds are simple to make; a chest, even a small one, takes greater skill."

"Proceed," he said in the most bland manner. She had no clue as to what he thought of her presumptuous ordering of the furniture destined for the servants' hall. It was customary, but how was he to know that? For that matter, it was not unusual for the architect to design all of the furniture for the house. Her father had maintained that architects were by far the best designers of furniture, having a better understanding of the house, the people who were to reside therein, not to mention a better sense of proportion.

"Well, you may concentrate on the necessary," she said, "important things like your table and chairs and your bed."

"First thing in the morning we shall begin the rounds of the furniture makers. I would see what is available before I commit myself." He rolled up the paper that had the floor plans sketched on it, and tucking it under his arm, he ignored Juliana's soft sound of protest.

She wondered if he applied this philosophy to the selection of a wife, looking about Almack's and the opera to see what was on the marriage market before settling on a likely choice.

It was a relief to see him depart, promising to return early in the morning.

"Arrogant creature," Juliana murmured, knowing that deep in her heart she did not actually believe it to be true.

After an afternoon of purchasing reticules, slippers, and other items necessary to a London wardrobe, Aunt Tibbles and Juliana spent the evening discussing the trends in furniture design, and where they would be most apt to find the best pieces.

"Do you suppose he has the least notion of what is wanted?" Aunt Tibbles wondered aloud. "What a pity he does not have a wife to assist him, for I have yet to see a man who can choose the proper bed and chest and wardrobe that will go well together in a room."

"You must help me persuade him that what I suggest will be the best for him," Juliana said earnestly, then made a face. "What an audacious and utterly pushing creature I must seem. 'Tis only that I have studied the matter to some length, and I doubt if he has purchased so much as a chair in his lifetime."

"Perhaps he is one of those rare individuals who truly knows his mind as to what he likes," Aunt Tibbles replied, sounding a bit dubious about the possibility.

Come morning, the ladies were neatly—and most practically—garbed, and awaited Lord Barry over the morning papers.

"Ah," he said briskly when he joined them in the morning room, "precisely what I appreciate, ladies who understand the value of time." He stood politely by the door while they set aside papers and rose from their chairs with a swiftness any man must admire.

Edmund watched both women, wondering what was in store for him today. He had studied a few pattern books, gone over that floor plan, and had to confess that Lady Juliana most likely was right. He would have to spring for the entire list, were he to have a home and not an empty barn. But he intended to have chairs that were comfortable and not like the ponderous things he'd seen in a recent issue of *Ackermann's Repository*. If a chap wanted to move one of those, it would take two men and a boy to do so.

"Where do we begin?" he asked. "I rather liked a few of the Hepplewhite chairs, and there is a Sheraton design I must admit appeals to me."

Lady Juliana wore the sort of expression he expected he did when presented with something he was sure to detest. Well, he had a fair idea of the type of furniture he wished, and just because she was a delectable young woman who disturbed him far more than she ought, he'd not yield an inch to her.

Once they were seated comfortably in the coach, he opened the pattern books to the correct pages. Her sigh of apparent relief was almost comical.

"These will do nicely, my lord. Quite nicely, indeed."

At Gillows he felt as though he had found an ally in the gentleman who met them at the door, prepared to assist in any way he might. Edmund presented his needs, pulled out the crisp copy of his house plans, and smiled a trifle wryly at the altered expression on the clerk's face.

This was not a casual purchase; it meant enormous profit, unless Edmund missed his guess. However, also knowing that profit was what gave incentive, he began his discussion, quite forgetting Lady Juliana in the process.

The clerk looked over at her once or twice, then totally dismissed her.

Juliana studied the furniture on display, then strolled over to page through the pattern books of pieces to order. Gillows was a respected name in home decoration. She could scarcely quibble with his desire for excellent help.

But, she thought resentfully, he does not even seek my opinion. Just like a man, he discusses the situation with another man, leaving the woman in limbo, when it is a woman he will have to please in the long run. When she had suffered about enough of this treatment, Juliana stepped forward to address the clerk.

"What I felt appropriate for the drawing room is a selection of lightweight chairs of the klismos design; you know," she added to his lordship, "those Grecian chairs with the lovely curved backs and elegant sword legs. Most women I know seem to admire them."

"Lightweight? Not difficult to move?" Lord Barry demanded. "I do not wish a chair that appears to have been carved from stone. That is well enough for the garden. I do not wish it in the house."

"Indeed," she assured him. "And a monopodium table by the window, to blend with them," pointing to a table with a single, beautifully carved support. "As well, you will surely wish one of the popular backless sofas from Sheraton's design studios." Juliana slipped the Sheraton pattern book from Lord Barry's arms and in short order found the illustration she sought—an elegant sofa with eagle heads at the top and bottom that looked to be a perfect complement to the chair designs.

The clerk appeared annoyed that Juliana had broken into his territory, so to speak. Juliana gave him a reassuring look. "Lord Barry is spending some time becoming acquainted with present furniture designs. Once he discovers pieces he feels will fit in with his style of living, he will need to order a great number of things. You certainly have an impressive array to offer."

She drew the clerk away from where his lordship now looked fit to explode, explaining that while they were definitely interested in a number of things, they intended to shop around a bit first.

When they had left the shop, his lordship still annoyed, Juliana turned to him before entering the coach and said, "You did say you wished to look over everything you might before ordering, did you not?"

And so the day went.

By late afternoon all three were tired and irritated. Only occasional bright spots, such as locating precisely the right bed his lordship wanted for the master bedchamber, saved the day from being a disaster.

Juliana had studied the bed, walking around it while trying to imagine the woman who would share it with Lord Barry. Would she appreciate all the efforts being expended upon her happiness and comfort? Somehow Juliana doubted it.

"I cannot begin to tell you how much I value the help you have given me today," his lordship said, unable to keep the fatigue from his voice.

"The opera will do nicely," Aunt Tibbles said bluntly, with no effort at roundaboutation.

"They are having a gala performance tomorrow evening. I managed to obtain tickets, almost forgot to tell you."

Juliana decided that if ever she saw a sheepish expression, that was it.

"We will be ready promptly," Aunt answered for both. "I do not hold with arriving late to the theater or opera. Bad manners, I say," she concluded with a snap.

"Why do you not join us for dinner beforehand," Juliana suggested politely. "I am certain that by then the kitchen staff will be quite up to company."

"I scarcely feel like company at this point, what with spending so much time at your sides." He rose after a glance at the mantel clock, obviously feeling it time to head for his hotel room and bed.

"Let us hope that you come to know your future wife as well," Aunt Tibbles declared in ringing tones. "Many a man has been snared by a winsome face, only to rue that day over the breakfast table."

"Perhaps it has escaped your attention since you returned to England," Juliana added gently, "but often a gentleman and his bride have met but a few times, shared a few dances, perhaps a few drives in the park, before they are wed. It does not strike me as the most advantageous background for a happy and solid marriage."

"And you would wish for something other than that?" he queried, interesting lights seeming to dance in his eyes.

"Indeed, I would," she daringly replied. Normally a young woman did not discuss such things with one not in her own family or confidence, but Lord Barry had made it clear he cared not the least for her and intended to look elsewhere for a bride. "I would like a husband who is thoughtful; a good and kind man, one who will love his children." She could feel herself blush a trifle at this allusion to the more intimate side of marriage.

"No insistence upon a handsome fellow, a dashing blade of Society?" his lordship inquired lazily from where he leaned against the door frame, seeming reluctant to depart.

"If I should be so fortunate as to have a handsome gentleman ask me to marry him, I would not hold his looks against him," she said, unable to resist a grin at the thought of turning down a proposal because the gentleman was too good-looking.

"Well, no doubt someone will come along one of these days. Perhaps when we are at Almack's, you and I might each find the proper mate?"

He bowed and left abruptly. It was a good thing, too, for Juliana would have been tempted to toss a cushion at him.

"Proper mate, as though he shopped for a piece of furniture to grace his drawing room. Now I ask you, dear Aunt!"

"Poor man," Aunt Tibbles said softly, with a shake of her head. "One of these days, he will realize what he feels and be quite confounded."

Juliana could pull no more regarding this intriguing remark from her usually loquacious aunt. She had to go to her bed no wiser than before regarding the lady Lord Barry supposedly loved. As to how her aunt found out about the lady, well, Aunt Tibbles knew everything going on in Society—sometimes before it happened.

Chapter Fifteen

They began the following morning. At an hour when ladies are usually still in bed, having a cup of hot chocolate, the three set out to the section of London where the fine cabinetmakers were to be found.

It was soon evident that Lord Barry had most thoroughly studied the books Juliana loaned him. As well, he had decided ideas as to what pieces he wanted to grace his new house.

"This is going to be difficult," she whispered to her aunt, who merely smiled in return.

"Always allow him to believe the choice is his own," she counseled. "No matter what, for it is *his* house, you must own."

"We shall see," Juliana replied with a tilt of her chin.

Aunt Tibbles smiled—one of those wise, patient smiles that elders bestow on the young and often foolish.

Not only did his lordship have decided ideas, he was in no rush to make up his mind. Juliana had counted on his desire to inhabit his house as soon as possible. Not that she wished to rush back to Beechwood Hall, but she had hoped that selecting furniture would be a speedy business, and she would be free to partake of a few of the delights found in the city.

"He examines everything in sight," she softly complained to Aunt, "and then declares he wishes to look elsewhere. Perhaps Anne Hepplewhite will have designs to please him. I wonder if he will like furniture designed by the woman who took over for her illustrious husband."

Juliana was surprised when Lord Barry found several pieces at the Hepplewhite display room that pleased him. Not only that, but he studied the book of designs and ordered a satinwood table with delicate painted decoration.

"It is much like a Sheraton design I have seen," Juliana informed in a quiet aside.

"It pleases me. Do you not like it? I thought my wife would enjoy it in our private sitting room, a nice little thing upon which to breakfast if she so desires." The amused glance he sent her was quite enough to make Juliana long to punch the dratted man.

She turned away from him at the reminder of his future wife, whoever she might be. "What about this mahogany tallboy? 'Tis not the latest thing, but then, you have said often that you prefer the traditional."

If he suspected her of goading him a trifle, he gave no indication, but crossed the room to study the elegant design of the tallboy. The grain of the mahogany was magnificent and the lines clean and simple. He bought it, as Juliana had suspected he might.

They went on to another display room, and Juliana grumbled to her aunt, "I do not see why we must go with him, for he rarely consults me on anything."

"Be thankful that you are here to prevent disaster," Aunt Tibbles advised.

This good sense bore fruit at the very next shop they visited. The clerk, who must have fancied himself an incipient interior decorator, began to shower Lord Barry with suggestions. He must have the latest in chairs, with chimeras—those imaginary monsters composed of incongruous parts—composing the arms and front legs. There absolutely *must* be lion paws on his table feet, griffons and sphinxes by the score on everything from candelabrum to torchère tripods to table legs. While Juliana thought them clever, she drew the line at having them peer from everything.

Lord Barry listened with great patience, looked over the offerings of that particular shop, then announced he would think about it and left.

"Presumptuous puppy," he growled, while assisting Aunt Tibbles and Juliana into the coach. "As though I could not decide on what I like or want."

"There are people who prefer to have a professional assist them in selecting their furnishings," Juliana dared to say.

"Like you, for instance?" He raised his brows at her and waited politely for a reply.

"I do not claim to be a professional at anything, sir. But I have studied a good deal, and I do know your house."

He accepted her gentle rebuke with a nod. "So you do. I suggest we return to your family home to go over what we have seen to this point. Perhaps you would be so kind as to make suggestions regarding possible placement?"

"Of course," she said, feeling just a wee bit smug.

Once they were settled in the dining room, with the plans spread out across the table, Juliana commenced her attack.

"I suggest we go room by room."

And they did—for over an hour. Lord Barry looked as though he was almost sorry he had made such a suggestion in the first place.

"You really think we need Etruscan chairs for that room upstairs? They do not look very comfortable."

"Pish tush," she said, thinking those chairs were not intended to be sat on for any length of time anyway. "And a wardrobe as well. Thomas Hope has an interesting cheval looking glass that should be perfect for the room. We did not go there today, but I think you ought to see his place on Duchess Street as well as his display room. I believe I can arrange for you to view them if you like."

It was decided that Lord Barry would visit the Duchess Street home that Thomas Hope had adorned with his furniture designs, not to mention a great number of other items Juliana had heard about.

Lord Barry left the house not long after, reminding the ladies that this evening they were to attend the final performance of the opera for the Season.

The evening was less than a total success as far as Juliana was concerned. She found the opera enchanting, if confusing. Those in attendance seemed far more interested in gossip than singing. But the music was lovely, the gowns amazing, and even his lordship's company was almost all she might wish. The gown from Madame Clotilde earned eloquent looks from Lord Barry, as did the elegant hair style devised by the maid Aunt Tibbles hired. Juliana was pleased—at first.

Lord Barry had properly attended them in the box he had rented for the evening. At the first intermission he had taken off, ostensibly to find them some lemonade.

"He is hunting, most likely," Aunt suggested.

"Ah, yes," Juliana said with a hint of acid in her tone, "that wife he will need—the very English wife to grace his home and produce those very English children."

"He will most likely have as difficult a time selecting a wife as he does his furniture, I've no doubt. Take comfort in that." Aunt shared a very knowing look with Juliana, who promptly blushed.

"Am I so very transparent, then?" Juliana said, as much as admitting her love for the impossible Lord Barry.

"No, of course you are not any such thing. I have had time to observe you when he is around. I am very good at observing women—and men, too, for that matter. Your eyes light up when he enters a room, and your gaze tends to follow him as he moves about." Aunt Tibbles watched the far side of the theater as Lord Barry chatted with a white-haired gentleman he must have met before coming north.

"She is very beautiful," Juliana admitted when she caught sight of Lord Barry bending over to greet the young woman who sat in the box, probably the daughter of said gentleman. "I'll wager she is a peagoose of the first water," Juliana concluded thoughtfully, wafting her fan back and forth.

"Now, now," Aunt admonished. "He asked for a typical English wife, and you know most wives hide their intelligence, using it when husbands are not about."

"That must be why he cannot consider me for the position of wife—I make no attempt to be silly or stupid."

"I believe he will come to view you in a different light," Aunt said in a vague reply. She didn't sound very convincing to Juliana, who resigned herself to a future without Lord Barry.

"Well, I hope she appreciates the marble dressing room bath, and that great bed in which he intends her to sleep with him—and the pretty little Etruscan room."

"The trouble with you," Aunt declared, "is that you have put too much of yourself into this house."

A gentleman entered their box at that moment, seeking to reestablish an acquaintance with Juliana, who it must be admitted, looked most fetching in the low-necked gown of white spider gauze trimmed with blush satin roses.

"Lady Juliana, I hope you remember meeting me at a party given by Lord and Lady Titchfield last winter. Lord Carlingford at your service." He bowed nicely over Aunt Tibbles' hand, then stood chatting about trivialities, taking care to include Aunt Tibbles as well as Juliana.

She bloomed under his attention. He was a handsome, well-set man with blond hair and hazel eyes. Never mind she preferred dark blue eyes and thick dark hair; she couldn't have that, so she had better settle for something else.

Within minutes Lord Barry entered, frowning at the intruder, who introduced himself with a certain *savoir-faire* possessed by those who frequent the highest strata of Society.

"Lady Juliana is in London assisting me with buying furniture for my new home," Barry said abruptly, casually placing his hand on the back of her chair, as though to stake a claim on it and her.

"I thought it the neighborly thing to do for a poor man without a wife to guide him," Juliana said sweetly.

"Truly most kind of you," Lord Carlingford said, leaving minutes later, most likely sensing the chill that had descended on the box.

"How could you!" Juliana said with fire spitting from very angry eyes. "I'll have you know he is of the highest *ton*."

"Looked dashed havey-cavey to me," he argued.

"He was introduced to me at a party given by the Titchfields—perfectly proper! I have not asked you to vet any potential husbands," she said with spirit. "As you pointed out once, I need to acquire a husband. Where better to find one than London, even if it is the end of the Season?"

He gave her a frowning, thoughtful look, then subsided onto his chair, murmuring something that sounded like, "Quite right."

At the next interval he set off again, this time promising for certain to locate that lemonade.

"I doubt he will have any luck," Aunt observed, "I believe he went in the wrong direction."

"I believe," Juliana said, a spark of mischief lighting her fine eyes, "that tomorrow we shall find a great number of things his lordship simply cannot do without. Once he has viewed the Duchess Street house, we will whisk him off from shop to display room to shop again until he is dizzy with all he has seen and is willing to do most anything to be finished."

"No, I disagree with you there," Aunt admonished. "Allow him to take his time, see what is to be seen, discover for himself what it is he desires in his home."

"Very well." Juliana had the oddest notion that her aunt had something else in mind other than furniture.

"While you are *au fait* with the latest designs in furniture, I believe you need a bit of practice with gentlemen, my dear. I sent a letter to Lady Jersey this morning, to be delivered after we went out. Dear girl, she replied promptly, and I am to see her in the morning."

"Which means about three in the afternoon, of course," Juliana said, thinking quickly. "We will have to be out and about first thing for you to be home in time. I believe I should like to attend Almack's. Maybe I could meet someone interesting while there. Oh, Aunt, see if you might do something for Lord Barry. I understand there is always a shortage of eligible men at these little assemblies, and he is presentable."

"Who is presentable?" Lord Barry demanded, entering the box with two glasses of lemonade in hand.

"Did you suppose we discuss you, my boy?" Aunt Tibbles said with a sparkle in her eyes.

He handed the glasses of lemonade to them, then made a dismissing motion with one hand, looking a bit nonplused.

"Actually, we did," Juliana interposed after a sip of the tart drink. "I had suggested that Aunt obtain a voucher for you, that you might attend the best marriage market in town. And I had admitted that you were presentable—there ought to be no objection. Unless you have concealed something from us?"

"I have already seen to that, my lady. The gentleman I chatted with earlier introduced me to Lady Sefton, who in turn agreed that it would be a shame were I to miss out on the remaining Wednesday evening assemblies. A single gentleman is such an asset, you know," he concluded with a wry grin.

"Lady Sefton," Aunt Tibbles added, "will automatically believe that a single gentleman, especially one who is known to possess a fortune, is in need of a wife. This ought to be most interesting."

"Oh, ho!" Juliana chortled with glee, "you will meet every flower of England who is in Town and eligible to be presented to a viscount on the lookout for a wife. I daresay you will dance your feet off."

The remainder of the evening, when they were not paying attention to the opera, was spent in excruciatingly polite conversation. At last the curtain fell.

Aunt Tibbles rose from her chair to announce, "If we are to rise early in the morning, I, for one, wish to have an early night." She extended her hand to Lord Barry and continued, "Thank you for the treat, my lord. It has been an elevating evening all around." With that obscure remark she led the way from the box and along the hall.

Juliana hurried after her aunt, thankful the evening had come to an end, even if she was further away from Lord Barry than ever. All she might do is trust in her aunt's advice. Goodness knew that Juliana hadn't the foggiest idea how to go about attracting the man she found so captivating, worse luck.

The next day they set out after a hearty breakfast—Lord Barry was apt to become absorbed in his furniture quest and forget all about nourishment—to visit the display room kept by Thomas Hope. When Mr. Hope learned Juliana's identity and that she had a commission from Lord Barry to decorate his house—which stretched the truth just a trifle—he graciously invited them to his house.

Lord Barry apparently found much to his liking, particularly some chairs.

"I think he is becoming accustomed to the newer styles of furniture, for he doesn't shudder or shake his head as much as he did at first," Juliana quietly said to her aunt.

From the Hope residence on Duchess Street, they again flitted through another group of shops and display rooms, sometimes peeping into the manufactory area where a particular table or chair was in the process of production. Juliana figured that they would not have been encouraged to do this had it not been for her background as an architect's daughter.

At last they collapsed in the drawing room at the Hamilton house. Aunt Tibbles rang for a substantial tea and insisted Lord Barry join them.

"If you intend to maintain this pace for any time, you will need sustenance, my lord," Aunt Tibbles declared. "Now then, what have you learned of benefit to you?"

"Well, I am rather glad to have Lady Juliana along—she does open a number of doors that might otherwise be closed to me. I find I like to see the furniture in process. There are so many beautiful woods in use."

"Mr. Hope says that mahogany should be confined to the parlor and bedchamber floors, leaving the satinwood, ebony, tulip, and rosewood for the more formal apartments, as they take kindly to inlay and fanciful treatment."

"Then it is well he will never know about the satinwood Pembroke table I bought for the upstairs sitting room."

"I thought it lovely, and after all, you are the one to be pleased," Juliana said, surprising herself by coming to his defense, even when she knew the table was to be for another woman.

"Yes, I am, true." He sipped his tea, frowning over something that must have just occurred to him.

"Well, I believe you have formed a good notion of what furniture is available. Now, if you will excuse me, I am off to see Lady Jersey. The vouchers, you know." Aunt Tibbles rose from the sofa and marched out, militantly going to her room on the next floor.

Juliana studied the teacup in her hand. The silence stretched on until she looked to see if his lordship intended to leave, as he ought.

"I owe you an apology of sorts, I believe." At her look of inquiry, he added, "For last evening. It was churlish of me to say what I did to Carlingford. I feel sure he's a nice enough chap." He paused, then went on, a rakish gleam in his eyes, "Although, I cannot imagine him to have the slightest interest in building houses."

Juliana compressed her lips, wanting to say something, yet not sure she dare.

"Spit it out, or you will certainly have indigestion."

"Odious creature," she said with a laugh. "I do not intend to make a lifework out of building houses. I merely wished to complete the last one my father designed—and you know it."

"What is there left to finish?" He leaned back in his chair, crossing perfectly splendid legs and looking far too at ease with the world.

"At your home? Some odd touches here and there, the last of the floors. You must," she reflected, "remember to purchase some carpets. And there are a few outbuildings to construct, but that need not matter to you, for you will surely be involved in the landscaping."

"You are so sure?"

"I have no doubt that you will be marching around with book in hand, telling Repton, or whomever you choose, precisely what you want and where."

"You believe that to be a bad thing?" His hands curled about the arm of the chair, the only indication that he was wary of her reply.

"Not in the least, or, I should say, not when you exhibit such excellent taste as you have done so far in furniture."

"Excellent taste? My, my. From you that is a very nice commendation, my dear Lady Juliana. I suspect you have high standards."

"In furnishings, I suppose I do."

"Not only furnishings. Lord Carlingford is fortunate to have caught your eye." There was a hint of sarcasm in his tone that Juliana could not like.

"He did not catch mine, sir. Rather it was the other way around."

"You both realize that it is highly improper for the two of you to be sitting in here without a chaperon, do you not?" Aunt Tibbles said, pausing on her way down to the ground floor and out to the carriage.

Lord Barry rose immediately and strode to the door. "I tend to forget myself when I am with Lady Juliana. Somehow she does not seem like a lady."

Before he had a chance to comprehend what he had just said, he bowed to them both and ran down the stairs. The door was shut with a vehement snap.

"As Lady Rosamund would say, I am *so* masculine," Juliana said with an exasperated look at her aunt.

"Never mind, dear girl; she doesn't have the sense God gave a flea. Stick to your convictions and all will turn out well in the end." With that, Aunt Tibbles whisked herself down and out the front door, closing it far more quietly.

Juliana wandered idly down the stairs and into the small bookroom to the rear of the house. There was but one window and its view was of a dainty garden.

"There is a gentleman to see you, my lady," Hilsom intoned shortly, managing to sound stuffy and disapproving all at once.

Annoyed that he should presume to imply what she ought or not ought do, Juliana rashly replied, "Show him in here, please." She ignored the butler's look of displeasure.

Lord Carlingford was ushered into the little bookroom within moments. Juliana was most surprised and rather pleased to see him. Hilsom left the door wide open and stationed himself immediately outside the door.

"I must apologize for being alone, Lord Carlingford. My aunt left moments ago on an errand, and I confess I was curious as to who might wish to see me, for I know no one in the city." She extended her hand in greeting and was thankful Hilsom, stickler that he was, remained close by. She'd not have his lordship thinking her lost to all propriety.

"I know your brother, and you have somewhat the look of him. I wished to bring you these flowers and inquire if you would like to drive out with me this afternoon?" He proffered a lovely bouquet of summer flowers to an entranced Juliana.

"She cannot," snapped Lord Barry from where he stood in the doorway, looking very much as though he owned the house and Juliana to boot.

"And why would that be?" Juliana asked, her tone most demure while she sniffed the flowers in her hands.

"Because I have need of your excellent taste. There is a sideboard I wish you to inspect. Saw it when I was over at

Gillows. Forgot to tell you." He strolled into the room, looking at ease with the world and quite to home beside Juliana.

"Oh, dear," Juliana said, wondering what sort of thing he had managed to discover now. While he had used fine judgment so far, that did not mean that someone might not influence him into a horrible choice. "Gillows again?"

"Perhaps tomorrow?" Lord Carlingford said with an appraising look at Lord Barry. "I had not realized that you were in such demand, my lady."

"Not me, precisely, just my knowledge," Juliana admitted. "I am well informed on furniture designs, and I know the floor plan of his lordship's new house, as my father designed it."

"How, er, interesting," Lord Carlingford said with a narrow look at Lord Barry that seemed dubious to Juliana.

"She is indispensable, you know," Lord Barry said in an odiously patronizing manner. "Wouldn't know how to go on without her advice. She will be occupied most days—at least until we have selected all the furniture needed for the house. It's a rather large place, you see, so it might take some time."

Juliana did not dare to say a word, or she might explode and frighten poor Lord Carlingford into the next county.

"In that case, I can but hope to see you at Almack's next Wednesday evening," Lord Carlingford concluded before making his farewell bow and leaving.

"Lord Barry," Juliana snapped, rounding on her patron with a wicked gleam in her eyes, "if you ever do anything like that again, I will take great pleasure in denouncing you to every presentable female within miles of here."

"Now see here, Juliana," he sputtered.

"Oh, no, you see here. You are only my patron. Why, you were behaving like a proprietary lover, sirrah!" With that pithy remark she stormed from the room and marched upstairs, leaving the dratted man where he was without so much as a good-bye.

Edmund shook his head, strolled past the butler and on to the front door, meeting Miss Tibbles coming in as he was about to go out.

"Now what?" she demanded. "You look upset."

"I believe I just made a fool of myself," he said, wondering how on earth he could have uttered such words and where they had come from in the first place.

"Is that all! Juliana perturbed?" she inquired at the sound of a door being slammed somewhere in the upper regions of the house.

"I believe she is a little annoyed with me at the moment," he confessed.

"Well, tomorrow is another day and I obtained the vouchers we desired. I have an invitation for Juliana to a little party this evening. It is last minute, of course, but it ought to make her more cheerful. Lady Jersey is having a few friends in this evening. The cream of Society will be there, and I hope Juliana will make new friends." Miss Tibbles gave Edmund a significant look.

"By new friends, I gather you mean gentlemen friends?"

"Naturally. I mean for her to find a good husband. Her mother will never be bothered, silly goose that she is. Juliana is my dearest niece and will inherit my portion once I'm gone. I care a great deal about her and her future. I mean to see a few great-nieces and nephews before my time is over."

With that she bid him good day, saying that they needed to decide what they would wear this evening to such a grand affair.

"Grand affair," Edmund grumbled as he strolled along the street in the vague direction of his hotel. He had been accepted as a member of his father's club and decided he would spend the evening there. Perhaps he might renew a few friendships made while at Oxford years ago. One never lost old school ties. It would help take his mind off a radiant Juliana in that white gauze thing with the pale roses nestled at her delightful bosom and looking like a piece of confectionery. How could any man with half an eye fail to appreciate such beauty? Of course he wouldn't know about the sharp tongue or devious mind that went along with that beauty. Edmund righteously decided he would be only to happy to tell any fellow who elected to court Juliana just what was in store for him. All in the name of fair play, naturally.

* * *

Juliana was delighted at the news of a party at Lady Jersey's that evening—even if it was the last minute.

"For the more people I meet, the better, do you not agree?" she earnestly inquired of her aunt.

"By all means," her aunt agreed, then said, "Now please tell me just what went on before I arrived back here."

Juliana dutifully explained, with much indignation and waving of arms as she stalked about her lovely room on the second floor.

"My, it sounds as though Lord Barry was a real spoilsport. You'd think he cared about you, the way he carries on," Aunt Tibbles said thoughtfully, watching her niece absorb this scrap of insight.

"Well, he cannot," Juliana declared. "All he wanted was to have me go with him to look at some sideboard." And then it struck her. "The blasted man did not even stay to take me to *see* the sideboard that was so very important that I could not go for a drive with Lord Carlingford."

"You did take a rather frosty leave of him, my dear," her aunt said mildly. She turned Juliana's attention to the treat in store for her this evening and a choice of gown, for Madam Clotilde had sent around two of the dresses that had been ordered.

The two women slipped out for a bit of shopping—reticules and slippers and gloves, mostly—then returned home to dine and prepare for the party.

Juliana wore a delicate sea foam sarcenet with an overdress of sheer aerophane crepe. A jeweled clasp caught a green riband at the front where the neckline dipped. A pretty ruffle that went around her neck saved the dress from seeming too daring. Juliana fingered her pearls where they nestled against her skin. "I look rather nice, if I do say so," she concluded before they were to depart.

"Pity Lord Barry could not see how feminine you look this evening. He'd not speak as he did," Aunt Tibbles said with a nod and a gleam in her eyes.

"I doubt if it would make a scrap of difference," Juliana grumbled before accepting her wrap and joining her aunt on what promised to be a wonderful evening.

Chapter Sixteen

"**I**f there is a maker of furniture east of Tottenham Court Road that we have missed these past weeks, I vow I cannot imagine who it could be," Juliana said, sounding rather cross as she paced back and forth in the Hamilton town house drawing room.

"It does seem as though I have viewed a goodly number of sofas and chairs, not to mention tables this past month and more," Aunt Tibbles agreed from the sofa, where she perched, waiting for his lordship to arrive for the day.

"I am fully convinced that every piece of furniture he actually needs for that house has been ordered—most on their way by now. And I do believe he must have met every eligible young lady to be found in London. So why?"

"The delay?" Aunt Tibbles queried. "More young ladies, perhaps? I did think Lady Caroline Putney, with all that chestnut hair and being quite a beauty, stood a chance."

"What about the heiress, Miss Smythe-Easton? He danced with her three times at Lady Sefton's party."

"What do you propose, dear?"

"We shall leave! Almack's is over and done. Even Parliament will soon be closing, the members heading for their country homes. Why not us? I have had a feeling . . ."

"It has become rather warm in London," Aunt Tibbles confessed.

"Well, he cannot require my advice any longer. I truly fail to see why—" She broke off when Hilsom entered the room, bearing a letter on the salver.

"Your mother has written, my lady," he said, sounding quite as stuffy as usual.

With a glance at her aunt, Juliana picked up the letter, hastily broke the seal, and gasped at the first lines she read.

"Do not keep me in suspense. Tell me the whole of it," her aunt demanded.

"Kitty has eloped with Sir Peregrine! They flew off to Gretna last week! How dreadful!" Juliana exchanged an anxious look with her aunt. "Had I been there, I feel certain I might have talked her out of such foolishness. Mama is rightly upset—although she worries more about the impression such news might have on Barbara's come-out."

"But Kitty and Sir Peregrine are much attached, planning to wed once mourning is over," Aunt argued.

"That is true, but still, elopement—it is not a good way to begin a marriage, I believe."

"What is it you so firmly believe this hour of the morning, Lady Juliana?" Lord Barry said from the doorway, Hilsom having allowed him to come on his own since he had practically been living in the ladies' pockets all this time.

"Kitty and Sir Peregrine eloped! It is my fault, for I did not convince her of the folly of such behavior. Had I remained at Beechwood, I could have stopped her."

"Do you really think so?" he said. "It seems to me they were determined on the course of their future and did not wish to wait for six months to begin their life together." He strolled across the room to make his bow to Aunt, then turned to face Juliana again.

"We are leaving at once," Juliana declared.

"What good will that possibly do? They are most likely well married by now and on their way home again. She will be living with Sir Peregrine, where she doubtless has longed to be for some time."

"What do you know about it?" Juliana said quietly, thinking he probably had the right of it.

"I have eyes in my head. You would think the same if you stopped being elder sister for a bit."

"What an abominable creature you are, to be sure," Juliana said with more spirit. "What did you wish today? More manufactories? Upholsterers? Decorators? I vow I have seen all there could possibly exist in London."

"Well . . . I thought perhaps a drive in the park."

"Nonsense," Juliana said impatiently. She wondered which of the young ladies he wished to make jealous by parading her in his new carriage. "Since we have done with the shopping and your leather-covered bergere chairs and the plum-covered sofa, not to mention that sideboard you finally ordered have been sent north, we are no longer needed."

"True," he admitted. "But I would miss your company."

"Very civilized of you to say so," she replied politely. With a glance at her aunt, Juliana moved forward to shake his hand, adding, "My solicitor will settle the final bill with you, if you please. The house is complete, I feel certain. Any details can be handled with my cousin, Henry."

"Your *cousin*?" This one word seemed to impress him a great deal.

"Henry is like a brother to Juliana, for so her father treated him," Aunt Tibbles said, watching the two who eyed one another so warily. "Trained the two together."

"What you do is, of course, up to you," he said. "The Season is drawing to an end; London grows dull, I suppose."

"You must have solved your dilemma—that of finding a wife?" she boldly inquired, knowing it was far too impudent a thing to ask, but aching to know the awful truth.

"I narrowed the field some, but if you mean—have I asked a lady to be my bride, the answer is no. I am not certain the one I want would have me."

"Fainthearted? I'd not have believed it of you," she said with a sorry excuse for a laugh.

"Women are not the only ones to nurse doubts, harbor fears, my lady," he concluded. "If you wish to leave now, I had best depart. I shall see you when we return to the country?" He paused by the door, hat in hand, to give her an oddly questioning look.

"Perhaps. I do not know what my future plans are."

Once he had left, Juliana turned to her aunt and said, "I wonder who the nitwit is?"

"Probably does not know he cares for her, what with him being tongue-tied and all," Aunt said blandly.

"Who would have thought it?" Then, depressed by the knowledge that even if he hadn't asked a girl to marry him, that he had actually selected her, Juliana briskly said, "Come, we have much to do. How quickly can we leave here?"

With a summons to Hilsom, then the maids, action commenced, and the move from London began.

Edmund strolled away from the Hamilton town house deeply in thought. What a dunderhead he was. Why had he not considered the possibility of Henry Scott being a relative, and an innocuous one, to boot? Now, he feared that he had burned his bridges behind him, treating Juliana with far too much familiarity and relying on her in a way that might not be pleasing to a potential bride.

"Idiot!" he declared, causing a passerby to stare at him in alarm.

Pulling himself together, Edmund decided he had best finish his business as soon as possible, then return to his new home. Perhaps he might find another lady of spirit and charm to grace the halls? Never mind that he had inspected the finest crop of the land at Almack's and found them all wanting one way or another. There must be someone.

It did not take long to conclude the payment for his house. He felt a fraud when the solicitor commended him for his prompt settling of his accounts—so many gentlemen allowed them to drag on for months, even years. Edmund just wished to be done with all that had to do with the project.

By the time he traveled to his home, he found that Beckworth, his newly hired butler, had efficiently disposed of all the furniture that had arrived, placing every item precisely where Juliana had indicated on the floor plan Edmund had providentially sent along. Even the drapers had come, measured, and returned to hang the various festoons and curtains required. The carpets Juliana had argued about with him—and won—most handsomely adorned each room. And that landscape paper in the drawing room was exactly right, just as she had predicted.

He missed her.

He walked slowly up the stairs, recalling his arguments

with Juliana over the design and stability of them. They
seemed most solid under his feet now. At the landing he
turned and wandered slowly along the hall, although he
knew where he was headed. Once at the door to the Etruscan
room, he entered, pausing to again study the paintings on the
wall, marveling at the freshness of the scenes and the exquisite detailing. Of course the wardrobe she had spotted
was perfect for the room, as were the dainty chairs, so right
for a lady.

He was not quite so sure of the looking glass, but if she
liked it, he supposed it could remain.

In the master suite he came to a dead stop. There against
the center of one wall was the massive bed he had ordered according to a Sheraton design he favored. It was quite splendid,
almost awe-inspiring, in fact. He walked over to it, sat down
to test the mattress, then stretched out, contemplating future
nights on this most comfortable of spots—all by himself. It
was unthinkable.

He missed her.

Rising from the bed, unable to halt the flow of wishful
dreaming that had taken hold of him, he continued on his inspection of the next room, the dressing room for the mistress
of this household.

She was everywhere—from the marble bath to the crisply
skirted dressing table, the gilt wall sconces above it, to the
delicate torchère near the bath, not to mention the amazing
wardrobe she had insisted he purchase. It had two generous
compartments for gowns to hang in—one to either side, centered by shelves for clothes to lay flat on and drawers for
other garments. Magnificent in mahogany.

Oh, how he missed her.

"My lord, I was just told you had arrived. Is it all satisfactory?" Henry Scott stood in the doorway, a quizzical expression on his face.

"Indeed, indeed," Edmund said, trying to seem pleased—
which he was, actually. Then, with a genuine smile, for he
had always wanted to like the chap, he walked over to clasp
Henry's hand. "There is not money enough to pay you for all
you have done here, but I will try to compensate you for your

good stewardship. You are a fine man. If there is a letter of commendation you might wish, you have but to ask."

Seeming a bit taken aback at this heap of praise, Henry studied his patron, then said, "I gather all went well in London? From the looks of it, you bought out a furniture manufactory or two."

"Yes. Lady Juliana"— Edmund had to clear his throat at the sound of her name—"was most helpful."

"She arrived home yesterday. I suppose you know about Kitty—now Lady Forsythe?"

"They returned?" Edmund paused in their stroll back to the stairs, for he had found it necessary to leave the room that contained so much of Juliana in it.

"They have. Kitty is as happy as a duck in a pond, taking capable control of the Forsythe home. Things needed a strong hand there, for the last Lady Forsythe had been gone aloft for some years. Since Kitty hasn't the slightest inclination to go to London, Lady Hamilton has forgiven the runaways."

"As I suspected she might do." The two men exchanged a look that said much about their understanding of Lady Hamilton and her desires for Lady Barbara.

"You said once—just in passing, mind you—that you hoped to find a wife while in London," Henry said most hesitantly.

Knowing what he did now, Edmund could see the fellow's dilemma. Henry cared for Juliana while she considered him no more than a brother. Edmund would not wish that position for himself.

"I certainly surveyed all that the *ton* had to offer at Almack's and the various balls and parties. But, no, I did not find a wife among them." If Henry thought the phrasing of that reply odd, he gave no indication. Edmund figured that he was quite safe with his foolish love for a woman who most likely wished him to perdition.

He had once said, with Sallust, that every man is the architect of his own fortune. Perhaps had he any common sense he . . . Was it Voltaire who had written that common sense is not so common? At any rate, Edmund could not think of a way out of his stupidity at the moment.

"Pity, that," Henry said with every evidence of sympathy.

"Mr. Teynham been around?" Edmund inquired, the beginning of an idea stirring in his mind.

"Not recently," Henry said, then gestured to the back of the house. "Would you come with me to have a look at the outbuildings that have been finished while you were gone?"

"Certainly," Edmund replied with no hint of the impatience he felt.

They strolled along over the neatly raked ground awaiting a coating of gravel to reduce the dust and mud.

"The ice house is half hidden over there, and before that is the kitchen gardens."

"Very neat brickwork on the walls, I must say," Edmund said with obvious approval ringing in his voice while he stood, hands behind him, studying the pretty pattern of it.

It earned him a curious glance from Henry, but they went on. With each building came strong appreciation of all that Henry Scott had done while Edmund was flitting about London, hunting for furniture and someone to take Juliana's place. Fat lot of good that had done him.

"Do you dine as usual with the family this evening?" Edmund said casually when Henry indicated he had finished the tour of inspection.

"Yes, I do," Henry replied, looking nonplused.

"Would you be so kind as to tell George Teynham I would like to see him on the morrow?"

With a wondering expression Henry agreed, then left.

Edmund returned to his house, standing in the entryway, trying to envision any other woman joining him here and he could not. And hoped it would not be necessary.

A loud knock on the door sounded, and Beckworth, as efficient as evidence had given, sailed across to open the door at once.

"We have come to welcome his lordship back to the country," trilled the unmistakable voice of Lady Rosamund.

"Is the dear man to home?" Lady Titchfield inquired.

Edmund nodded wryly to Beckworth, and in moments found his ears assaulted with enthusiastic praise of the furnishings, the chairs and sofas, not to mention the mahogany dining table with its delicate ormolu inlay work.

"Such taste!" Lady Titchfield exclaimed when she viewed the landscape paper on the drawing room walls. "Such divine proportions," as she fingered the tails of the draperies. "Simply elegant!" she concluded.

"Any woman would be proud to be mistress of such a house," Lady Rosamund blushingly offered.

"Dare we ask if you found a special lady while in London? Lady Juliana spoke of Almack's and all the world knows that is the premier place to find a wife," her ladyship said with a narrow glance at her daughter.

"No, I fear I am still unattached. Perhaps I am too exacting in my tastes," Edmund said with a smile.

"Well, your taste is exquisite in furnishing, so you must be looking for someone very special to adorn this lovely home," Lady Titchfield coyly declared.

"I am in no hurry," he said, guiding his guests along to the next rooms and hoping they would leave when the proper time came.

"Lady Juliana said she is going to go south to live with her brother and his wife," Lady Rosamund said while staring at Edmund's favorite horse painting by Stubbs.

"Really," he replied. "Did she mention when? I intend to give a small party and invite the neighbors who have been so gracious to me. Do you think they would enjoy seeing the house, now it is finished?"

"Indeed," the two ladies agreed in unison.

"Naturally, as daughter of the architect, and one who assisted in much of the planning, it would be appropriate for Lady Juliana to attend, would you not agree?"

"Indeed," they again allowed, this time with less enthusiasm.

"Once I have set a date, I will speed an invitation to you. Promise you will come?"

"We would not miss it for the world," Lady Titchfield said, then looked startled when Beckworth opened the front door for her and she discovered she was being guided to her carriage by Lord Barry. In moments they were gone.

There was no time to lose. If Juliana thought that she was going to move away before he had a chance to discover if there was any possibility for them, she was sadly mistaken.

"Beckworth, I would send a message to Mr. Teynham at Beechwood Hall. Do I have someone who could ride there at once?"

"Indeed, my lord," the efficient gentleman replied.

Edmund thought for a few moments, then marched to the library where he picked up the pen he found on the desk. After dipping it in ink, he scratched a brief epistle to George that ought to bring him on the run.

Once the note had been sent, Edmund hurried up to his dressing room to change his clothing and prepare for the visit from Mr. Teynham.

George must have broken all records for speed; he came before Edmund would have thought possible.

"Welcome, my friend," Edmund said with more enthusiasm than he'd expressed for days.

"Well, what can possibly be so important that I must rush here with all possible dispatch?"

"Something rather serious, I fear," Edmund said, thinking that was about half the matter. After issuing a few instructions to Beckworth, Edmund led George along to the library, which still smelled faintly of paint and varnish. Looking up, Edmund caught a glimpse of the carved figure of Terpsichore that had reminded him of Juliana. That it did, down to a certain twinkle in the eyes.

"All right, out with it, Barry." George Teynham had no more patience than did Edmund, which gave him hope.

"Do you recall my saying I wished to look for a wife while in London?" At Teynham's quizzical look, Edmund shook his head. "A lot of empty-headed twits is what I found. Not one of them can hold a candle to a particular lady I would wish to inhabit this house."

"Not to mention your bed, eh?" Teynham said with a sly smile.

"You have no idea? I do not refer to Lady Rosamund. Rather it is Juliana I desire." Edmund slid his hands into his pockets and paced back and forth before the new and elegant bookcase he and Juliana had found in a most unprepossessing shop just off Tottenham Court Road. "There is not a room in this entire house that does not have her touch."

"That is understandable, but scarcely a reason to wed the girl," her uncle argued.

"That would be true if I didn't love that dratted woman beyond belief," Edmund said with a forlorn look to the man he hoped would help him with his little plot.

"This is interesting," Teynham said, finding one of the green leather bergere chairs much to his liking and settling back for more discussion of this intriguing topic.

"She'll not come here unless there were a raft of others about, I'll wager. So I thought to invite everyone in the neighborhood to see the new house—with Juliana as a special guest, to represent her father, as it were, and her own efforts as a decorator."

"I suspect you have the right of it there," Teynham said reflectively. "How may I help?"

Edmund gave a whoop of delight, then pulled up a chair for a council of war. "Here is what we shall do." There followed a carefully detailed plan that ought to cover anything that might possibly come up. "She will come?"

"Of course."

"There is no way in the world I shall attend his little party to show off his new house. I know what the place looks like already," Juliana declared vehemently.

"Silly goose, not with all the furnishings in place," Barbara chided. "You must come. You are guest of honor. It simply isn't done for the guest of honor to refuse!"

"Barbara is correct, Juliana," Lady Hamilton said firmly. "You will attend and wear that spider gauze creation from London. I vow, we must go to that mantuamaker next spring, Barbara. She is truly a wizard."

Juliana crept up to her room, utterly in despair. Not a word had come about any engagement Lord Barry might have entered into in the past days. Yet, she feared to attend, for she just knew her heart would ache with the love she felt for that miserable worm. Oh, was ever a woman's lot so wretched? To love and not be loved in return?

The evening of the party came all too soon to suit Juliana. She slipped on her spider gauze, ignoring the remarks from her mother's maid that she looked like an angel. Rather, she donned her pearls, gloves, then picked up the little ivory fan Lord Carlingford had given her just before he had asked her to marry him . . . and been refused. It was just as she had told Lord Barry. Lord Carlingford had asked her after quite a few meetings, much like other Society meldings.

Barbara chattered all the way to Lord Barry's home, Lady Hamilton studying her eldest daughter with a perplexed frown, as though seeing her for the first time.

"Here we are," Barbara gaily announced, following her mother from the carriage with an eager step.

Juliana forced her feet to march up the steps which she had watched being built, to the front door she had designed. It opened, and a highly correct butler ushered them in with great civility.

"Susan, Dowager Lady Hamilton, Ladies Juliana and Barbara Hamilton," he said with what appeared to be great respect.

"Welcome, Lady Hamilton, and Ladies Juliana and Barbara," Edmund said with a polite bow.

Juliana avidly drank in the sight of him dressed in his London splendor. Buff breeches topped by a cream waistcoat and deep gray coat was devastating. He proceeded to escort them to a place of honor in the drawing room. Once they were seated most comfortably in the graceful chairs with their saber legs, he went to the front of the room. He commanded silence effortlessly, just standing.

"I welcome you all to my new home. A few of you have been here before," he said with a bow to Juliana and Rosamund, "but those who have not may wish to inspect the place at your leisure. Musicians will play for any who care to dance. Food is arranged for any who desire food."

He looked straight at Juliana when he uttered those last words, and she thought her heart would cease working. Desire food? *Food* did not figure the least in her desires.

"Before you all drift away, I want to express my gratitude to Lady Juliana Hamilton for all she has done to create this house for me and furnish it in the highest style, to make it a truly English house, by a truly English lady. My lady?"

He held out his hand, and Juliana rose from her chair as though she was a puppet and someone had pulled her strings. She walked none too steadily to stand beside him, casting him a questioning look. She had not expected to see him, here, especially, again.

"May I extend to you a small token of my appreciation?"

Her eyes widened as he removed a slim box—a jeweler's box, it was—from his inside coat pocket. He opened it, revealing an incredible diamond necklace.

"I realize that a gentleman does not usually bestow such a thing on a lady not his wife, but with her uncle's permission I could find nothing more appropriate than diamonds to express my feelings at all she has created for me—a diamond of a house in the setting of my land."

There was amused and delighted applause when he handed Juliana the box, then unclasped her pearl necklace, setting it aside, and placing the cool gold chain about her neck. She felt as though on fire.

"How dare you, sirrah?" she whispered. "This is most improper!"

"I have just begun to dare," he whispered back.

She smiled as though she was not burning with the touch of his hands on her bare skin or with unanswered questions.

Out in the spacious entry three musicians struck up a minuet, and people took it as a cue to begin strolling about the house, exclaiming over the clever objects Juliana had helped Edmund discover in London.

Juliana stood, feeling wretchedly awkward. "What can I say? This is far too much, and you must know it. What am I to do with you?"

"Well," he said and frowned, then motioned her to follow him. He casually clasped her hand, drawing her through the throng of people until they were in the peace of the library. He firmly closed the door behind them, slipping the lock into place with well-oiled care.

"What is it?" she asked, suddenly worried that something had been found wrong with the house and she had not been told. "You are displeased with something?"

"In a manner of speaking," he said musingly.

"What is it?" she demanded. "Tell me!"

"Well, I would like to marry, but I feel the nursery wing of the bedchamber floor is totally inadequate. I cannot contemplate asking a woman to wed me, then find this flaw in an otherwise perfect house. I would very much like to have you remedy the matter."

"What is wrong with the nursery suite?" she asked indignantly, instantly leaping to the defense of her own design for that area—one arrived at after consulting with other mothers, nursery maids, and her own nanny, now retired but with sensible ideas.

"You see, Juliana, I cannot think of any children I would wish to place there . . . except ours." Edmund met her gaze, recognized the startled confusion in her eyes, and decided it was time for the next step in his plan.

He swiftly crossed to her side and pulled her into his arms, noting she did not resist him. It gave him courage and hope. Not waiting for her to deny him what he sought, he kissed her with every ounce of expertise he had accumulated in his years on this earth, which was not inconsiderable. When he withdrew, he was satisfied to view her bemused expression, well loved and loving in return.

"Juliana, my love, I have missed you as I would miss my very breath. I cannot live in this house without you at my side. You would haunt my every step, my every waking moment. Please—promise you will not consider Lord Carlingford or any other man to be your husband. Only me. No one else in this world can love you half as much as I do."

Juliana, enchanted by this speech as much as she had been swept away by the passion of his kiss, could at first only nod her acceptance of so handsome a declaration.

The doorknob rattled, and Lady Rosamund could be heard wondering why the door was locked when everyone wished to see the wonderful library with the carvings of the muses.

Edmund pointed to Terpsichore and said, "There you are, my love, smiling down at me every time I walk in here. Now I will be able to have you everywhere."

Juliana thought of that perfectly splendid bed upstairs and whispered her agreement to his offer. And she hoped that no one would find the spare key to the library door for some time. She had some important things to finish in this house after all.